FIG1

Gr

**FIGHTING COMMAND text ©
GRAHAM JOHN PARRY**

COVER ARTWORK © G. J. PARRY

All Rights Reserved

This is a work of fiction. The names and characters, places and events, are the product of the authors imagination, or are used in an entirely fictitious context. Any resemblance to actual incidents, localities or persons, alive or dead, is wholly coincidental.

**For my Wife and Children
with love**

Table of Contents

NOVELS by Graham J. Parry

1 .. The Phoenix Rises
2 .. Open Sea
3 .. Lion's Den
4 .. Gnat's Whisker
5 .. Plans Afoot
6 .. Recall
7 .. Scapa Flow
8 .. Ad hoc Flotilla
9 .. Hands to Stations
10 . Lookout's Call
11 . Discovery
12 . Signal
13 . Heavy Going
14 . A Distant Shadow
15 . Small Echo
16 . In For A Penny
17 . Heavy Artillery
18 . Senior Officer
19 . Convoy
20 . Engage At Will
21 . Call His Bluff
22 . Damage
23 . No Way Back
24 . Gunfire
25 . Battle Weary
26 . All Change
27 . Restless Seas

> They did not look for Glory, nor
> ribbons on their chest,
> But fought together side by side,
> gave only of their best.
> And when the battle's course was
> run and they could fight no more,
> They humbly asked, do not forget ..,
> the bloody waves of war.

1 .. The Phoenix Rises

It was early in the September of 1944, when Lieutenant-Commander Richard Thorburn strode purposefully towards a fitting out berth in Portsmouth's Royal Navy dockyard. Drawing level with the bows of a small destroyer he slowed to let his gaze run down the length of the ship's upperworks. Standing with hands on hips he let a quiet smile tug the corners of his mouth. The dockyard, he thought, had excelled themselves.

The ship had suffered battle damage on D-Day. An out of control U-boat had lunged to the surface and collided with her forefoot. Having initially been passed over as too lengthy a repair to undertake, forty-eight hours after returning to harbour a brief underwater inspection had shown only the bows and a small section of keel needed replacing. And although the dockyard promised a quick turn around, a lot of manpower had then been diverted for emergency repairs to landing craft returning from the Normandy beaches. But all said and done, Thorburn thought the reconstruction had been skilfully handled.

He took a deep breath and passed a hand over his weathered face. That battle had certainly come at a cost, but after three months of waiting, she was nigh on ready for sea.

There was a good deal of warmth to the morning sun, and with it the pungent smell of fresh paint hung thick in the still air. He pushed back the peak of his cap, and at that very moment he found himself hit by an overwhelming sense of pride. H.M.S. *Brackendale* had been his to command from the day of her launch back in 1940, and across the years she'd survived everything the enemy had thrown at her. And a bit more besides when his own ship handling had not been all that it should have. The Ship's Crest caught his eye, boldly displayed on the bridge superstructure just beneath the screen. A pony's head framed by a gold hunting horn, dedicated by a New Forest 'fox hunt' to which this class of ship owed its name. He stepped back and took another long look at her swept lines. In outward appearance very little had changed, still a compact, agile destroyer, the epitome of Royal Navy architecture. But beneath that smart exterior the years of conflict had taken their toll. Delve beneath the fresh paintwork and an experienced eye would detect all the dents and scars of war.

Thorburn straightened up and squared his shoulders. Whatever her faults he felt more than justified in holding a deep affection for this weary, battle-hardened little warship.

A bead of perspiration trickled down his forehead. He wiped it and settled his cap, wincing as it tightened round the livid scar on his temple. He swore quietly. That U-boat had a lot to answer for. The wound had taken a long time to heal, longer than predicted and had left him nursing occasional headaches, some of which were annoyingly potent. Not that he'd let it be known, least of all to the doctors at the hospital where he'd been assessed for duty. With his future career currently under possible review, the last thing he needed was for the Admiralty to find an excuse to move him elsewhere. He'd made a point of not admitting to any ill effects.

He gathered himself and strode off towards the ship's stern. Drawing level with *Brackendale's* sea boat, he shot a veiled glance at the quarterdeck. It revealed a hurriedly assembled side party jostling together to pipe him aboard, and he momentarily lowered his head to hide the smile.

A few more paces and then, to the wailing call of the Bosun's whistle, Lieutenant-Commander Richard Thorburn, R.N., D.S.O., strode down the gangway and stepped aboard his small 'Hunt' class destroyer.

Striding along the main deck, the ship's First Lieutenant was late to join the side party. Delayed by the dockyard foreman requiring a signature, he nonetheless managed to arrive as the captain stepped over the side. Straightening his tall, wiry frame to attention, Lieutenant Robert Armstrong saluted.

'Welcome aboard, sir.'

'Thank you, Number One. How're things?'

Armstrong saw him glance towards the stern, his critical gaze roving over unfinished modifications. Empty paint cans and packing cases lay discarded next to the depth charge rails, chisels and brushes lying haphazardly to one side.

'Coming along nicely, sir.'

Thorburn raised an eyebrow. 'Really? Wouldn't exactly be my turn of phrase.'

Armstrong blinked, said nothing. Was there a hint of irritation in the reply? If so it didn't bode well. The Captain had been away attending a mandatory Board of Inquiry. And even though *Brackendale's* collision had happened during combat, the circumstances surrounding the event still needed Their Lordship's approval. He wondered if everything had not been as clear cut in testimony as it had in reality? A captain's entire career could hang on the whim of one 'out-of-sorts' senior officer.

But then he saw Thorburn smile, a mischievous twinkle in his eyes.

'God, but it's good to be back. Come on, Number One, my cabin. You can bring me up to date.'

Armstrong relaxed and breathed out. That broad smile seemed to indicate all was well, and he quickly dismissed the side party. He followed Thorburn across to the starboard side, dodged the ship's motor boat, and clambered up the ladder to the fo'c'sle. There the Captain stopped and looked up at the Range Finder Director Control tower.

'Is 'Guns' aboard?'

'Yes, sir,' he said, 'checking the ammunition hoists.'

'And the crew?'

Armstrong hesitated and Thorburn was quick to fix him with a raised eyebrow.

'C'mon, out with it. Who's not back?'

'Two of the starboard watch depth-charge crew. Lieutenant Labatt's pulling his hair out.'

Thorburn pursed his lips. 'Mmm . . . , keep me informed, we might need replacements.' He paused, and Armstrong then found himself fixed by an inquisitive pair of eyes. 'You referred to '*Lieutenant*' Labatt, Number One. Has his promotion come through?'

Armstrong grinned. 'Yes, sir, and his mess bill now far exceeds the meagre rise in pay.'

The Captain smiled at the reference to some kind of celebration, then dropped the smile. 'Other than that?'

'Starboard watch cleaning ship, port watch

due back tomorrow.'

'Good,' Thorburn said, and then pointed to the top of the mast. 'And what's that bloody thing up there?'

Armstrong glanced at the masthead, searching for some obvious discrepancy. Everything seemed to be in order. 'Sir?'

Thorburn jabbed his finger skywards. 'That thing looking like a clothes dryer.'

'Additional wireless antenna, sir. Supposed to be a big improvement on the old one.'

Thorburn shook his head. 'I won't hold my breath,' he muttered, and strode into the passage leading to his cabin.

Armstrong loped along behind him, head down, and smiling at the Captain's belligerent comment. He wasn't one to mince his words.

Thorburn let himself in, and Armstrong stood back, waiting respectfully in the doorway. He watched Thorburn take a swift look around and toss his cap onto the desk, and then he beckoned for Armstrong to take a chair.

'No need to stand on ceremony, fill me in on the details.'

Armstrong sat and reached over to the captain's 'in-tray'.

'It's all in there, sir,' he said, and dropped a folder on the desk.

Thorburn opened the report, grimaced, and began to flick through.

The First Lieutenant, knowing full well what

was inside, leaned back and kept his mouth shut. He'd learned many years ago that the man across the desk had his own ways of dealing with paperwork, especially if it interfered with the running of his ship. Better not speak until asked and he took the opportunity to take a long, unobserved look at his Captain. The wound to his temple still looked raw, but he appeared to be his usual self, although the lines on his forehead seemed a little more prominent. But the eyes were as clear and sharp as ever, and there was no obvious lack of energy. He thought back to when he'd first joined ship. Thorburn had been a revelation, a breath of fresh air when compared to other captains Armstrong had served under. Young for a Lieutenant-Commander, Thorburn had a ready smile and a genuine warmth which touched all those with whom he came into contact. Above all, it quickly became apparent that his Captain was a very capable seaman with an instinctive knack of ship handling. More importantly, the man knew how to fight a ship, and from Armstrong's first hand experience, it was not with the reckless abandon the top brass at the Admiralty had branded him with.

But, and Armstrong hid a thoughtful smile, when it came to paperwork, well . . . , each to his own.

Below the waterline, Lieutenant (E) Bryn Dawkins, R.N.R., *Brackendale's* veteran Chief Engineering Officer, squatted on his haunches in the middle of the engine room and peered under the starboard bank of pipes, dials, valves and wheels. Something had caught the Welshman's eye, a discrepancy in the spotless perfection of his domain. It was a piece of discarded waste cotton and he shook his head in disbelief.

'Moore!' he called to the Leading Stoker, 'fish that bloody bit of rag out.' He jabbed an oily finger at the offending article.

'Ginger' Moore wiped a greasy palm down his overalls and stepped over to the main panel. He bent beneath the myriad array of pipes and flicked the rag out and back towards the Chief.

'That's the ticket,' Dawkins said, and scooped the filthy remnant over to a waste bin. He looked again at Moore. 'You'll have a word then, won't you boyo? This shouldn't have happened.'

Moore straightened, nodding. 'Right, Chief, but it might have been the dockyard.'

Dawkins gave him a wry smile. 'Might have been,' he conceded, 'but it won't harm to remind 'em, will it now?'

He turned his attention to the gauges and polished vigorously with a cloth kept only for that purpose, and then pursed his lips in thought. The engines were the ship's beating heart, and in itself the cotton waste wasn't really a problem. But it only took a small strand to enter an oil-way, seize a bearing, and the ship might be brought to a standstill. And after all the hustle and bustle of dockyard repairs, he was well aware the Captain would definitely be inspecting ship, sooner rather than later. It wouldn't do to let him find fault.

Bryn Dawkins, a product of the Royal Navy's engineering excellence, knew how to apply himself, and bent to the task in hand.

Chief Petty Officer Barry Falconer stood under the barrels of the forward gun mount and stared out over the harbour. He found it hard to believe that *Brackendale* had once again emerged from the hands of the dockyard and been transformed into a seagoing concern. A faint smile creased his lips. As one of the longest serving Coxswains in the Royal Navy, he'd seen more than his fair share of warships. There'd been battleships, cruisers, and Fleet destroyers, finally followed after many years by an assignment to this unpretentious, undersized little destroyer.

And it was shortly after their first patrol that Falconer knew he'd found his true calling. The proud 'Geordie' from the banks of Newcastle's River Tyne had become a destroyer man, through and through. This tiny warship had stolen his heart and from that moment on all his energies had gone into making her the best she could be.

Not that he'd admit his feelings to anyone. It was enough that he knew, and from thereon in, let no man raise a word against her. A stiff breeze stirred the waters of the harbour and *Brackendale* tugged at her moorings, and again the smile came, unbidden. It was as if the ship knew it was time, pulling at her tethers for the freedom of the sea.

The Cox'n squared his shoulders. He too was ready.

Richard Thorburn cleared the last of his paperwork to the out-tray and leaned back in his chair. His temple ached, whether from the strain of reading or the gradual healing process he was unsure. He managed the ghost of a smile. What didn't ache? The old wound to his shoulder blade still played him up, and occasionally his right knee could unexpectedly give way to leave him with a painful limp. He'd learned to live with it, knowing he'd been lucky not to have suffered anything worse. The faint smile evaporated and he breathed in. At thirty-one years of age, and with four long years of war under his belt, he was in relatively good shape. He and the Ship's Company had participated in more than their fair share of action, and for the most part, any wrong decisions he'd made had been outweighed by the good ones. Mistakes had come at a cost, but as with every chosen path, rarely were there improvements unless different solutions could be found. And he believed, deep down, that he'd never caused a man's death aboard *Brackendale* by reckless leadership. Honest mistakes . . . , yes, but never through deliberate misuse of his authority.

Footsteps sounded from overhead, muffled voices from the wheelhouse. An almost hidden vibration could be felt beneath his feet and he guessed the Chief had the screws slowly turning over, testing the boilers and machinery of the engine room.

Thorburn reached for his cap, checked his appearance in the mirror . . . , and frowned at the reflection. He leaned closer. Was that a few grey hairs? He grinned. The strain of command beginning to show? Well that's what he could claim if anyone had the temerity to bring it up. He carefully patted his cap into place, tugged the jacket straight and turned for the door. It was time he inspected the ship, unannounced, no warning, just the old Captain making his rounds. There would probably be a few terse remarks left in his wake, but better that than something important overlooked.

He noticed the ache in his temple had subsided.

2 .. Open Sea

The next day, morning on Friday the 8th, Richard Thorburn stood on *Brackendale's* bridge and smiled at the ship's gentle corkscrew. The men of the port watch had arrived back aboard ship from first light onwards, and by 09.30 they'd all stowed away and been accounted for. At that point in time, Thorburn had formally requested permission to test the ship at sea. It took a while, but after sorting the inevitable 'red tape', they'd been cleared for sea trials. Wasting as little time as possible, he'd brought the ship out of the Solent's eastern arm, and then headed south from Hayling Island. It was a glorious day, waves sparkling in the sunlight, glinting off the occasional breaking crest. To his left, over the port bridge-wing, seagulls caught a lift on rising thermals, wings spread to the soft breeze. He grinned. Of all the many times he'd weighed anchor or cast free from the shore, he'd never lost that thrill of meeting the open sea.

But the moment had come to lift her skirts, and he gave the order for twenty knots. His navigating officer, Lieutenant David J. Martin, more commonly referred to as 'Pilot', passed the order to the wheelhouse, and moments later the small destroyer picked up speed and powered out into the English Channel. A fine vibration reverberated through the deck plates, and overhead abaft the bridge, *Brackendale's* White Ensign whipped and snapped to the strengthening wind. He glanced at Armstrong and was met with a broad smile, and they both nodded in satisfaction.

From the centre of the bridge overlooking the forward gun mount, Thorburn moved to his right, stepping across to the starboard wing.

He looked astern at their foaming wake, and at Hampshire's southern coast rapidly receding into the distance. He thought how warm and peaceful it all looked, even in the midst of war.

The momentary illusion was quickly dispelled. A low flying formation of Hurricanes roared their way out from inland, gained height, and powered off towards the south.

He stepped back to the bridge-screen and grabbed a handset for the engine room. Lieutenant Bryn Dawkins answered instantly. 'Engine room.'

'How are we, Chief?'

The Welshman's warm brogue came through loud and clear. 'All's well, sir.'

Thorburn pursed his lips, hesitant to push his luck. 'I'd like to try emergency full ahead?'

'Whenever you want, sir.'

'Right, give it all you've got.'

'Aye aye, sir,' Dawkins said, and Thorburn clipped the handset back on its bracket. He looked up over the screen, sensing the next step in acceleration, heavy spray lifting from the bows. *Brackendale* swayed and straightened, punching the waves, white water surging down her length. He let her run on, the turbines extracting every last ounce of power from the boilers as the small warship knifed through the seas. Only when a full five minutes had elapsed did he ask the question.

'What's our speed, Pilot?'

'Twenty-seven knots by the log, sir,' Martin said.

Thorburn smiled in appreciation. Bryn Dawkins had surpassed himself.

'Very well,' he said, and decided there was nothing more to prove. 'Half ahead together, make revolutions for fourteen knots.'

Brackendale eased from her headlong run, slowing to his command. He moved to the bridge-chair and contemplated whether to give "Guns" a brief practice shoot. He thought better of it, and instead turned to Armstrong.

'I'll require all officers for debriefing on our return to harbour. If there are no major faults I want to sign off and report for duty. I've had enough of the dockyard to last me a lifetime.'

Armstrong touched the peak of his cap. 'Aye aye, sir. I'll let them know.'

Thorburn watched him depart down the ladder and called to Martin. 'Take us home, Pilot, it's time we got back to the war.'

'Starboard twenty,' Martin ordered to the pipe, and Thorburn sat back and relaxed. A couple of hours and they should be safely tied up alongside. He hoped fervently for a string of good reports when his officers assembled. He tapped a pocket, found his pack of Senior Service and extracted a cigarette.

He smiled and struck a match, a moment to be savoured.

At 13.25 hours, in the building known as Portsmouth's 'Semaphore Tower', Commodore James Pendleton, R.N., D.S.C., leaned back from his desk and frowned at a solitary sheet of paper. He stroked his handsome beard with a thumb and forefinger, a habit he'd long since failed to notice, and put his signature to the bottom. The formal typewritten message informed him that H.M.S. *Brackendale* had completed sea trials and was fit for duty. He glanced at the desk diary, eyes narrowed in thought. It had taken almost fourteen weeks, but from a strictly naval aspect that brief message was good news. Another destroyer available for deployment, and for that he was more than grateful.

A knock on the office door interrupted his thoughts.

'Come,' he growled, and then smiled at the sight of his elegant assistant.

First Officer Jennifer Farbrace breezed in with a new folder, cleared a space, and laid it carefully on the polished mahogany table.

'The report you requested, sir.'

Pendleton reached forward, hesitated, and then very deliberately picked it off the desk before leaning back in his chair. He thumbed rapidly through the contents.

'Thank you, young lady,' he said, and placed the folio to one side, the frown returning as he met her calm gaze. He tugged impatiently at the full beard. 'Has Thorburn been informed?' he demanded, making no attempt to hide his impatience.

Jennifer gave the slightest shake of her head and a faint smile danced across the delicate lips.

'Not yet, sir, no. You wanted Lieutenant Creswell to divert the Harwich supply convoy. I can tell Lieutenant-Commander Thorburn if you'd rather.'

He pursed his lips, momentarily studying her lovely profile. She stood quietly, showing no sign of being put out by his behaviour. And he also recognised that it was indeed Creswell's duty to inform Thorburn, and the man was dealing with more than his fair share of orders.

'No, that's alright, Miss Farbrace. Leave it to Creswell, but do let me know the moment Thorburn arrives.'

'Of course, sir,' she said with a quick smile, and turned for the door, pausing to look back. 'Will you need me in attendance?'

He shook his head. 'No . . . , might call you later though.'

'Yes, sir,' she said, and quietly closed the door.

From somewhere out in the harbour, the distinctive double hoot of an American destroyer echoed across the water. He sighed, came to his feet, and then wandered over to the tall sash window that overlooked the docks. In comparison to the organised chaos leading up to D-Day, the transformation of the harbour seemed almost unbelievable. It was relatively empty. Hospital ships made irregular appearances, disembarking casualties to waiting ambulances where nurses and orderlies tended the stretchers, hurrying to and fro. And warships continued to take advantage of the facilities, to replenish ammunition, refuel and make hasty repairs.

As the strong sun shimmered off the still waters, Pendleton subconsciously itemised the vessels on view. There were minesweepers and corvettes, three Fleet destroyers, and a cruiser smoking from her funnels as she built up steam. A pair of Admiralty harbour tugs busied themselves with a merchantman, nudging her into the nearest quay. Most noticeably, four Landing Craft Tank, fully loaded with Sherman tanks, nosed their way out of harbour towards Gosport's headland, part of the never ending supply of reinforcements needed for the Army's push south through France.

He turned his gaze to the right and squinted in the sunlight. There at a distant berth sat a small destroyer and he pursed his lips in thought, recalling other times when he'd had good reason to personally welcome the return of that little warship.

Commodore James Pendleton sighed and turned back to his desk. He squeezed his thickening waist into the chair and looked again at that new folder lying on the table. The humdrum routine of Portsmouth harbour faded into the background and he rubbed his forehead. Why, he pondered, was there always so much paperwork?

Thorburn drained the last dregs of tea from his cup and glanced at the time. It showed two in the afternoon and he shook his head, exasperated by the endless wait for news. The meeting of ship's officers on *Brackendale's* return to harbour had passed off with no serious issues raised, and within two hours of mooring alongside he'd signed for the ship and the last of the dockyard people had gone ashore. Pendleton's office had been informed of the successful outcome, and yet, here they were still waiting for their orders. Not that it surprised him. From the Admiralty's point of view, Thorburn had never managed to shake off the notoriety of being a bit of a rebel, someone they had no real use for. Except of course, he thought with a wry smile, in exceptional circumstances. He'd long since come to terms with it, but with every passing hour another opportunity to get back to sea slipped by. What troubled him most was whether those in authority wanted to replace him, give the ship to someone more 'worthy'. It wouldn't be unusual for an out of favour captain to suddenly find himself squirreled away into some desk bound backwater. At the same time, he knew that old man Pendleton was very much on his side and that the Navy still had need of experienced captains at the helm.

Looking round the cabin he wondered if it wasn't time to report in person, tackle the Commodore head on?

There was a knock on the door.

'Yes?' he said sharply, unintentionally voicing his irritation, and immediately regretting the lack of self control.

A duty seaman stuck his head in. 'Telephone call, sir. In the dock office.'

'Thank you,' Thorburn said, a moment of optimism coursing through his veins. He grabbed his cap and strode out to the portside gangway.

In the heavily timbered hut that served as a dock office, the works foreman nodded to a desk in the corner. He crossed the room and snatched up the receiver.

'Thorburn,' he said into the mouthpiece.

'Connecting you now, sir.'

There was a click followed by a humming line.

'Thorburn,' he said again.

'Creswell here, sir. I have orders for you.'

'Go on.'

'You are requested to attend Commodore Pendleton's office at 15.30 hours.'

Thorburn felt a flutter of anticipation, but hid the emotion from his voice. 'Very well, half-past three.'

'Yes, sir. 15.30,' and the line disconnected

With deliberate care he replaced the receiver. At last, he thought, Pendleton wouldn't order him in without good reason. One way or another, good or bad, he was about to find out what the future held.

Aboard ship, the newly promoted 'Lieutenant' George Labatt, the youngest officer in the ship's company, walked into the wardroom and ordered tea. Not that age detracted from his ability. He'd joined *Brackendale* as a Midshipman in 1940, and now, with four long years of war under his belt, he'd made Lieutenant. But his normal cheerful smile had been replaced by a frown and he slumped despondently into a leather armchair. Two members of his depth-charge crew were still adrift after a two week leave, both men from London, and both with homes in the Old Kent Road.

'Your tea, sir,' the steward said, and set the cup on the table.

Labatt nodded his thanks, but then shook his head, brooding over the absentees. They were good characters, and popular amongst their mess-mates. Going by their past records it wasn't in their nature to wilfully transgress and his first thoughts had been for their welfare. That aside, it left him two experienced men short, not an ideal situation.

He looked up as Lieutenant 'Guns' McDonald breezed in. Tall, well built, and always immaculately dressed, he was the image of every woman's ideal sailor.

McDonald nodded by way of greeting. 'George,' he said amiably, 'I hear the skipper's in the dock office.'

Labatt sat forward, suddenly alert. 'Why?'

'Telephone call I think.'

Labatt dropped his gaze and took a sip of tea. There might be a dozen different explanations as to why, but for the Captain to personally step ashore to answer a dock office telephone, that could be quite significant. Especially as *Brackendale* had successfully completed her sea trials.

McDonald ordered tea and toast and then settled for the bench seat, rummaging through the morning papers.

'Aha . . . , here we are,' he said, picking up the Daily Telegraph. 'Jerry on the run. War over by Christmas.'

Labatt raised his eyebrow. 'You don't believe that, do you?'

McDonald shook his head. 'Not at all, but it makes for a good headline.'

'I hope Higgins and Reid don't believe it, they're still adrift.'

Guns looked over the top of the newspaper. 'Have you told Number One?'

'Yes, he wasn't impressed.'

'I don't suppose he was,' McDonald chuckled. 'They better have a good excuse.'

True, thought Labatt . . . , if they ever returned. He finished his tea and left McDonald to his paper. It was time to work on rearranging the depth charge team, that way he would have an answer to the inevitable questions. He remembered when he'd first joined *Brackendale* as a Midshipman. The skipper had patiently taken the young Labatt under his wing, given him responsibility, and nurtured the officer within. And the one thing he had learned across the years was that the Captain didn't suffer fools gladly. Do not be found wanting, get to the root of the problem and solve it.

He made for the boat deck and strode aft to the depth charge racks, and a determined smile returned to the boyish face.

Out in the waters of the Labrador Sea, southwest of Greenland, a German submarine, the U-699, located and sank a Canadian flagged five-thousand ton merchantman. It was highly unusual to find an unaccompanied vessel in this stretch of the ocean and it took the U-boat's commander a considerable length of time to ensure he was not being led into a trap. With precious few torpedoes remaining in his arsenal, only one was used in the attack. Manoeuvring into the perfect position and using an almost ideal 'firing solution' the S.S. *Silver Moon* went to the bottom in less than six minutes. Of her twelve man crew there were no survivors.

In the immediate aftermath of the sinking, the U-boat turned away from Greenland's coastal seaboard and followed orders to relocate and patrol the waters south-west of Iceland.

For twenty-five year old Kapitänleutnant Helmut D. Eckermann, who was nearing the end of a two month patrol, that solitary sinking marked the high point in what had been a wasted expenditure of torpedoes against fast moving vessels. And he well knew that without the pre-patrol addition of a Schnorkel, U-699 would have been lost many weeks ago. But now that the diesel motors could breathe while the boat remained submerged, Eckermann had so far eluded the enemy anti-submarine patrols. His luck had held . . . , for the moment. It would be four or five days before his boat reached the new patrol line, and even then, U-699's recall to base could not come soon enough.

Helmut Eckermann shook his head in sorrow. The Kriegsmarine's U-boats no longer wreaked havoc on the enemy's convoys. In recent months he had lost many comrades. Not a week passed without hearing of another boat destroyed, sometimes two in the space of a few days. Someone had coined the phrase "iron coffins". Eckermann was determined not to join them.

In the hours that followed, U-699 slid on beneath the waves.

3 . . Lion's Den

Thorburn climbed the stairs to the fourth floor of the administration block and turned down the corridor for Pendleton's office. In the aftermath of D-Day, the building appeared busier now than it had prior to the invasion. The clatter of typewriters emanated from every doorway and he dodged a number of Wrens scurrying between rooms.

At the door marked, "Commodore J. Pendleton", he tapped lightly, turned the handle and stuck his head through the opening of the outer office.

The sparkling eyes of Jennifer Farbrace looked up from her desk and he smiled. The two of them had been seeing one another on and off for a long time now. It had developed into an 'understanding', but it was only in recent months that Thorburn had recognised the inevitable truth behind their 'liaison'. A month after D-Day he'd summoned up the courage and asked her if she would marry a humble Lieutenant-Commander. A week later they'd formally announced their engagement. But nonetheless, within the confines of official duty, protocol must take precedence

'Good afternoon, Miss Farbrace,' he said with all the formality he could muster.

'Afternoon, sir,' she answered with equal formality, but the smile deflected the severity in her voice.

He stepped in, pulled the door closed, and removed his cap.

Before he could say anything more she raised

a hand in warning and a small frown wrinkled her delicate eyebrows. She nodded towards the inner office door that stood slightly ajar.

'The Commodore's waiting, sir.'

'Ah,' he said, 'I see,' and tucked the cap under his left arm. 'I'll go in then.'

Jennifer nodded, the frown still very much in evidence.

'Exactly, sir.'

Thorburn straightened to his full height, tugged his jacket into place and winked at her sombre expression.

'Into the lion's den,' he whispered, and left her to smile behind a guarded hand. His knock on the inner door produced a rasping, 'Come!' and he stepped smartly over the threshold.

Pendleton sat with elbows on his desk holding an open folder. Thorburn stopped short and stood to attention.

The Commodore's sharp eyes lifted from the page.

'Relax, Richard. How's the head?'

Thorburn instinctively reached up to touch his left temple.

'Good, thank you, sir.'

Pendleton nodded. 'Glad to hear it, take a seat.'

Thorburn dragged a chair towards the desk and sat while the Commodore finished reading. He eventually closed the folder and tossed it to one side. Easing back in the chair the old sailor stroked his beard, eyes raised to the ceiling.

Thorburn swallowed, anticipating bad news. Maybe his worst fears were about to be realised, to be relinquished of command and provided with a dreaded desk job.

Pendleton ran a hand through the greying head of hair before looking at Thorburn and pointing to the folder.

'That's the official report from the Board-of-Inquiry. Exonerated, m' boy. No fault could be ascribed to your actions, and there's a footnote congratulating you and the ship's company on sinking the U-boat.'

Thorburn sat dazed, astonished by the turn of events. One minute he thought he'd been written off, bound for duty ashore, and now, not only had he been granted a full reprieve, their Lordships had actually praised him. He met Pendleton's eyes.

'I thought . . . ,' he muttered, and shook his head.

'Thought you were being hung out to dry, eh? No, not yet. We're still got a bloody war to fight.'

Thorburn felt the tension leave him. 'Yes, sir.'

'Now,' Pendleton said, 'according to my information, you're ready for sea.'

'Dockyard did a good job.'

'Good . . . , I'm sending you back south to the beaches. There's a combined op about to take place and the army have asked for naval help. So, that said, we've decided to send in the battleship *Warspite,* and possibly *Erebus,* the monitor. They're going to have a look at Le Havre, knock out some German gun emplacements. To that end I've volunteered you to cover a force of minesweepers clearing the way.'

Thorburn scratched his chin. 'How far from shore?'

Pendleton gave a mirthless grin. 'As far as you're concerned, too close. Probably ten to twelve miles out, but the minesweepers will let you know.'

'When do we sail, sir?'

'Tomorrow, if all goes well. The plan is for you to join them a couple of hours before sunset, see for yourself before dark. It's busy down there, a lot of re-supply still going on, all centred on 'Sword' and the Mulberry harbour, west of your area. Having said that, the other hazard now is the number of sunken vessels. Your lookouts will be earning their keep.' He grinned.

Thorburn half smiled with him, and then asked, 'Who am I reporting to down there?'

The Commodore frowned, and checked his paperwork. 'Ah . . . , here we are. H.M.S. *Hornbill,* Lieutenant-Commander Tim Roberts. It's a flotilla of five and he's been Leader since May.' Pendleton cleared his throat and looked up from beneath the bushy eyebrows. 'You are the senior officer, but I'm sure you'll show him your full co-operation.'

'Of course, sir, there to help.'

'Good,' Pendleton beamed, 'never doubted it.' He leaned back in the chair. 'Well that about covers it. Miss Farbrace has your orders, and I'm sure you have a lot to tend to.'

Thorburn realised the meeting was at an end. 'Yes, sir,' he said, and turned to go.

'One more thing, Richard.'

Thorburn looked back.

'The Germans are laying acoustic mines. The advice to all captains is hold your speed beneath ten knots. The resonance from your propellers then minimises the acoustic signal, less chance of setting one off.'

'Right, sir, I'll bear that in mind.'

Pendleton nodded thoughtfully. 'You'll do well not to forget it. Good luck, Commander.'

'Thank you, sir,' Thorburn said, and walked out.

In the outer office Jennifer was sat at her desk shuffling paper, and she stopped to reach for a manila envelope. 'Your orders,' she said, and stood to join him. 'Back to Normandy then.'

'Yes, seems that way. Playing nursemaid to a bunch of minesweepers.' He knew it was a flippant remark, but it was a deliberate attempt to make light of the situation.

She smiled automatically, but there was a sombre expression in her eyes. 'Be careful, Richard. We've lost a lot of ships down there.'

There was a knock on the outer door and a messenger stepped in. 'Package to be signed for ma'am.'

Jennifer nodded at the interruption but didn't look away. 'You'd best be off,' she said, and surreptitiously squeezed his hand. 'I'll see you when you get back.'

Thorburn grinned. 'That's a date,' he said, and released his fingers from her grip. For a long moment her eyes held his, no words, just thoughts.

The messenger gave an insistent cough. 'If I could have a signature, please, ma'am?'

Jennifer made a face, turned to sign, and Thorburn used the moment to take his leave. He stepped out into the corridor, his mind already wrestling with the logistics of replenishing ship.

Hundreds of miles across the wind tossed waters of the North Sea, heavy rain and high winds battered the German port of Bremerhaven. The few ships that lay strategically spaced within the basins rocked uncomfortably to the driven waves. The deluge all but obscured the bombed out buildings, and scudding clouds darkened the sky, adding their own melancholy to the sombre spectacle of a ruined city.

Within those rubble strewn port facilities, at the underground headquarters of Marineoberkommando der Nordsee, a signal had arrived from Grand Admiral Karl Dönitz. It was addressed to Admiral Mathias Krause, Knights Cross, and ordered him to sail for the west coast of Norway where he would set up a temporary U-boat

Command Headquarters in the non-operational light cruiser, *Aldenburg*. Once there, Krause was to asses all available resources and prepare to take control of operations.

Having thoroughly read and digested the orders, Krause snorted his disdain, dropped the decoded message onto his desk, and reached instead for his glass of cognac. He took a large mouthful and set it back down with a bang. The *Aldenburg*, he knew, unlike the *Tirpitz*, had managed to evade observation for nine long months and currently lay hidden beneath an overhanging escarpment in the fjords. He sighed, already resigned to his enforced departure.

'Bergmann,' he said to his Assistant Executive officer. 'I have been ordered to Norway. You will accompany me.'

From his desk in the corner of the office, Kapitän-zur-See Ralf Bergmann looked up. 'As you wish, sir.' He hesitated. 'Forgive me for asking, Herr Admiral, but why you?'

Krause looked directly at Bergman and gave him the only possible explanation. 'When I was a young Lieutnant I spent four months in U-boats. I think Dönitz has been told. But he forgets I am older, much has changed.' He closed his eyes, conjuring up long forgotten memories of simulated underwater attacks.

'I doubt my experience will be of use now.' He laughed, an explosive bark of contempt.

'Believe me Bergmann, Dönitz is gambling on

a miracle. He tells Hitler what he wants to hear, he does not speak the truth. The war at sea is lost and Dönitz knows it . . . , he knows.'

Krause shook his head. 'But an order is an order and we obey.' He tilted his head. 'What ships do we have?'

Bergmann peered at the stack of paper on his desk and extracted one from beneath the pile. He opened it and scanned the list.

'Ready for sea? Only four.' He hesitated. 'There are two U-boats also. Would they not be a better choice?'

Krause rolled his blood-shot eyes to the ceiling, immediately dismissing the idea of an underwater passage. 'The ships, what are they?'

'One Zerstorer, two Elbing, and an M-class torpedo boat.'

Mathias Krause tapped the desk in thought. 'Who commands the Zerstorer?'

'Kapitänleutnant Herman Richter, for two years, sir.'

'Mmm . . . , let me have Richter's service record, and have him report this afternoon.'

Bergmann nodded and crossed the room to a filing cabinet.

Krause leaned back and rubbed his forehead in thought. Reaching Norway would not be easy. British and American forces had a stranglehold over North Sea waters. The recent heavy losses in U-boats bore witness to the facts, and contributed to his own reluctance in using one.

Even Dönitz accepted a short lifespan from his men; the rate of attrition exceeded his ability to train new recruits.

Matthias Krause swore softly, heaved himself out from behind his desk and turned to the door.

'I'm going up for some fresh air,' he said, and stepped out into the corridor. At the far end he mounted the concrete stairway where a soldier saluted and opened the narrow door. He moved out and stood under the tall arched entranceway. It gave him a panoramic, though rain swept view of the harbour, and there, berthed alongside the northern quay sat one of the few remaining Zerstorer class of destroyers. He wiped his mouth with the back of his hand and smiled. It was a twisted smile, mirthless, and reflected the misery of his innermost thoughts. Ingrid, his wife of twenty-eight years had been killed during a bombing raid on their home in Stuttgart. His eldest son Karl had lost his life at the battle for Stalingrad, and his youngest son was believed to have succumbed to a depth-charge attack when his U-boat was hunted to destruction in the Straits of Gibraltar.

Krause stared silently through the teeming rain, alone with his thoughts. He had no illusions about what the future offered. The Fatherland could not hold out for much longer. Russian armies closed in from the east, British and Americans from the west. And what would happen at the war's end? Did he really want to live in a subjugated Germany?

Heavy raindrops battered the doorway and he turned back for his underground office. The corridor smelt of decaying damp and he thankfully entered the warmth of the room.

Ahead of him, Bergmann laid a file on the Admiral's desk. It contained the service record of Kapitänleutnant Herman Richter and the state of readiness of the destroyer, *Bruno Keplar* The time for decisions approached.

Back aboard *Brackendale*, Thorburn called his officers to a meeting, and when the First Lieutenant reported they were all accounted for, he followed Armstrong to the wardroom. He stepped inside and moved to stand with his back to the fireplace. The general hubbub of voices fell away and faces turned expectantly to hear their Captain's words.

'Gentlemen,' he began, 'tomorrow we'll be returning to the French coast. We're to link up with a minesweeping flotilla in order to give them a bit more protection.'

He glanced at the familiar faces of his six commissioned officers, but also, crucially, Chief Petty Officer Falconer, the man who bridged the gap between officers and Ship's Company, a foot in both camps so to speak. At the back of the group he found Surgeon-Lieutenant 'Doc' Waverley stood with his arms folded, and Thorburn felt himself being professionally scrutinised by an inquisitive pair of eyes. Of all those present Doc Waverley might be the only one that fully understood the possible after effects of a wound to the head. Thankfully, Thorburn knew he could be trusted not to break patient confidentiality, nor, more importantly, their long standing friendship.

'The minesweepers,' he continued, 'have been deployed on a specific task. *Warspite* and *Erebus* will be moving down to bombard Le Havre, help the army with an assault on the town.'

Labatt let out a low whistle. 'Fifteen-inch guns on the battleship.'

Guns McDonald nodded. 'Same on the old *Erebus*, serious artillery.'

Thorburn nodded. 'Let's hope the shore batteries don't have an equivalent range, we could well be in the firing line.' He looked pointedly at Labatt. 'Anything on our absentees?'

'Not yet, no, sir.'

'Might be as well to liaise with Number One, think about reorganise your people.'

'Yes, sir,' Labatt said, and Armstrong nodded.

'Well,' Thorburn said, 'that about wraps it up. Are there any questions?' When none were raised he gave them a slow smile. 'Holiday's over, tomorrow we go back to war.' And with that he took his leave of the wardroom and headed for his cabin. It was time to sort out his sea-going uniform.

Early on Saturday the 9th, with the coming of first light, two seamen arrived at the head of *Brackendale's* gangway. On the main deck a sentry charged with the ship's security shouted a challenge and the pair reluctantly shuffled to a halt. The elder of the two took a step forward.

'Come off it, Nobby, it's me an' Alf.'

Signalman 'Nobby' Clarke had no doubts about their identity, but orders were orders. He'd been one of the Ship's Company for what seemed a lifetime, promoted Leading Signalman in the past, but had then lost it after a drink fuelled altercation ashore. He was loyal, trustworthy and good at his job. He'd made a mistake, kept his nose clean since, and was due to get his senior rating back shortly. As far as Alf Higgins and Sid Reid were concerned, and he knew them as well as anybody, both had been posted as Absent-Without-Leave. Shipmates or not, Clarke wasn't about to let them aboard without the duty Petty Officer's say so.

Footsteps approached from the boat deck and Chief Petty Officer Falconer appeared.

'What's all the noise about then, Clarke?' he asked, peering up at the quayside. 'Oh, I see,' he said. 'Our bloody waifs and strays. Where've you been?'

'In hospital,' Higgins said.

'What, the pair of you?'

Reid nodded. 'Yeah. The Corporation were

clearing some ruins next door to the pub and a bomb went off. Big 'un too. Wiped out half the workers and took out our end of the pub. We'd only just ordered our bleedin' pints'

The Cox'n relented. 'Well don't just stand there, get yourselves down here.'

They hurried down the gangway and stepped on deck.

Falconer eyed them suspiciously. 'Can't see no injuries.'

Higgins delved in a pocket and produced a crumpled piece of paper. 'Suspected concussion. That's from the 'ospital doctor. They kept us in overnight, 'ad to be signed out so we did.'

The Cox'n glanced at the discharge note and passed it back. 'Hang onto that, you'll need it when you report to the First Lieutenant. Now get yourselves below.'

Higgins grinned. 'Aye aye, Cox'n,' he said and they both turned for the fo'c'sle.

Falconer had one more question. 'What was the pub?'

'The Prince of Wales,' Reid said. 'Right bloody mess it was.' He shook his head and then hurried after Higgins.

Falconer smiled to himself. He could put out a call and soon have that verified, but he didn't really doubt their story. There were a lot of similar incidents happening all over the country.

He left Clarke to continue his watch and went off to find the Officer-of-the-Day. Those two would be up before Number One, sharpish.

That same day, at precisely 13.00 hours, the last wires securing *Brackendale* to the iron bollards were hauled inboard and Thorburn gave the order for 'slow ahead together.' The screws began turning, contra-rotating from out to in, oily scum swirling astern. The ship gathered speed..., three..., four knots, moving gently to port in preparation for negotiating the harbour boom nets. The Union flag disappeared from the jack-staff and the White Ensign rose abaft the bridge, the visible sign of cutting all ties with the land.

A cruiser lay moored off the starboard bow and Thorburn checked that Armstrong stood ready with the saluting party. The pipe shrilled as they drew level with her quarterdeck, and from somewhere high on the cruiser's upperworks, the haunting notes of a bugle returned the compliment. By 13.20 hours they had cleared the eastern arm of the Solent and bade farewell to the Isle of Wight.

Thorburn took his seat in the bridge-chair and glanced at Martin. 'Put us on course for Le Havre, Pilot.'

'Aye aye, sir,' Martin said, and leaned to the pipe. 'Port five, steer one-six-five degrees.'

Thorburn looked at his watch. They were on their way, heading south-southeast and back to the beaches. The faint drone of high flying aircraft made him look up, glasses raised. A large formation of Lancaster bombers were heading south, and to the west American Mustangs swept round a flight of Liberators. Beyond them were B17's, the distinctive Flying Fortress, darkening the sky, and he could just make out what appeared to be Thunderbolts as their escort.

Lower down, at around one or two-thousand feet, Spitfires roared overhead, the throaty growl of Rolls Royce engines lingering in the air, and a tightly grouped squadron of Hurricanes powered past in their wake. He lowered the binoculars and leaned back in the chair. Crucially for the lookouts, all Allied aircraft bore black and white painted stripes to aid recognition. It saved Guns a lot of time in having to call 'disregard' every few minutes.

And now they were clear of land they began to encounter ships, a lot of ships, many pushing south, heavily laden with equipment for the Army. Destroyers fussed over their charges, and a sloop threaded her way through a disjointed line of what appeared to be ammunition carriers. Corvettes were in abundance, hurrying as best they could to shepherd the merchantmen into some semblance of order. Plenty of vessels steamed north on return journeys to their original ports of embarkation, and Thorburn watched a sea-going tug towing three damaged landing craft. It was all a constant reminder, if needed, that the battle for Normandy still raged on.

Armstrong came to stand by the chair. 'Bit busy, isn't it?'

Thorburn smiled at the understatement. He nodded. 'Getting to look a bit like a Cowes Regatta.'

The First Lieutenant chuckled and pushed his cap back. 'Piccadilly Circus comes to mind.'

Leading Seaman Allun Jones, lookout in the port wing, interrupted, binoculars raised. '*Warspite* at Red ninety, sir.'

Thorburn came to his feet and stepped across to the port-wing. At this range the battleship looked every inch the indestructible old lady she truly was. He lifted the binoculars and studied her silhouette, focussing on the formidable fifteen-inch guns.

Armstrong spoke quietly. 'They say she was the first to open fire on D-Day.'

'So I believe,' Thorburn said, glasses centred on the battleship's bridge. 'If I remember rightly she was launched and commissioned in time for the Battle of Jutland.'

'And since this one started, you can add Narvik, the Med, Sicily and Salerno. Years of service, major battles.'

Thorburn lowered his glasses and nodded. 'Let's hope we don't do anything to jeopardise her future career.'

'No, sir,' Armstrong said with a tight grin. 'Might find ourselves in a spot of bother.'

They watched her stately progress for a while longer, but with *Brackendale* pushing on they eventually lost visual contact and she receded astern.

At 15.25 hours, *Brackendale* began her final run in towards the war torn coast of Normandy. On the bridge Thorburn lowered his glasses and nodded to Martin.

'Slow ahead, Pilot.' He caught Armstrong's eye. 'Tell Asdic I want a full underwater search pattern, three-sixty degrees. And have the bridge repeater on.'

Studying the smoke strewn higher ground inland, Thorburn carefully scanned the coast from Le Havre off the port bow, and round to Arromanches on his right, surprised by the amount of activity visible. According to reports the Allied Army's progress south into German occupied territory had not been as straightforward as planned, and there'd been a significant increase in casualties.

Armstrong called from the port wing. 'Our minesweepers by the look of it, sir.'

Thorburn joined him and brought up his glasses. The five ships were deployed in line abreast and obviously in the process of sweeping. 'We'll station ourselves astern of that last ship,' he said, and turned to the compass platform. 'Port ten, Pilot. Put us five-hundred yards astern of their right flank.'

'Aye aye, sir,' Martin said.

'And watch our speed, conform to theirs. Unless I order otherwise, no more then eight knots.' He glanced at Clarke on the Aldis lamp. 'Make to *Hornsbill*, "Suggest I provide cover between you and the shore?" . . . Got that?'

'Yes, sir,' he said, and the lamp clattered under his well practised hand.

A flicker of light blinked in reply.

'*Hornsbill* signalling, sir. Reads, "Very welcome. Beware mines exploding in harmony." Message ends, sir.'

Thorburn grimaced at Armstrong and nodded to Clarke. 'Acknowledge.'

4 . . Gnat's Whisker

The remainder of the afternoon passed with the minesweepers following a strict pattern of patrol, west to east, turn towards the shore, and back from east to west. Each run brought them closer to Le Havre's shore guns, but not near enough to provoke a response. Later, daylight faded into twilight, before the darkness of night settled over the sea. Far inland orange and red pulses glowed bright and receded, the distant sound of explosions marking the battle's fluctuating fortunes. Thorburn paced the bridge, unable to relax.

Approaching midnight, warships that had established a protective cordon round the Mulberry Harbour let loose at enemy aircraft. The Germans weren't bombing, the night time sorties were all about dropping acoustic mines. From the pattern of anti-aircraft fire the planes were flying west to east. Every conceivable colour of tracer lit the night sky, and the occasional bright yellow flash indicated a direct hit.

But before coming in range of *Brackendale's* guns, the formation appeared to turn south and head inland. In ten minutes it was all over and a strained silence settled over the ship. Only the monotonous 'ping' of the Asdic bridge-repeater disturbed the quiet.

Minutes later, midnight came and went, and Sunday the 10th of September had arrived, the day the Combined Chiefs of Staff had earmarked for the assault on Le Havre.

At 02.15 hours Thorburn was sat in the bridge-chair when a radar operator came through on a voice-pipe.

'Radar -Bridge!'

Thorburn answered. 'Bridge.'

'Green four-oh. Five echoes! Course three-five-oh, fast moving. Range eleven-thousand.'

Thorburn came to his feet. 'Gun crews close up.' The order was instinctive, but almost unnecessary, they'd been at Action Stations since before dusk. He checked *Brackendale's* bearing . . . , holding steady and tracking slowly east parallel with the shore. He leaned to a pipe.

'Guns?'

'Sir.'

'Ready with starshell.'

'One in each turret.'

'Good. Wait for the word.'

'Aye aye, sir.'

'Radar-Bridge! Range eight-thousand.'

'Very well.' He peered round the darkness of the bridge. Subtle shadows moved where lookouts watched their sectors, and the signalman stood poised at his lamp, fractionally darker than the background sky. Martin was bent over the chart table, the dimmed light affixed to the bulkhead glowing orange against his jaw.

'Range ..., seven-thousand.'

'Very well.'

They waited, the ship seeming to hold her breath.

'Guns-Bridge?'

'Captain.'

'I have five E-boats at Green four-five, six thousand.'

Thorburn took a breath. 'Fire starshell!'

The fo'c'sle guns inched to starboard, and then one barrel lifted to blast a shell skywards. Moments later the flash of an incandescent white light hung in the night air. A second went up from the quarterdeck, burst beyond the first and swayed in the breeze.

And there in the distance, with nowhere to hide, were the enemy boats.

'Open fire!' he called, and *Brackendale's* guns

crashed out an opening salvo. The blast from the muzzles beneath the bridge made him wince, momentarily numbing the senses. He bent to the wheelhouse pipe, voice raised above the din.

'Revs for ten knots, Cox'n.'

'Ten knots, aye aye, sir.' And the small destroyer gathered speed, holding an oblique angle to the enemy boats.

Thorburn watched them closing in from off the starboard bow, wishing he was able to apply more speed, but heeding the stark warning of mines. *Brackendale's* shells were in amongst the enemy now, columns of spray marking near misses, but still they came on.

On the multi-barrelled pom-pom, Taff Williams found the leading E-boat and hit the trigger. The guns hammered into action, the four synchronised barrels pumping shells across the void. Tracer swept the sea, vivid red, green and orange. Enemy tracer deceptively lazy at distance, but whipping in with a hissing whine. He held focus, leading the boat, watching his tracer converge on target. He made three or four hits before the boat jinked sideways to dodge the blows. He swore, but the sights landed on the next boat, and he fired again, his body jarring to the beat.

Oerlikons and machine-guns joined the fight, thumping rounds at the fast moving flotilla. And the main armament roared on, spitting flame, each gun capable of twenty 4-inch shells a minute.

Thorburn saw an E-boat turn aside at speed and circle out towards *Brackendale*'s stern. He turned to shout at the pom-pom but the gunners had already seen it, bracketing the boat with tracer. He trained his binoculars abeam, picking out individual E-boats, all of them now sparkling with gunfire. The range had decreased rapidly, only a matter of time before they launched torpedoes. He wasn't about to wait for the inevitable.

'Hard-a-starboard!'

In the wheelhouse below Thorburn's feet, the Cox'n acknowledged, 'Hard-a-starboard, aye, sir!' and spun the spokes clockwise. The rudder followed suit, biting at the waters, and *Brackendale* swung to face the enemy. As she came south towards the French coast, bow on to the danger, Thorburn again bent to the pipe. 'Midships . . . , steady.'

Jones called, urgent. 'Two torpedoes, sir!'

Thorburn peered ahead and raised his glasses. 'I see them.' They were tracking to port, wide of the mark, fired in haste.

A stream of tracer lashed the bridge, bullets rattling, ricocheting off steel panels. Below the port bridge-wing, the Oerlikon banged into action, the first time the gunner had seen the enemy.

An explosion of orange-yellow light caught Thorburn's right eye, and a triumphant shout went up from the pom-pom crew. The flanking E-boat attacking the stern had all but disintegrated.

'Bloody marvellous,' he said under his breath, but kept focus ahead.

Abruptly, the four E-boats peeled apart, two to the left, two right, going wide. It left him facing a pincer movement, not clever. Then the fo'c'sle guns traversed to starboard; McDonald had made the decision to engage the right hand pair, the bigger threat. Those two had not yet fired torpedoes. That left Thorburn with the two off the portside, one of which had already launched.

He lunged for the port wing and yelled to the pom-pom. 'E-boats! Port side,' and pointed with an outstretched arm. A figure turned his face to the bridge, vaguely seen in the darkness, then looked out to sea, and waved his understanding. The mounting swung round, steadied across the port beam, and banged into action. Scarlet tracer lit the air.

Thorburn sprang back to the compass platform and gripped the housing, squinting through acrid smoke, teeth bared. *Brackendale* was threading the eye of a needle and he couldn't risk more speed.

'Christ all bloody mighty,' he mouthed, aware he was almost out of options. Green tracer snaked towards the bridge, and then in that moment he found an answer. To hell with orders.

When the E-boats next fired torpedoes he would ignore the ten knot limit and accelerate hard, risk the acoustic mines. More tracer speared in from port, and the constant bellow of the fo'c'sle guns made him clench his teeth. A starshell burst overhead, not from *Brackendale*, her guns were fully engaged. He glanced astern. It was one of the minesweepers, and he caught the moment she fired a second. It too burst bright, drifting slowly, casting flickering patterns across the sea.

'Torpedoes, port seventy!' yelled a lookout.

Thorburn reacted. 'Full ahead both!'

Falconer acknowledged and the wheelhouse telegraph rang.

Below the waterline, Bryn Dawkins, blind to the battle going on outside, saw the sweep hand swing round to 'full ahead', and obeyed the call. The twin propellers answered the increase in power, and *Brackendale* surged ahead.

'Torpedoes closing, sir!'

Thorburn nodded with grim determination. He'd made his move and urged the ship on to maximum speed. Those skippers would not have foreseen that in their calculations. A glance to port. The E-boats had already turned away, careering across the waves, skipping and bouncing as they desperately fought to escape. In the light of the swaying starshell, tell-tale tracks could be seen converging on the port beam. He tried gauging the exact distance between torpedoes and stern. Only seconds in it either way.

Lieutenant George Labatt had his eyes glued to the twin streaks racing in towards the quarterdeck. The after gun mount roared, thumping a pair of shells over the opposite side, deafening in such close proximity. *Brackendale's* seething wake boiled out from beneath the stern rail, foaming and curling with the power of the screws. Instinct told him to move away from the impact, but he held his nerve, knowing the crew looked to him for resolve.

Behind him Higgins said, 'This'll be close.'

Labatt breathed in, clenched his teeth, accepting the observation. The deck trembled to the power of the engines and he willed her on. The bubbling twin wakes arrowed in, touch and go. Six-hundred yards . . . , five-hundred, sliding away, might catch the stern. He watched, mesmerised, and then the ugly tubes swept past, inches to spare.

'Sod that for a lark,' Higgins said with feeling, and Labatt nodded. 'One way of putting it,' he said, and turned for the bulkhead voice-pipe.

'Quarterdeck-Bridge?'

'Captain.'

'Torpedoes missed astern, sir,' he said with all the control he could muster.

'Close was it?'

Labatt grimaced. 'Gnat's whisker, sir.'

'Thought as much. Watch out to starboard, there are two more attacking.'

'Aye aye, sir,' he said, and rubbed his forehead. The 4-inch guns belched smoke, another pair of shells whipping away, and he turned to look. The E-boats were small dancing targets, surrounded by splashes. If 'Guns' didn't get them soon, he thought, we'll all be trying to dodge more torpedoes.

On the bridge, Thorburn ducked under a hail of bullets. A green tracer ricocheted and dropped between his feet, fizzing brightly. Then amidst the mayhem an excited shout.

'E-boat destroyed, sir!'

It came from Able Seaman Cockroft, lookout in the starboard wing.

Thorburn snatched a glance beyond him and caught sight of disintegrating wreckage. It spiralled through the air before splashing into the water.

'Nice work,' he said aloud, and then saw the last E-boat turn to attack. A storm of shells latched onto the fast target, *Brackendale's* gunfire reaching a crescendo. Surely it must succumb?

And so it proved. Struck by a series of shells, the boat lost power, bow wave dying. Tracer hammered the hull, lashing the foredeck, slamming at the cockpit. A ball of fire erupted from the afterdeck and the E-boat swung round and stopped, low in the water. Its guns lay silent, a body draped over the mounting.

'Cease fire!' he called, and then to the wheelhouse pipe, 'Port twenty, slow ahead, five knots.'

Falconer's answer echoed from the brass cup. 'Port twenty, revolutions for five knots. Aye aye, sir.'

The ship's speed fell away. Thorburn shuddered, an involuntary reaction. His decision to risk the mines had paid off, more by luck than judgement. And somehow, the heavy gunfire had also not triggered a single mine. A moment later the last remaining starshell blinked out and darkness returned. Other than the repetitive ping of the Asdic, silence descended over the ship.

The muffled gasps of a wounded man broke the spell.

Armstrong called out. 'Get this man to sick bay.'

Thorburn interjected. 'Damage report, Number One.'

'Aye aye, sir,' Armstrong confirmed and moved off to the port ladder.

Thorburn again leaned to the wheelhouse pipe. 'Midships . . . , steer oh-one-oh degrees.'

'Wheel's amidships. Bearing oh-one-oh degrees, sir.'

'Very well.'

The metallic rattle of brass shell-cases came from the fo'c'sle gun mounting, the crew clearing them over the side. The Lewis machine-gunners on the bridge followed suit.

Thorburn ignored it all and raised his binoculars. A brief check of the dark seas on the port bow pinpointed the minesweepers, and he counted all five pushing east in good order. There was relief in knowing they were unharmed. But the inevitable question now was, what would the Germans try next? The ship had been at Action Stations since before dusk, and add to that a short but ferocious battle, and the men would be flagging. He heard footsteps and looked round to find Armstrong.

'Three casualties, sir, Doc said they'll be okay. Chief and I had a quick walk round. Looks as if we've only got minor damage. We'll know better with daylight.'

'Good,' Thorburn said. 'I think we ought to see if we can get some hot drinks on the go. And some sandwiches wouldn't go amiss. Long time till breakfast.'

'I'll see to it now, sir.'

'Radar-Bridge.'

'Captain.'

'Strong echo bearing three-four-five. Range nine miles, sir.'

Thorburn glanced north in the darkness. That would be *Warspite* on her approach. 'Very well,' he said, and sank back in the chair. 'Time?' he asked.

'Oh-three-ten hours, sir,' Martin answered.

'Thank you, Pilot.'

A short while later there was movement at the back of the bridge and two seamen came forward with mugs of tea, and a heap of sandwiches.

'Radar-Bridge?'

'Bridge.'

'Second echo, bearing three-six-oh, range nine-miles.'

'Very well,' Thorburn said. That would be *Erebus*, the old monitor ready to play her part in the bombardment.

'Sir?'

He looked round, accepted a scalding mug of tea, and then selected a thick cut, bully beef sandwich with the other hand. He took a bite and chewed. A sip of the heavily sugared tea followed, warming as it went down. Another bite. Simple fare, he thought, but very welcome nonetheless.

'*Hornsbill* approaching, sir.'

Thorburn took another chunk out of the sandwich and wedged his mug precariously against a pipe bracket. He moved to the port wing and watched the sweeper closing on *Brackendale's* stern quarter.

'Mister Martin,' he said, heavy emphasis on each syllable. 'Let the wheelhouse know we've a ship coming alongside. Need to keep her steady.'

'Aye aye, sir,' Martin said, and could be heard passing on the instruction.

With deliberate care, *Hornsbill* edged forward until Thorburn felt he could almost reach across to the minesweepers bridge. He heard the telegraph ring from inside her wheelhouse and moments later the two ships were matched for speed. In the darkness he thought he detected a figure move to the adjacent bridge-wing.

'Hello, *Brackendale*!' came a shout.

Thorburn swallowed a last bit of sandwich and called across.

'At your service. Everything alright?'

'Yes, thanks to you. Nice shooting.'

'We aim to please,' Thorburn answered. 'How can we help?'

The voice from *Hornsbill* grew stronger. '*Warspite* and *Erebus* will be towed forward into the area we've just cleared. That's to reduce any chance of them setting off undetected mines. Our orders are to sweep two more corridors to within twelve miles of Le Havre.'

Thorburn frowned. That could put them all within range of shore guns. He called again.

'Might I suggest we cover you with smoke, if required?'

'That would be most welcome. I would advise you to remain astern of our sweeps until action is needed.'

Thorburn deliberately laughed aloud. 'I won't need telling twice. Good luck.'

'And you. Au revoir.' The shadowy figure withdrew from the bridge-wing and *Hornsbill* swung away, heading north to rejoin the flotilla.

'Pilot?'

'Sir?'

'Put us four-hundred yards astern of tail-end-charlie.'

'Aye aye, sir.'

Thorburn went back to his chair and eased the mug from its temporary home. The sweet tea still had some warmth and he drained it. A thought struck him.

'Number One.'

'Sir?'

'Has radar reported anything wrong with the set?'

'Not that I'm aware of . . . , no sir.' It was a straightforward answer, but the query in his voice was unmistakable.

Thorburn elaborated. '*Warspite* and *Erebus*. Radar didn't notify us until they were nine miles out. It's perfect weather for reception. I would have thought contact would have been made at more like eleven miles.'

'I'll check, sir.'

'Yes . . . , do that. And let me know.'

Armstrong headed for the ladder.

Thorburn sat and listened to Lieutenant Martin coaxing *Brackendale* round to take station well astern of the flotilla.

It would be a while till dawn.

5 . . Plans Afoot

At the German port of Bremerhaven, with darkness not yet transformed into day, Admiral Mathias Krause stepped aboard Richter's destroyer and gave orders to get under way. Driven clouds marked their departure, and strong winds whipped the sea into flying foam. Two minesweepers cleared the channel beyond the harbour, making hard work of the weather, and Richter's destroyer followed at a safe interval astern.

Krause remained on the bridge, and rough though it was, welcomed the sensation of being back at sea. It had been three years since he'd last felt the power of the waves. And the prevailing conditions were nigh on perfect, with gale force winds predicted during the next twenty-four hours. No Allied aircraft would be flying in this weather, and the chances of being spotted by a submarine were negligible. Kristiansand on Norway's southern shores would be their first port of call; after that, push on north of Bergen towards Trondheim and the crippled *Tirpitz*. But it would be to the fjords a hundred kilometres south of *Tirpitz* that Krause was headed, where the *Aldenburg* had remained hidden for all these months. That is where Krause intended to make his presence felt.

He stayed on, smoked a cigar and accepted a coffee before retiring to Richter's cabin. Soon, he thought, as he stretched out on the bunk, soon he would take command of the *Aldenburg*. He closed his eyes, and even though the destroyer banged and twisted through pounding seas, Admiral Mathias Krause fell into a dreamless sleep.

For Richard Thorburn the remainder of the night passed in relative calm, only the distant sound of onshore gunfire making its mark, accompanied by intermittent ruddy glows pulsing inland. There was no reaction from the shore guns, not even when the minesweepers had closed to within the twelve mile limit. And the tedious sound of the Asdic gave no hint of enemy submarines.

With the coming of pre-dawn, the sweepers were ordered to withdraw from operations and Thorburn brought *Brackendale* northwest in their wake. As the sun rose he heard the sound of heavy aircraft engines, and then watched as sixty plus Royal Air Force bombers pummelled the eastern fortifications.

At 06.40 hours, *Warspite* and *Erebus* opened fire, each of their 15-inch guns blasting a 2000 lb shell at the casemated German weapons on the perimeter defences, a part of Hitler's so called 'Atlantic Wall'.

Thorburn focussed his glasses on the cliff top to the east, where the ground heaved to the colossal weight of explosives. Lurid orange-red detonations erupted in giant mushrooms of dense smoke, and he found himself almost feeling sorry for those on the receiving end. Almost, but not quite. If, he thought, all this saved Allied lives, then enemy losses under such a punishing bombardment was a thing to be celebrated, not something to agonise over.

The naval salvos continued, on and off, for almost two hours. Thorburn held the ship at 'Defence Stations', which kept half the crew on high alert, but allowed the other half to eat a much needed breakfast and get what rest they could under the noise of the big guns. When the 15-inch broadsides eventually ceased, the sound of field artillery could be heard supporting the ground attack. Lieutenant Armstrong took the opportunity to use the daylight and make another inspection of the ship. As he'd previously reported the only damage sustained was that of small arms fire.

The clatter of the Aldis lamp made Thorburn look round.

'*Warspite* signalling, sir.'

Thorburn moved to the port wing and waited for more. The big lamp on *Warspite's* compass platform flashed again, a rhythmic blink of light.

'Message reads, "All ships to hold station." End of message, sir.'

'Very well, acknowledge,' he ordered, and turned to Armstrong who was stood at the forescreen. 'We're not finished yet by the seem of it.'

'No. Maybe they're waiting for more targets?'

'Quite possibly,' Thorburn said, 'but I'm not sure there'll be much left to hit.'

'Not nice if you were caught in that lot,' Armstrong said thoughtfully, and they settled into an amicable silence.

Not for the first time, they stood together at *Brackendale's* screen and watched a battle unfold.

At the far northernmost extremity of the British Isles, in Scotland's Royal Navy "Orkneys and Shetlands Command", Rear-Admiral Lawrence T. Collingwood, R.N., D.S.O., D.S.C., stood in his office and stared hard at an oversized Admiralty chart. His lean, angular face gave the appearance of a thinker, and the prominently hooked, eagle-like nose gave emphasis to his searching gaze. Piercing blue eyes surveyed the chart.

Rain rattled the windows, a gust of wind driving in across the waters of Scapa Flow. He ignored the squall and concentrated on the wall chart hanging opposite his desk. His thoughtful study roamed over the fine detail of Norway's jagged coastline and he rubbed a finger down the bump on his nose. Collingwood shook his head. It was a vague, subconscious gesture, an outward reflection of inner turmoil. He reached for his burr walnut pipe and tapped the stem against his teeth. Right now he thought, at this point in the war, that coastline and its surrounding waters was a problem he could do without. An order had arrived from the Admiralty instructing him to provide an offensive patrol between Iceland and Norway, primarily aimed at circumventing any attempts by German forces to intercept the next Russian bound convoy.

He tamped down the bowl of tobacco, struck

a match and drew smoke, wondering how best to resolve this latest predicament. His problem lay with Churchill's order to continue the Russian runs. The ships at his disposal had been depleted by the need to add additional escorts to those convoys. The question now was how to bolster his meagre reserves? That was the issue. A thought struck him, and he conjured up a long forgotten incident that had made a lasting impression at the time. He stood for a while longer, pondering the alternatives, and then turned to reach for the telephone.

A Wren answered from the main switchboard. 'Sir?'

'Put me through to Portsmouth, Commodore Pendleton. He'll be in Semaphore Tower.'

'Yes, sir,' she said, and silence ensued as she sought to connect.

Collingwood dropped the handset on its cradle and paced the room. Patience, he knew, was vital when dealing with the intricacies of wartime communications.

And it was a full five minutes before there was a response. 'Commodore Pendleton for you, sir.'

'James,' Collingwood growled into the mouthpiece. 'How the devil are you?'

'Busy.'

'Never doubted it. Sorry to take up your time but I need some help.'

'If I can,' said Pendleton, and Collingwood thought he recognised a hint of reluctance in the abrupt reply.

'You used to have a chap by the name of Thorburn, bit of a maverick. Any idea of his whereabouts?'

There was a short pause before Pendleton answered. 'He's off the coast of Le Havre. He's on escort duty with *Warspite's* minesweeping Flotilla.'

'Is he, by God? So he's actually on patrol at this moment?'

'Yes, and will probably take part in an attack on the harbour if the army make a breakthrough.'

Collingwood stared at the wall chart. 'Are there expected to be any problems?'

'Well we hope not. But I've already had reports of minor damage after a skirmish with E-boats overnight.'

'Ahh . . . ,' Collingwood said, 'but no reason to suppose there'll be anything untoward?'

'No,' Pendleton said, 'they were just waiting for daylight to do a thorough assessment.'

The Admiral cleared his throat. 'Well, I have to over-rule on this one. I need *Brackendale* as part of a new flotilla.'

'I see,' came the slow reply. 'No options then?'

'Afraid not, orders from on high.'

A prolonged pause followed before he heard a disgruntled Pendleton say, 'I thought we had enough ships up your end?'

Collingwood managed a dry chuckle. 'No, not

true. And even if it were, it's not the big bloody battleships I need, or even flag waving cruisers. I'm simply short of ships. Offensive patrols have to cover a lot of ocean so I want frigates, destroyers, and even sloops at a push. But more than that, James, I also want men who'll use their intuition, who can smell the enemy.'

There was a brief silence before Pendleton sighed. 'In that case I'll tell him myself. *Brackendale* could be ready to sail tomorrow, at first light. Will he report to you?'

'Yes, he will. Sorry to spring this on you but it is rather important.'

'Understood,' Pendleton said, 'but I'll have to detach another destroyer to fill the gap. The way things currently stand, that won't be straightforward, but I'll see what I can do.'

'Very well,' Collingwood said. 'Thank you, James . . . . Goodbye,' and he gently replaced the receiver. He leaned back in the chair and rubbed his jaw. A small piece of the jigsaw had just slotted into place.

First Officer Jennifer Farbrace, on hearing the conversation come to an end, surreptitiously replaced the receiver in its cradle. A worried frown furrowed her normally unblemished brow. Scapa Flow might also involve the Russian Convoys. But she had a friend up there in the main communications centre. Jennifer could always find out more later on.

Commodore James Pendleton shoved back his chair and came to his feet. He stalked over to the window and planted his hands squarely behind his back. Why, he wondered in annoyance, did Collingwood have to stick his oar in right now? Thorburn had resumed command no more than seventy-two hours ago, returned to the fold one might say, and Pendleton felt more than a little aggrieved at having his most experienced and trustworthy Lieutenant-Commander whisked away from under his feet.

He strode back to his desk and lit a cigarette. Like it or not, he'd never disobeyed an order and wasn't about to start now. A signal would have to be sent.

'Miss Farbrace!' he snapped to the outer office.

Jennifer appeared, notebook in hand. 'Sir?'

'I need to send a signal, take this down. To *Brackendale*. "Immediate. Return to base," and I want her oiled and re-ammunitioned on arrival. We'd better warn the yard.'

'Yes, sir,' she said, pen hovering above the pad. She raised an eyebrow in query.

'What?' Pendleton demanded, still having not regained his composure.

'Should her captain report to you?'

He hesitated, knowing full well he was out of order. Remorsefully, he offered her an apologetic smile and nodded.

'Of course, sorry ..., yes. Get Richard to attend

my office, soonest.'

'I'll see to it myself, sir,' she beamed, and slipped out of the door.

One-hundred and fifty sea miles west of Scapa Flow, at a place called Loch Ewe in the Northwest Highlands, eighteen fully laden merchantmen began making preparations for the dangerous passage to Murmansk. The sea loch covered an area almost eight miles in length and three miles in width. In the middle of the loch sat a small island, the Isle of Ewe, and it was to the southwest of that strip of land that the merchant captains assembled their vessels. Two of the ships were tankers transporting a total of 12,400 gallons of aviation spirit, and no-one begrudged their crews the enhanced extra pay received for such hazardous duty. The remaining vessels carried 69,321 tons of mixed cargo, consisting primarily of emergency supplies of food, medicines and ammunition to support Russians troops in their efforts to conquer the fast retreating German army.

To the north of the little island, Captain John Hennessey, R.N., D.S.C., in the destroyer H.M.S. *Scitalis*, had been given the task of shepherding those ships almost two-thousand seven-hundred miles to the precarious sanctuary of Kola Inlet. He was thirty-two years of age, fair hair cut short, ruddy complexion, and built like a scrum half. It would be his fifth Arctic convoy of the last twenty months and the last convoy of '44 to take the 'Summer Route', before the ice field encroached east of Greenland, and spread south from Spitzbergen. The longer route by far, but John Hennessey was thankful the 'Winter Route' had not yet come into play. For the best part of a 'winter' voyage, convoys travelled well within the range of the Norwegian based Luftwaffe.

In the seclusion of his cabin, Hennessey read through his orders and again checked sailing times and points of rendezvous. He took particular note of the schedule for the Convoy Conference, what personnel would be in attendance, and which of the skippers would be allocated to lead the columns. He made a few notes in preparation for his briefing and tucked them into his briefcase. Having dispensed with the paperwork, he reached for his cap and went out on deck. Around the bay, five other convoy escorts were preparing for sea, and he let his gaze linger on each in turn.

The nearest, a cable's length astern, lay H.M.S. *Standing*, and beyond her *Salient*, both of which carried four, 4.7inch quick firing guns mounted in individual shields, two forward and two aft. A little to the south H.M.S. *Transient* swung to her mooring, and then came the American 'Fletcher' class destroyer, the *Franklin George*. Lastly, and somewhat at odds with the sleek naval designs of the warships, the seagoing tug, *Bulger,* would hold station as a vital aid to those who might need her services.

Hennessey grunted to himself and turned to make his way forward to the bridge. It wouldn't be long before all twenty-four vessels ventured out to sea and began the long and dangerous passage to the Russian port.

In conjunction with the convoy's preparations, the Town class cruiser, H.M.S. *Stirling*, armed with twelve 6-inch guns, triple mounted in four turrets, lay at anchor on the southwest coast of Iceland. She was under the command of Captain Charles Taylor-Mitchell, R.N., D.S.O., D.S.C., a congenial, cheerfully ebullient man, whose relaxed style of command sat well with both officers and ratings alike. No stranger to the 'Russia' runs, Taylor-Mitchell and the Ship's Company formed a tough and experienced unit.

Two days before the convoy was due to weigh anchor, *Stirling* had arrived at Reykjavik in preparation to become an outlying roving escort. As the ships of the convoy passed by on their northerly track the cruiser would join up and remain with the merchantmen for the duration of the voyage.

6 .. Recall

Richard Thorburn stood up from the bridge chair and turned to Armstrong. 'Time for a quick wash and shave. You have the bridge.'

The First Lieutenant nodded and ran a hand over his chin. He obviously had similar thoughts. 'Aye aye, sir.'

'Keep a sharp eye on *Warspite*, you never know what might come next.' Thorburn warned, and made his way down to the cabin.

His reflection in the mirror didn't sit well. Tired eyes, more than a day's stubble on his jaw, and the scar on his temple still inflamed. He ran hot water into the basin and immersed his face. The heat did its job, soothing his salt encrusted skin. He towelled off, vigorously, except the area round his wound. Then he chose a fresh blade for the razor, lathered well, and gave himself a close, smooth shave. He rinsed and dried, and studied the final result. Much better, he thought, and indeed he felt better. A fresh shirt, a comb through his unruly hair, and he smiled. New man. He slipped an arm into his jacket, then looked round to a knock on the door.

'Come.'

Surgeon-Lieutenant 'Doc' Waverley, the slightly plump, red-faced, but trustworthy 'gentleman', entered and held out a message slip. 'I've just decoded this.'

Thorburn finished buttoning his jacket. Decoding signals was one of the Doctor's other duties, willingly performed, casualties permitting.

He took the slip, read it and met the surgeon's eyes. 'Immediate recall,' he said, 'something's brewing.'

Waverley nodded. 'My thoughts exactly.'

'Right then, thanks Doc. I'd better get back to the bridge.'

'How's the head, sir?'

Thorburn picked up his cap and placed it squarely on his head, ignoring the pain as the band tightened over his gashed temple.

He forced a relaxed smile. 'The head? . . . , just fine Doc, never give it a thought.'

'Glad to hear it,' the Doctor said, although his expression showed a hint of disbelief. 'Looks a bit raw. I probably have something for that if you need it.'

'Yes, Doc,' Thorburn grinned, checking for cigarettes, 'I don't doubt it. One of your secret potions mixed together in the dead of night.'

Waverley pulled a face and shook his head, arching a raised eyebrow. 'Far be it for me to indulge in such quackery,' he chuckled. 'I do it in daylight, in plain view.' And with that he spun on his heel and left.

As soon as he'd gone, Thorburn eased the cap back, just enough, and then made his way out to the starboard ladder. Arriving on the bridge, he strode forward to where Armstrong leaned over the chart table.

'I have the bridge, Number One. I suggest you clean up, we're going back to Portsmouth.'

The First Lieutenant looked at him in surprise. 'Now sir?'

'Yes, a signal from Pendleton. Immediate.'

'Right, sir. There's nothing to report, we're holding station as ordered. I'll get below.'

Thorburn moved to the compass platform. The ship was barely moving, a couple of knots, enough for steerage. He bent to the voice-pipe. 'Port twenty.'

'Port twenty, aye, sir.'

'Speed eight knots.'

'Revolutions for eight knots, aye aye, sir.'

Brackendale peeled out from the flotilla, turning slowly to the north.

'Steer three-five-five degrees.'

'Three-five-five, sir.'

'Very well,' he said, and motioned to the signaller. 'Make to *Prince of Wales*, "Fresh orders, returning to base." Send it.'

The lamp clattered and Thorburn turned back to the compass. He stayed with it as *Brackendale* pushed past the most northerly area of danger from acoustic mines. The Channel here was too deep for them to be effective. He moved to the port wing and raised his binoculars at the French shoreline. As far as he could see through the lens, dirty columns of smoke spiralled into the air. The field of battle was wide and all encompassing, and it looked to be a grim business. The thought struck him that it looked to be anything other than, 'over by Christmas.'

'*Prince of Wales* acknowledges, sir.'

'Very well,' Thorburn said, and ordered an increase of speed to fourteen knots. He then issued instructions for the Asdic team to confine their search from dead ahead to Green nine-oh. The possibility of U-boats off their port side was minimal, there were simply too many Allied warships on the lookout to the west.

Armstrong reappeared and gave a boyish grin. 'That's better,' he said, rubbing his clean shaven chin.

Thorburn frowned, leaning towards him for a closer inspection. 'Mmm..., I suppose it'll have to do,' and he grinned. 'Blunt razor probably, it happens when there's a war on.'

The First Lieutenant gave a petulant, exaggerated lift of his chin, and looked away. 'It was one of Gillette's finest, and the ladies have never complained.'

Thorburn laughed, and then felt the ship twist to a long swell coming in from off the port beam. She heeled to starboard, hanging over, bows dipping in the trough, and then swayed back to an even keel before lurching to port. It would make for an uncomfortable passage for those in the confines of the lower decks. He looked over to the chart table.

'How long, Pilot?'

Martin glanced round from his calculations. 'If we hold at fourteen knots, sir..., about five hours.'

Thorburn went over the signal in his mind. It had been prescribed 'immediate', but not 'with all despatch'. Economical cruising speed would suffice.

'Very well, I suggest you might want to clean up, get some rest.'

Martin looked crestfallen. 'I'm alright, sir. I still need to plot the latest shipwreck positions.'

Thorburn gave him a raised eyebrow. 'I think,' he said pointedly, 'your Captain has enough experience to manage our return to the Solent. I'll make sure you're on the bridge before entering harbour.'

Martin hesitated, looked down at his chart, and reluctantly laid his pencil against the ledge. 'Right, sir, I'll . . . , I'll get below.'

'Yes,' Thorburn said, and trained his binoculars beyond the bows. Two veteran 'V and W' destroyers were crossing *Brackendale's* path from east to west. They were at extreme range, making a good thirty knots judging by the bow wave. He lost interest, checked the sea off the starboard beam, nothing to see. He lowered the glasses and peered briefly at the compass. Three-five-five degrees. More than adequate for the time being. He moved forward to the bridge-screen and wondered what Pendleton had in store for them? A trip to the Med would be nice.

Brackendale pushed on into a spell of bright sunshine. Armstrong took over the compass platform, and Thorburn took his seat in the chair. He estimated their arrival as early afternoon, enough time left in the day for a thorough inspection of the ship. He eased his cap again and raised his face to the sun. There were times, he thought, when a man had to enjoy the simple things in life.

At 14.15 hours, Thorburn stood at the screen and watched the last of the wires being tightened and made fast. On the fo'c'sle, Armstrong turned and shouted.

'All secured for'ard!'

Thorburn crossed to the starboard wing and looked aft. Labatt was pointing at an uncoiled length of cable and urging a seaman to stow it properly. A fender was hastily repositioned, and then all became still. Labatt turned and waved to signal the bridge all was in order.

Lieutenant Martin, having piloted the ship to her designated berth, had been waiting impatiently for that last instruction.

'All secured fore and aft, sir.'

Thorburn stepped back to the centre of the bridge-screen. 'Very well, ring off main engines.'

For a moment he dwelt on the signal received as they entered the Solent. It had ordered *Brackendale* to a refuelling rig and requested state of ammunition. Food, water, and basic provisions to be topped up. It all sounded urgent.

A movement on the quayside caught his attention, a staff car threading its way through the numerous piles of stacked crates and boxes. It came to a halt ten feet short of the bow. The passenger door opened and out stepped First Officer

Jennifer Farbrace.

She looked up and Thorburn, surprised by her appearance on the dock, raised a hand in greeting, then made for the quarterdeck where a gangway was in the process of being settled into place. He met her as she drew level with the break in the fo'c'sle. They exchanged salutes, and he smiled.

'What brings you down to the sharp end?'

She turned to fall in step. 'Orders,' she said. 'Pendleton wants to see you.'

'Does he now?' He grinned. 'I'm honoured. Know what it's all about?'

'Vaguely,' she said, 'but I think you should wait and get it from the horses mouth.'

They reached the bonnet of the staff car.

'Should I change first?' he asked.

Jennifer shook her head. 'Not enough time.' She laughed and gestured at the car. 'Just for you, he's waiting.'

The driver opened a rear door and Thorburn waved her in. He slipped round the boot and squeezed himself onto the back seat. The driver found a gear and the car moved off, bumping along the pitted access road and out towards the red brick administration buildings. Her small hand found his on the leather seat and he met her eyes. It was enough, her lovely face shone with contentment.

The driver pulled up outside the entrance to Semaphore Tower and minutes later Jennifer opened the door to her office. She walked through, knocked on the inner door and looked in.

Thorburn heard her say, 'He's here now.'

Pendleton's voice barked from within. 'Then send him in . . . , send him in!'

She backed away and inclined her head at the door. 'All yours.'

He grinned, whipped his cap off and dropped it on her desk. Stepping closer he whispered, 'Sounds like I'm about to be clapped in irons.' He strode inside and came to attention.

'About time too,' Pendleton snapped, tapping on his desk. 'What took so long?' he demanded.

Thorburn frowned, slightly taken aback. 'I wasn't aware of it being that urgent, sir.'

'Well it was . . . , is. I have priority orders for you.'

Thorburn didn't know what to say for the best so remained silent.

'Mmm . . . ,' Pendleton mouthed. 'Well, not to worry.' His eyes drifted round the office in silence. He rubbed his nose.

'I'm sorry to say we'll be losing you, Richard.'

Thorburn felt his heart sink.

'Our loss,' Pendleton said, 'Rear-Admiral Collingwood's gain.'

Thorburn frowned, not sure he understood.

'Sir?'

Pendleton leaned forward. 'Collingwood, Richard, remember him? Got himself promoted, he's up at Scapa Flow.'

Thorburn gazed at Pendleton, his mind turning back to the summer of '42. It had been 'Commodore' Collingwood then, the man who'd sent him across the Channel to engage a raider. After the battle Collingwood had congratulated him, and then before departing had said, 'I might call on you again.' Thorburn hadn't set much store by it.

'What does he want?'

Pendleton chuckled and slapped his desk.

'You, Richard,' he said, grinning.

'And *Brackendale*, sir?'

'Of course, m'boy, that's the whole idea.'

Thorburn blinked, thinking through what had been said. 'But I thought Scapa had more than enough destroyers.'

'Don't believe all you hear,' Pendleton said. 'Either way, you'll soon know. You leave in the morning.'

Pendleton came out from behind the desk and Thorburn realised the meeting was over. He stood and accepted the Commodore's handshake.

'Good luck, Richard. I wish you well.'

'Thank you, sir,' Thorburn said, and for a moment he met Pendleton's searching gaze. This gruff old sailor had been instrumental in forging Thorburn's career, putting his own judgement on the line. When others had voiced grave doubts about the abilities of, at that time, such a newly promoted officer, Pendleton had been the one to stand against the general consensus. 'I've not forgotten you argued my case with the Admiralty. I'm indebted.'

Pendleton cleared his throat. 'Nonsense, Commander. Now I'm sure you have a ship to tend to.'

Thorburn realised he'd been dismissed and inclined his head. 'Aye aye, sir,' he said and turned for the door.

Behind him the deep baritone voice said, 'And do try to keep that bloody ship of yours in one piece.'

Thorburn glanced over his shoulder with a broad smile. It was a long standing joke between them, the first bit of advice Pendleton had ever given him.

'Of course, sir, I always do,' he said, and gently closed the door.

Jennifer confronted him with worried eyes. 'When are you sailing, Richard?'

'Tomorrow,' he said. 'I'll be aboard in an hour. Do you know what it's all about?'

She shook her head, white teeth nibbling her bottom lip. 'No ..., but I know it's Scapa and that might be convoy duty.'

'Ahh,' Thorburn murmured, 'the Arctic run, interesting.' He met her eyes and she came forward, standing close. The familiar fragrance of her gentle perfume filled the air, a subtle aroma that reminded him of more intimate moments. He lifted her chin and forced a grin. 'Stop worrying, they say the war'll be over by Christmas.'

Jennifer pouted. 'Talk's cheap and you know it. And somehow you always seem to end up in the thick of things.'

He chuckled. 'But I do find a way through, don't I?'

She shook her head, both anger and concern reflected in her gesture, lost for words. Eventually she sighed and fixed him with a long look. 'You worry me, Richard.'

He shook his head, wanting to allay her anxiety, but she stopped him by placing a hand on his chest.

'This war's gone on for so long,' she said, 'and you've had more than your fair share. I just feel . . . ,' she looked down, hesitated, and then with a defiant toss of her head met his eyes.

'You have to come back, Richard. I'm wearing your ring now, stop taking unnecessary chances.'

He stared at her, surprised by her reaction. It wasn't like her to get emotional, she'd always been strong, and he felt a pang of guilt. He'd been so consumed by his desire to get back to sea it hadn't crossed his mind she might be worried.

'I won't,' he assured her, and bent to meet her lips. She folded into his embrace, holding the kiss, and he felt the trembling warmth. Her eyelashes fluttered against his cheek before he slowly eased back to hold her at arms length. She was struggling to hold back tears.

As gently as he could, he said, 'Time I was going.'

Jennifer straightened and swallowed. 'Of course.' There was the glimmer of a tearful smile. 'Go on, I'll see you at Christmas.'

Thorburn nodded and squeezed her hand. 'Bye then.' He let go and turned for the outer door, opened it, and gave her a last glance.

She mouthed a silent, 'love you,' and with a final nod he took his leave. Outside in the busy corridor he replaced his cap, patted it lightly into position and took a deep breath. He was not one for long drawn out goodbyes, too many emotions involved, not at all what a man should succumb to. Luckily, he knew she understood, and he let it go, put it to the back of his mind. He had a lot to sort through and not a lot of time in which to do it. He strode off down the corridor.

7 .. Scapa Flow

In Loch Ewe, the captains of eighteen merchant vessels walked purposefully towards a large wooden shack where they'd been summoned to attend the Convoy Conference. As was their nature when confronted with the rules and regulations of the Royal Navy, the men took their seats at the roughly hewn table with a quiet reserve, saying little other than to pass greetings with the mutual respect skippers of their standing afforded one another.

What few words were exchanged quietened into silence as each man delved into a worn attaché or briefcase, wherein they produced the lists of men and cargoes that each would be transporting to a far flung Russian port.

At 16.00 hours, the Senior Naval Officer (Loch Ewe), Commodore T. R. Sheldon, R.N., D.S.C., entered the room. He was accompanied by Captain John Hennessey who moved to stand with his back to a large blackboard. One of Sheldon's Aides then issued each captain with a copy of Convoy Orders and allocated them a position in one of the columns. The routine information for executing changes of course, distance between columns and ships in line, were all touched on before he then turned to introduce Hennessey.

'Gentlemen,' John Hennessey began. 'For those of you who have sailed the Russian route before, you will note that we are not a big convoy. But we are an important one. The cargo each of you has loaded within the last couple of weeks has been specifically asked for by the Russian generals in the vicinity of Kola Inlet. Our understanding is that a major operation to attack German forces in northern Norway will take place shortly after we arrive. When these supplies are unloaded the Russians will push them straight to the front line, no more than seventy miles northwest.'

He turned to the blackboard and drew a rough outline of Norway's west coast, then tapped it with the stick of chalk. Looking round at the assembled captains, he continued. 'I'm telling you this because I want you to know that for future convoys, the chances of getting through without mishap will be significantly improved.' He could see a few of the captains nodding their approval and took comfort from their support. 'Simply put,' he said, 'the sooner the Russians drive the Germans away from the Norwegian coast, the better it will be for all concerned.'

A big man down the far end of the table lifted his head and cleared his throat. He looked to be in his late fifties, greying hair, lined forehead, and with that tell-tale weather beaten face that indicated so many years at sea.

'It really makes no never mind to me,' he said, choosing his words, 'but am I to understand that just for once we might actually be helping ourselves rather than the bloody Russians?'

Hennessey couldn't hold back the smile. These men seldom complained, although ever since the infamous PQ17 there had been a wary distrust of the Royal Navy's part in convoy escort duties. Many of them wondered if the years of convoying to Russia hadn't all been a terrible waste of men and resources.

'In a roundabout way, Captain,' he said, 'you've hit the nail on the head.'

The clear, dark eyes never wavered. 'Then I for one will be happy to make this voyage.' He lowered his head and sat still.

Hennessey glanced round the table, waiting to see if there were more questions. When nobody moved he decided to end the briefing with a better piece of news.

'I think you should know that when we reach Reykjavik the cruiser H.M.S. *Stirling* will join us in support. You'll not see much of her, but she'll remain very much within range.' And with that he brought the briefing to a close.

'Well . . . , that's it, gentlemen. I hope we all have a good trip.'

A murmur of acceptance rolled round the table and orders were tucked away, to be studied in greater detail aboard ship. Slowly, the Masters of eighteen ships filed out of the room and made for the harbour launch.

At 07.30 hours on Monday the 11th of September, *Brackendale* steamed out of Portsmouth harbour, entered the Solent, and turned east for the Dover Straits. With the sun above the horizon and the south shoreline clearly visible, the little destroyer swept past the lighthouse off Beachy Head and altered course to head north of east and up the coast to Dungeness.

The ship slewed across an oncoming wave and then thumped into the following trough. On the bridge, Thorburn stood at the screen swaying with her movement. Salt laden spray lifted from her bows and he grinned into the wind. He was back in his element, at sea, where he belonged, and he was glad of it. There was a businesslike purpose to their voyage, taking passage round the east coast and then on to the far north. Their destination . . . , the Royal Navy's great anchorage of Scapa Flow.

Exactly what awaited on their arrival, only those who gave orders were any the wiser. For now, for Richard Thorburn, it was enough to be at sea.

Following an uneventful thirty-five hours, it took *Brackendale* until 18.30 on Tuesday the 12th, to reach the southern entrance to the Fleet's most northern harbour. As the ship nosed towards the boom defences, a small cutter opened the anti-submarine nets, and promptly closed them once Thorburn had conned the destroyer through the gap.

'Where now, Pilot?' Thorburn asked.

At the chart table, Martin checked his notes. Two signals had arrived in the last few hours. The first gave details for refuelling at an oiler, and informed them of which mooring buoy to tie up to. The second signal was specific to the Captain and ordered him to attend a briefing at 08.30 hours the following morning.

'The oiler's berthed at No2 jetty, sir. I suggest port ten and then steer two-eight five.'

Thorburn bent to the pipe. 'Port ten.'

'Port ten, aye aye, sir.'

Brackendale swung towards the west and

Thorburn watched the compass.

'Midships,' he said. 'Steady.'

'Midships, aye sir. Steady on two-eight-seven degrees.'

Thorburn corrected the bearing. 'Steer two-eight-five.'

'Two-eight-five, sir.'

'Very well,' Thorburn said and straightened to study the anchorage.

Armstrong came to stand at the screen. 'Bigger than I thought,' he said.

'Not been here before then?' Thorburn asked.

'No, it was always down south for me.'

'Same here,' Thorburn agreed, 'I was in the China station and then the Channel. Never got the opportunity.'

Armstrong pointed northeast across the main anchorage. 'I think that's where Prien sank the *Royal Oak*.'

'Mmm,' Thorburn nodded, 'and this is where *Hood* was before *Bismarck* happened.' He felt the enormity of recent history. So much had been initiated from this famous stretch of water.

'Oiler off the port bow, sir,' Martin warned.

Thorburn returned to the job in hand, looking ahead to see the workmanlike shape of a fleet refuelling vessel berthed at a pier.

'Slow ahead,' he said into the voice-pipe, and *Brackendale* eased down in preparation for securing alongside. He could see movement on the oiler's deck as hands assembled to receive heaving lines, and his own seamen stood by with fenders and wires, ready to make fast.

'Port ten,' he said.

Falconer acknowledged. 'Port ten, aye sir.'

'Midships..., steady.'

Brackendale slid gently towards the oiler's side and Thorburn narrowed his eyes, watchful.

'Stop both,' he ordered, and tensed. She was going in too fast.

'Half astern together!' he snapped, and just when he thought he'd overcooked it, the propellers found purchase, dragging them to a halt.

'Stop port, slow ahead starboard.'

Heaving lines snaked across as fenders touched, and the trailing wires were hauled in.

'Stop starboard,' he said bending to the pipe, and in answer to the telegraph the rhythmic pulse of the shaft died away.

'All secure, sir.'

'Very well.' He moved to the port wing and spotted Dawkins standing on deck waiting to oversee the refuelling. 'We'll leave it to the Chief,' he said, and turned to Armstrong.

'I'll be in my cabin, Number One. Let me know when we're done.'

Following the destruction of S.S. *Silver Moon*, Kapitänleutnant Helmut Eckermann had pushed east as fast as the prevailing conditions allowed. And luck was with him. At night on the surface, in ideal conditions, U-699 had pressed on making almost thirty kilometres to the hour. Even in daylight, with the Schnorkel deployed, he'd managed to achieve ten. They'd survived two enemy aircraft sightings, both long range American Liberators. At 21.35, following hours of maximum effort, Eckermann climbed to the bridge and ordered the lookouts below.

He gazed at the night sky, picking out the familiar pattern of stars, relieved to have made it to their new station. The plot showed U-699 located one-hundred kilometres west of the Faroes. Now he would go deep on the electric motors, let the crew rest and maintain a minimal listening watch in the control room.

He gave a final warning from the bridge. 'We go to eighty metres, take us down.' With that, he lowered himself into the tower, secured the hatch overhead and dropped to the deck. His First Officer looked at him with raised eyebrows.

'Relax, Kurt, we will rest. Only a listening watch, slow ahead. The men deserve it.'

Kurt Keller gave him a tired smile and nodded. 'They will be pleased, Herr Kapitän.'

Eckermann yawned and rubbed his eyes. 'Good, you will tell them. Eight hours, after that . . . , we move the final kilometres and begin our new patrol.'

Keller unclipped the microphone and informed the crew.

Eckermann left them to it and went to

his cabin. He knew sleep would not come so soundly, but he could rest. He lay on the bunk and poured a brandy. It might help.

8 . . Ad hoc Flotilla

At Scapa Flow it was precisely 08.00 hours on Wednesday the 13th when Thorburn turned up his collar against the rain, took his seat in the ship's motor boat and settled down for the short run to the quayside. The rain, coming in with such force it flattened the waves, left them all but lost in the deluge.

But, thankfully, it was only a short trip and before long the engine throttled back, the boat slowed, and a stone dockside appeared ahead. Thorburn felt the gunwale touch and stood, instinctively hunching his shoulders. He jumped from the boat, landed on greasy steps and hauled himself up to the hard.

A Royal Marine saluted. 'If you'll follow me, sir,' he said, and without waiting for a reply, turned and strode off.

Thorburn lowered his head and splashed through deep puddles. It took but a few minutes to arrive at a plain two-storey brick building and the Marine opened an unvarnished door. Once inside the man pointed to a flight of stairs. 'Up to the first floor, sir. The Admiral's office is down the end.'

Thorburn thanked him, took the stairs two at

a time, and walked to the door at the end of the corridor. He knocked.

A young Lieutenant opened up and stood aside. 'Can I take your coat, sir?' he asked. 'If you'll wait a moment, I'll let the Admiral know you're here.'

Thorburn nodded and peeled off his coat. The man hung it dripping on one of a dozen hooks, half of which already had a variety of sodden rainwear, and then he tapped an inner door and entered. There was a muffled exchange of words and the Lieutenant reappeared.

'You can go in now, sir.'

Thorburn removed his cap and stepped inside. A group of officers stood talking quietly at the far end of the room, and Thorburn immediately recognised Collingwood listening intently to a man wearing a Captain's insignia on the cuffs of his jacket.

The Admiral's prominent beak swung round as he saw him enter. 'Ah . . . , Thorburn. Come and join us.'

He walked forward and the conversation ceased, faces turning to greet the newcomer.

Collingwood shook his hand with a firm hold. 'Been a while since we last met. I hear you've kept Jerry busy,' he smiled, and began the introductions. 'This is Captain Alexander McGregor of *Zeus*.'

Thorburn offered his hand. 'Sir,' he said respectfully, vaguely remembering the name from some past exploit. The row of medal ribbons was impressive.

McGregor grinned, exposing a mouthful of badly discoloured teeth.

'Glad to have you aboard,' he said. 'I'm informed you tangled with a U-boat.'

Thorburn accepted the statement and guessed the Admiral had given everyone the details. He nodded, but shot an accusing glance at Collingwood who held up his hands in mock dismay. 'Not me. One of your fellow officers,' and he gestured behind him.

And Thorburn blinked in surprise. Lieutenant-Commander Peter Willoughby stepped forward with a broad grin.

'Hello, Richard. Glad you made it.'

Thorburn smiled with genuine warmth. They'd known each other for years, and it was Willoughby who'd come to his assistance on D-Day. It was also Willoughby who'd witnessed the aftermath of the collision with the U-boat. He looked older now, face lined, weather beaten, but unbowed and smiling. As they shook hands, Thorburn raised an eyebrow.

'So I take it I have you to thank for letting the cat out of the bag?'

Willoughby's familiar laughter filled the room and he glanced mischievously at the Admiral. 'I might have mentioned something in passing.'

It was Collingwood's turn to grin. 'Far be it for

me to listen to such exaggerated tales,' he said, and then continued with the introductions. He pointed with an outstretched hand. 'Jeffrey Parker of the Frigate *Pegwell Bay*, and this is Francis Gilliam of *Seaham*.'

Thorburn nodded to each in turn and shook hands. Parker stood tall and rangy, with prematurely grey hair and piercing hazel eyes. His handshake was firm and solid and he gave the overall impression of a very experienced officer. Gilliam, on the other hand, was the archetypal naval officer. Dark hair slicked down with a neat parting, medium height, immaculate uniform, and an easy going, welcoming smile. He noted they both wore the wavy stripes of the Volunteer Reserve. Not that he thought anything of it. This far on from the beginning of the war, half the small ships in the Navy were captained by reservists. If they held command they'd earned the right.

Collingwood clapped his hands and moved to his desk. 'Right then, now we're all acquainted, down to business. Be seated, gentlemen, and I'll put you in the picture.' He waited while they found a chair, perched himself on a corner of the desk, and rubbed his forehead to gather his thoughts.

From the corner of his eye, Thorburn watched Captain McGregor pull a chair forward and sit slightly to one side.

'I've brought you here as reinforcements,' Collingwood began. 'What was, and theoretically still is, the Northern Patrol, has been somewhat depleted over recent weeks.' He paused to stare at the floor. When he looked up, Thorburn could see there was a determined set to his jaw.

'There's a convoy being prepared for Russia, bound for Murmansk.' He looked at the floorboards again, swinging his free leg. 'It's slightly unusual in that the cargo being transported will be on the front line within hours of arrival. The Russians, along with their Norwegian counterparts are readying themselves for a major offensive into German held Norway.' He slid slowly down from the desk to stand and face them.

'The convoy will be well escorted and they'll have additional support with the deployment of *Stirling*.' He grinned. 'For anyone not familiar, she's a twelve gun Town class cruiser.' He paused for a moment and rubbed his forehead.

'That said, I've been charged with establishing a new offensive patrol line which will encompass an area east of the Faroes and north as far as the Arctic Circle. And you, gentlemen,' he said, with a half smile playing round his lips, 'are the Royal Navy's answer to that request.'

Thorburn frowned to himself. That was a sizeable area to patrol with only five ships.

Collingwood continued. 'Our main concern . . . ,' he corrected himself, '*your* main concern, are the U-boats.' There was hard authority in the way he spoke. 'Now let me say this.

Although we're rather an ad hoc flotilla, short notice and all that, every one of you has experience of hunting U-boats. You may not be aware, but since D-Day, the French ports have quickly become isolated and we've taken steps to make life difficult for boats to gain access to the pens. The latest intelligence report suggests surviving boats have been diverted to the Norwegian fjords.'

Thorburn snatched a quick glance round those seated beside him. All were listening intently. He caught a movement from McGregor, who came to his feet.

Collingwood said, 'I'll let the Captain take the floor.'

Tall and broad shouldered, the man took centre stage and paused to eye his captive audience.

'The Admiral and I have discussed this at length. Uppermost in our minds has been how best to deploy five ships to cover such a large area.' He glanced at Collingwood before continuing.

'There are two imperatives, gentlemen. Although each of you has radar the first thing we require is that any given ship will remain in visual contact with at least one of the others in the flotilla. Assuming therefore we deploy in line astern, or line abreast, and allow seven to eight miles between each vessel, we'll have the ability, taking account of radar, to patrol an area approximately fifty miles by twenty.'

He looked down and scuffed a polished shoe across the floor.

'Secondly,' he said, raising his head to eye each of them in turn, 'that will permit any adjacent ship to assist another in engaging a contact, multiplying the chances of a successful outcome.' He swept the room with his eyes. 'That, in a nutshell, is the broad outline. Any questions?'

Thorburn breathed in, measured, giving himself time to digest the information. His first impressions were favourable, but he wondered what maintaining visual contact meant when two ships closed a contact. He raised a finger.

McGregor caught the movement. 'Yes, Commander?'

'Why the need to stay within sight of one another, sir?'

'We intend to maintain radio silence, so it's either 'flags' or 'lamps'. We'll be too close to Norway and possible attack from the air. Luckily, surface forces are not part of the equation, the *Tirpitz* is out of action. There are a few destroyers, but without battleships or cruisers to lend support they're not likely to put to sea. Our intelligence people estimate a total of no more than seven German destroyers, all widely dispersed along the Norwegian coast.

But visual communication also gives us the ability to respond quickly in case of need. If we maintain the recommended intervals, then maximum speed offers close support in a matter of minutes.'

Thorburn still felt he needed more detail and pressed his case. 'And if two of us converge for an attack, sir, how do the rest maintain visual observation? The wrong pairing could leave one ship out of sight beyond the horizon.'

McGregor nodded. 'True . . . , and should that situation arise, the outlying ship will maintain radar surveillance and, only if absolutely necessary, revert to wireless communication until a line of sight is re-established. I stress, only if absolutely necessary.' He then nodded to Willoughby. 'Yes?'

'Can we assume we're not the only flotilla out there on patrol?'

McGregor hesitated and turned to Collingwood. 'Admiral?'

Collingwood stepped forward. 'That is a correct assumption,' he said. 'There is one other group in the far north, patrolling the waters off Jan Mayen Island. Our little expedition will commence operations northeast of the Faroes.'

Willoughby relaxed into his chair. 'Thank you, sir.'

McGregor raised an eyebrow. 'Any more?' He waited. 'No? Well I don't doubt we'll think of something soon enough. But in the meantime I suggest you all replenish as necessary. If you can squeeze in a few more depth charges, that'll be all to the good. We'll be on our way at 05.00 hours.'

He looked round at Collingwood, but then with a flash of discoloured teeth, turned back to grin at them. 'And we'll have ample time to put my philosophy into practice . . . , we'll exercise my ideas on the way to our station.'

Collingwood stepped forward. 'Thank you, gentlemen, I think that about covers it. You best see to your ships.'

Thorburn came to his feet with the others, the briefing at an end, and turned for the door. Ahead of him Willoughby glanced back, a broad smile on his face. He paused to let Thorburn catch up.

'We're off again then, Richard. Another day, a new dawn . . . , another battle.' He laughed and Thorburn smiled. As always, Willoughby was only truly happy when action seemed imminent. His one thought, to close with the enemy.

'Don't count on it, Peter. I think there'll be a lot of patrolling and little in the way of action. That's a big expanse of water McGregor's talking about.'

Willoughby snorted his disbelief. 'What? Those U-boats will be popping up left, right and centre. They want an argument with the Royal Navy, I'm only too happy to oblige.'

It was Thorburn's turn to grin and he slapped Willoughby on the shoulder. 'Well, I think you've found the right man to lead the way. I seem to remember that McGregor's rumoured to be a bit of a firebrand.'

Willoughby rolled his eyes theatrically. 'Into the valley of death, eh?'

'Hope not,' Thorburn said slowly. 'We've seen a bit too much of that recently.'

Willoughby dropped the smile and nodded. 'You could be right,' he said, and then brightened. 'but maybe a little skirmish would suffice?' There was a twinkle in his eye.

Thorburn gave him a push through the door and they shrugged into their still damp coats. Caps on, they made their way down the concrete stairs and outside into the teeming rain. Heads down, they retraced their steps to the quayside where motor boats from the ships awaited their captains.

Willoughby peered through the rain and stuck out a hand. 'All the luck, Richard. I'm off.'

Thorburn found his friend's eyes beneath the peaked cap. 'Mind you leave some for the rest of us,' he said, and shook the hand with a firm grip.

'Not if I can help it,' Willoughby chuckled, and turned away. He dropped lightly into his ship's boat and a minute later vanished into the swirling rain.

Thorburn recognised his own motor boat edging in, dropped into the waist and ducked beneath the hood. The helmsman throttled up, turned out from the quay and moved north for *Brackendale's* mooring. Thorburn lowered himself onto the bench seat and thought back to the briefing. Five small warships to patrol an enormous tract of sea. He wondered if Collingwood and McGregor really believed in the plan they'd hatched or whether all this was just a token gesture? If the U-boats deployed in numbers there could be a massacre in the offing.

As *Brackendale* loomed into view through the sheeting rain, he stood, readying himself for the Jacob's ladder. Tomorrow, he thought, before sunrise, their Northern Patrol would set off for the North Sea. It was hard to shake the feeling that something . . . , he couldn't put his finger on it and let it be.

Time to climb aboard.

9 . . Hands to Stations

Five kilometres off Norway's west coast the *Bruno Keplar* answered a challenge from a small picket boat. Richter's senior lamp-man read out the message.

'Herr Kapitän, this boat will be our guide. We are to follow.'

'Confirm,' Richter said, and turned to his Navigating Officer. 'Our course is that of the picket boat. Obey their signals.'

'Jawohl, Herr Kapitän.'

Richter returned to the screen and motioned for a bridge messenger. 'Inform the Admiral we are entering the fjords.'

The man clicked his heels and hurried away,

and for a moment Richter watched as his ship fell in with the picket boat's alteration of course. He lifted his binoculars and studied the approaching headland, a foreboding buttress of craggy heights. Not a place to be trapped in. The sooner clear water was back under the keel, the better.

Krause entered the navigating bridge as the destroyer swung slowly left between towering walls of grey rock. When it straightened from the turn he caught the flicker of a signal lamp from the small picket boat ahead of the destroyer's bows.

'Time to leave you,' the lamp-man read. '*Aldenburg* is ahead and to starboard.'

Krause raised his binoculars. The dark waters broadened out until the fjord resembled a gigantic lake, and there, a thousand metres to the right, well hidden from prying eyes, lay the cruiser. It was concealed from above by a huge granite overhang, and from the open side by cleverly installed camouflage nets replicating grey granite. He allowed himself a small smile of satisfaction. At the very least, he'd managed to achieve the first part of his orders. Now, whatever the problems, he must turn this ship into a U-boat command headquarters.

'Richter,' he said with quiet authority, 'I will have the ship's boat readied for my transfer.'

Within minutes the destroyer slowed to a

stop, five-hundred metres from the *Aldenburg*, and the motor boat touched down onto glacial waters. The companionway was swung out over the side, and Krause, closely followed by Bergmann, walked down the steps and dropped into the boat's cockpit. The Admiral chose to stand, hands clasped firmly behind his back while the helmsman coaxed the boat across the fjord. The boat slowed beneath the huge hanging nets to hook on at the foot of the cruiser's steps.

Before mounting the steps, Krause took a moment to look up. In comparison to the destroyer the sides of the cruiser appeared enormous, taller than he remembered for a warship of this type. Maybe it was a sign of age he thought grimly, and stepped across to the platform.

When he finally planted a foot on the main deck, the side party snapped to attention and a Fregattenkapitän saluted him aboard.

Bergmann dispensed with the formalities and Krause allowed himself to be led to the commander's cabin.

Mid-morning on Wednesday the 13th, and the skippers of eighteen merchantmen gave orders to weigh anchor. Propellers began turning, pushing the ships slowly forward, and in compliance with their Convoy Orders, each vessel took station in a single long column before steaming out through the boom nets.

Captain John Hennessey, in the Fleet destroyer H.M.S. *Scitalis* led them north through the relatively sheltered coastal waters between the Outer Hebrides and Scotland's craggy west coast. Two hours later the ships passed Stornoway lying off to port, and a short while thereafter, Hennessey and the captains of the other escorts chivvied and cajoled the convoy into three columns of six. With patience and a good deal of tactful persuasion, the eighteen merchantmen finally took their places, and the destroyers deployed around the convoy for the long voyage ahead.

At Scapa Flow at precisely 05.00 hours on Thursday the 14th of September, a familiar call echoed through *Brackendale's* tannoy. 'Hands to stations for leaving harbour! Special sea-duty men, close up!'

Thorburn reached across the bunk for his binoculars. The sound of sea boots thumped along the decks, followed by shouted commands, then relative quiet. There was a knock on the door.

'Come,' he said.

Armstrong stuck his head in and stepped over the threshold.

'Ready to proceed, sir.'

'Thank you Number One, I'll be right up.'

And so, *Brackendale* slipped her wires and turned to join the line of warships. McGregor's destroyer led them out of Scapa's southern reaches before then turning east into the North

Sea. The forecast for cloudy skies had proved correct, though visibility was good. But Thorburn was only too aware that the mercury had begun to drop.

He stood on the raised platform of the compass housing and watched the purple-grey headlands slide past, the ship rocking easily in the wake of the vessels ahead. He crossed to the port wing and looked aft down the quarterdeck. *Rosefinch* swayed in line astern, the soft sheen of her bows glinting across the void. He wondered what Willoughby was thinking? Probably relishing the thought of getting to grips with the enemy.

He turned back and moved to the forebridge, settled himself into the chair, and jammed a booted foot onto a bulkhead bracket.

'*Zeus* signalling, sir.'

'Read it,' Thorburn said.

'Signal reads, "Take station line abreast. Speed fourteen knots. My bearing oh-two-five degrees." End of message, sir.'

'Very well, acknowledge.'

The Aldis lamp clattered a brief reply.

Thorburn turned his head. 'Pilot?'

'Sir?'

'We'll be altering course to oh-two-seven degrees, and be prepared to ring up fourteen knots.'

'Aye aye, sir.'

From McGregor's flag deck, Thorburn caught a brief flicker of light and the signalman said, 'Execute, sir.'

'Now, Pilot,' Thorburn called, and Lieutenant Martin bent to the voice-pipe.

'Port ten, speed fourteen knots.'

Thorburn came to his feet and leaned his elbows on the folded down screen. Up ahead the three leading ships began their turn north and *Brackendale* followed round, but on a wider arc. Without looking he knew *Rosefinch*, last in line, would deviate even further out to starboard, positioning herself off *Brackendale's* right flank.

'Midships,' Martin ordered, and then, 'steady . . . , steer oh-two-seven degrees.'

Thorburn glanced ahead over the port bow and noted *Zeus* steadying onto her new course. *Brackendale*, steering two degrees off the designated bearing now had to conform to the Leader's instruction.

'Steer oh-two-five, Pilot.'

'Port five . . . , steady . . . , steer oh-two-five degrees.'

The small destroyer eased onto station and Thorburn relaxed. *Brackendale's* first Northern Patrol had begun in earnest. He looked around at the small flotilla and smiled. They made for a brave sight, ploughing on through a short chop, white spray coiling from their bows. Hulls rose and fell to each passing wave, pennants and ensigns flapping in the wind. And no doubt, he thought with a wry smile, McGregor would soon put them through their paces.

Kapitänleutnant Helmut Eckermann edged U-699 cautiously towards the surface, the electric motors giving the boat just enough forward momentum to counteract what felt like heavy seas.

'We are at periscope depth, Herr Kapitän.'

'Can you hold us steady, Kurt?'

'I am not certain. The waves are big I think.'

Eckermann stared at him and narrowed his eyes. 'You will do your best, no?'

'Of course, Herr Kapitän. Always.'

The U-boat swayed awkwardly, rocking from beam to beam.

Eckermann grimaced and raised his eyes, imagining what the overhead conditions must be like. But there was always a form of safety in rough seas, the enemy would not detect one small dot on the ocean.

'Periscope up,' he said, and reached for the handles. He bent to the eyepiece, and cursed. The waves were indeed breaking into flying spume and he found only a constant stream of seawater obscuring the lens. He turned slowly through the entire compass bearing but the horizon remained hidden from view. A minute later he stepped away and nodded for the periscope to be withdrawn.

'We are in trouble, Kurt. No horizon, only waves. The Schnorkel will give us too little air.' He shook his head, frustrated by the sea. The batteries had less than five hours available and without the Schnorkel he must surface the boat. The storm conditions were of no concern, a U-boat could not be capsized by bad weather. The greater danger was air reconnaissance, and he frowned, torn between surfacing and trying to wait for better weather. But if the wind was strong enough, aircraft might not fly. He must take the chance, better to accept the danger and fire up the diesels.

'Full ahead both, Kurt, and take us up,' he ordered, 'we will ride the waves.' He laughed at his own recklessness, disregarding the risk.

U-699 lunged to the surface between wave crests, corkscrewed wildly and thumped through green seas. Eckermann slammed the hatch open, stepped onto the bridge, and was then forced to cling to the rail as a solid wall of water threatened to sweep him away. Coughing his lungs clear, he clipped on and braced himself against the forward casing. Lookouts swarmed up after him, each man concentrating on his own sector, binoculars raised. Their horizon was limited, no more than six kilometres at most, but it was enough for Eckermann.

'Start the diesels!

The electric motors disengaged, immediately followed by a rumbling bark as the diesels powered up. The boat surged ahead, knifing the waves, heavy spray whipping across the conning tower.

But Eckermann had achieved his aim. The men were rested, the boat breathed fresh air, and the batteries warmed to a new charge. He raised his binoculars to the grey skies. Every passing minute was precious, a small victory gained.

U-699, limited by circumstances beyond Eckermann's control, had nonetheless begun to search again.

Early evening found *Brackendale* forging on through rising seas. Ahead of the port bow the distant outline of the Faroes began to take shape, a grey smudge on the horizon.

'*Zeus* signalling, sir.'

'Tell me,' Thorburn said.

'Reads, "Alter course to oh-one-oh", sir.'

Thorburn nodded at the new bearing, ten degrees east of north. That would have been his own choice.

'Very well, acknowledge,' he said, and turned to Martin. 'New course Pilot, bearing oh-one-oh.'

The order went down to the wheelhouse and the ship eased away to starboard. She began to corkscrew, the waves coming in on her port beam. It made for an uncomfortable passage and Thorburn braced himself at the screen.

'Midships,' Martin said.

Thorburn glanced astern at *Rosefinch*, and grinned. The sea hit her in the same manner, plumes of spray engulfing the fo'c'sle.

'Steady, steer oh-one-oh.'

Brackendale settled to the new course, the pitch and roll more rhythmic, allowing a man to find his balance. The signal lamp from *Zeus* flickered again.

'What's she saying?'

'Reads, "Commence operations", sir.'

Thorburn nodded. 'Acknowledge,' he said. 'Commence zigzag, Pilot,' and then in case anyone on the bridge had any doubts, he said, 'let's have the Asdic repeater on.'

A moment later the solid, haunting 'ping' of the underwater search beam resonated round the platform.

He turned to the starboard wing and raised his binoculars, watching *Zeus* push well south, almost over the horizon. Of *Pegwell* and *Seaham* there was no sign, but down there somewhere beyond *Zeus*, eight and sixteen miles respectively. So, he thought, with the Flotilla formed in line abreast and tracking more or less north-northeast, the hunt was on. He wondered what chance they had of finding the proverbial needle in a haystack?

Thorburn lowered the glasses and moved back to his chair. He decided to stay awhile, for an hour or so, just for the hell of it. The reality was, they might be doing this for days. It would be interesting to see how McGregor's plans came to fruition.

Brackendale, now the most northerly warship

of the flotilla, dipped her nose, shipped green seas, and shook herself free. A cold spray hit the bridge, and Thorburn wiped his face, relishing the bracing chill. And it was a reminder, if ever it were needed, that no matter what seamanship a man gathered under his belt, it was the sea and not these warring ships that held the final say if you let your guard down. To the northwest beyond the Faroes, a mass of dark cloud showed the passing of a heavy squall. He leaned back. This was only the beginning.

10 . . Lookout's Call

On the *Aldenburg*, Krause had spent hours familiarising himself with the ship's layout. From his personal viewpoint the cruiser had an extremely important asset that smaller warships were not able to entertain. The ship mounted an Arado float plane for reconnaissance while at sea. And although he accepted he was not at sea, the ability to send out aerial patrols gave him an immediate sense of freedom. With a range of over a thousand kilometres he could order his own flights to monitor the surrounding seas.

With that in mind he had the pilot report for duty and instructed him to fly as far west as fuel permitted. He was to use cloud cover to maximum effect and was not to engage enemy forces under any circumstances, only to report what he saw.

A short while later the placid surface of the fjord churned into a white wake and the seaplane, throbbing to the beat of a BMW radial engine producing nine-hundred horsepower, took off for the Norwegian Sea and the Atlantic beyond.

Krause watched it fly out and then continued meeting the officers and senior crewmen, and getting to grips with the incessant amount of veiled complaints. It was obvious that their morale was rock bottom, enforced idleness undermining what little faith they had in the outcome of the war. Privately, he thought it hardly mattered. The cruiser was not here to fight, only to wield command, and as he was beginning to understand, command what? A few U-boats with mostly youngsters in charge. The more experienced men had long gone. Famous names such as Günther Prien, Otto Kretschmer and Joachim Schepke, all with thousands of tons of Allied shipping to their names. But not to be frustrated by a lack of experienced men, he'd ordered Bergmann to compile a list of all U-boats nominally under his command.

Later, as the day's routine drew to a close, he returned to his spacious cabin and ordered Bergmann to turn it into an operational briefing room. Charts were hung, reports brought together, and the latest known position of every boat in the Atlantic and Norwegian seas plotted.

He was studying notes when the Senior Wireless officer entered.

'Signal for you, Herr Admiral.'

Krause raised a weary eyebrow. 'What now?'

'Secret, from Grand Admiral Dönitz,' said the officer, holding out the decrypted copy.

Krause frowned, straightened, and plucked it from his hand. It was a long message, and he initially read through at speed, but then settled to absorb it in detail. Eventually he looked up and gave Bergmann a piercing glance.

'A situation has developed. Dönitz wants all boats fit for operations to put to sea. They are to form a patrol line. It will extend north to south, from Jan Mayen to Iceland.'

Bergmann looked puzzled. 'Why the urgency?'

Krause peered at the signal to find the relevant part. 'A fast convoy is heading for Murmansk and Hitler directs it must be stopped.'

Bergmann gave a cynical laugh. 'Stopped? A fast convoy must be stopped? We do not sink slow convoys, what chance with a fast one? And what of their escort? Always there are aircraft carriers and too many destroyers.'

Krause looked at him coldly. 'For some reason,' he said, choosing his words with care, 'this convoy has no aircraft carrier. Dönitz feels that much damage could be done.' He squinted in thought. 'He could be right.'

Bergmann gave a slow shake of his head and in an overt show of disdain, shrugged his shoulders.

'Enough!' Krause barked. 'We have three boats within these fjords that are ready for Murmansk. We can start with those. Dönitz diverts three more from their patrol areas, and according to your summary there is a U-699 stationed somewhere east of the Faroes. When did he last report?'

'Not heard from for two days, Herr Admiral.'

'It is of no consequence. In the meantime you will have our three commanders report for an operations briefing, tonight at nine.' He thought for a moment and then said pointedly, 'No radio transmissions, we will use messengers to relay orders, you understand?'

Bergmann met his eyes and nodded. 'I will see it is done.'

Krause watched him leave, came to his feet and began pacing round the cabin. His thoughts centred on one other U-boat just arrived from La Rochelle. The boat was undergoing essential maintenance at the depot ship while being rearmed with torpedoes. If . . . , he thought, if he cancelled all crew leave that boat could be deployed by morning. It would not make him popular, and he gave a lopsided smile, he was not here to be liked. Dönitz wanted maximum effort and Krause was not a man to shy away from duty.

He moved back to his desk, made a note for Bergmann, and chose a cigar. The U-boats would be hunting soon, and if just one found the convoy? He nodded in thought; the wolves would be away by dawn. Sitting quietly and enjoying the solitude with his cigar, a sudden thought made him reach for the telephone. The duty officer in charge of the Arado's hanger answered.

Krause waved away cigar smoke. 'Has the pilot reported yet' he asked.

'We've heard nothing, Herr Admiral.'

Krause looked at his watch. 'What is his expected flying time?'

'Already thirty minutes overdue.'

'Inform me if you hear anything.'

'Jawohl, Herr Admiral.'

Krause let the handset slip into the cradle and sank back into the chair. The cigar was no longer so enjoyable.

Thursday night came for the Northern Patrol and *Brackendale* pushed on, riding the sea with an easy rhythm, fine spray occasionally feathering from the bows. On the bridge, Thorburn balanced against the ship's motion. They'd avoided the remnants of a gale to the north that had passed from west to east, and the state of the sea was relatively calm. The moon shone, and visibility had stretched to an acceptable four to five plus miles. South of *Brackendale*, *Rosefinch* lay hidden in the darkness, but she was well in range of the radar. That conformed with their orders; a shaded signal lamp would still be picked up by the lookouts. He stepped across to where Martin stood in the dim light of the chart table, swivelling his dividers along a plotline. A faint cross clearly marked an intersection of longitude and latitude and he pierced it with a sharp point. He dropped the dividers and scribbled a few calculations on the edge of the chart.

'Alright, Pilot?' Thorburn asked.

'Just checking, sir,' Martin said without looking up.

'Very well,' Thorburn said, and moved back to the bridge-chair. He settled and turned up the collar of his jacket. The wind might have eased, but there was a distinct chill in the air.

'Object! Bearing Green-one-oh! Range three-thousand!'

Thorburn came to his feet and brought his binoculars up over the screen. He focussed a few degrees right of the bows and studied the dark waters for thirty seconds. He drew a blank so checked the bearing.

'Fine off the starboard bow you say?'

'Yes, sir. Green-one-oh.'

He looked again, this time taking account of *Brackendale's* course and assuming the object would move even further to starboard relative to the original sighting.

'Asdic?' he inquired calmly.

Labatt, who was Officer-of-the-Watch, replied. 'No reports, sir.'

Through his glasses Thorburn could find only the smudge of breaking waves. He lowered the binoculars and glanced round at the lookouts.

'Anyone got this in view?'

The lookout on the port bridge-wing, Leading Seaman Allun Jones, gave the answer. 'No, sir.'

'What speed are we doing, Mr Labatt?'

'Fourteen knots, sir.'

Thorburn narrowed his eyes, sifting through the possibilities. If it was a surfaced U-boat, radar would have picked it up. If it was submerged, Asdic would have it . . . , hopefully. Wasn't always guaranteed.

Brackendale heeled to an oncoming wave, righted herself and steadied. He lifted the glasses and searched again, this time ninety degrees to starboard. Dark sea, pale streaks of foam, but nothing substantial.

'Who made the sighting?' he asked of the bridge in general.

'I did, sir,' came the answer from the starboard side.

Thorburn turned and found Able Seaman Cockroft.

'And what did you see?'

'Couldn't tell for sure, sir. Might have been a short mast.'

'A sail, then, or rigging?'

'No, sir.'

Thorburn swallowed, following his thought process. 'A periscope?'

'I don't think so, sir.'

Thorburn grimaced in the darkness. Cockroft

was a reliable lookout and it was obvious that he'd only had a fleeting glimpse, a split second observation. But the man had been certain in his own mind, certain enough to risk criticism if it turned out he was wrong. And Thorburn wouldn't fault a lookout for doing his duty.

'Very well,' he said, mind made up. 'Sound Action Stations.'

11 . . Discovery

Labatt shot him a glance of surprise and pressed the alarm.

In an instant the small destroyer came to life. Men who moments before had been sound asleep, grabbed for their boots, helmets, life jackets and duffle coats. They scrambled down ladders, mounted others, slammed watertight doors, and raced to their stations.

And it was the First Lieutenant, out of breath from mounting the bridge ladder, who was on hand to take the reports. The calls flooded in, each department keen to announce their readiness. Finally, Armstrong turned to the Captain.

'Ship ready for action, sir.'

'Thank you, Number One. I have the bridge,' Thorburn said, and stepped up onto the compass platform. He bent to the wheelhouse pipe.

'Starboard twenty, Cox'n.'

Falconer acknowledged. 'Starboard twenty. Aye aye, sir.'

Thorburn studied the compass as *Brackendale* heeled to port and commenced the turn. He watched and waited, a sailor's instinct guiding his judgement.

'Midships,' he said, to catch the swing.

'Wheel amidships, aye, sir.'

The ship swayed upright. 'Steady,' Thorburn warned.

'Steady on oh-three-five, sir.'

Thorburn made an adjustment. 'Steer oh-four-five.' *Brackendale* settled, new course established, north-east towards an unidentified target.

A quick check of the bridge personnel and Thorburn raised his old Barr and Stroud binoculars. They must surely come across something soon.

'Radar-Bridge!'

Thorburn leaned to the pipe. 'Bridge.'

The voice of the operator, Bellingham. 'I have a small echo off the starboard bow.'

'Range?' Thorburn snapped.

'Four thousand yards, sir.'

'What do you mean, small?'

'Size of a ship's boat, sir.'

Thorburn rubbed his jaw, frowning. 'U-boat?'

'Not a strong enough signal, sir.'

'What's your best guess?

There was a pause as the man thought it through and Thorburn gave him the time. Bellingham was experienced at his job. 'Could be an

E-boat, sir.'

Thorburn breathed in. He doubted that was possible this far out from German held ports.

'Guns-Bridge!' It was McDonald via a voice-pipe.

'Captain,' Thorburn answered.

'I can see what looks like a float plane.'

Thorburn wondered if he'd heard right. 'Say again.'

'A seaplane, an Arado if I'm not mistaken.'

Thorburn shook his head in the darkness. If an E-boat was unrealistic, a seaplane mid-ocean was inexplicable. 'Are you sure?'

'I am, sir. It's just sat there, rocking on the water.'

Thorburn tried to visualize a small seaplane floating silently on the sea, miles from anywhere. Why . . . , what had happened? And was there anyone in the cockpit?

'Number One,' he said. 'Make sure the Oerlikons are ready.' The safety of the ship came first, he didn't want any unnecessary injuries.

Armstrong moved to both bridge-wings in turn and could be heard warning the gunners.

'Guns-Bridge . . . , two thousand yards, sir.'

Thorburn braced a thigh against the compass binnacle and very deliberately brought up his binoculars. He slowly swept the waves ahead. And as *Brackendale* lifted to a roller he caught the glint of something solid. The ship dipped and he lost the sighting, but then another wave and he found it again. McDonald was correct, it really was a seaplane drifting with the swell. It appeared to be leaning to starboard, wing down.

'One thousand yards, sir.'

'Very well,' Thorburn said and lowered the glasses. 'Slow ahead,' he ordered.

'Slow ahead, aye, sir,' from the Cox'n.

Brackendale eased from fourteen knots down to five, and less, no longer taking the rollers in her stride but corkscrewing awkwardly.

'Number One,' Thorburn said. 'I intend to bring that thing alongside the starboard quarterdeck. Have a party ready to make it secure.'

'Aye aye, sir,' Armstrong said, and made a move for the ladder.

'And make sure one of you is armed,' Thorburn called after him. He hoped the First Lieutenant appreciated the possible threat. He turned his attention to the ship. Time for the asdic team to earn their keep, and he reached for a bulkhead handset.

'Asdic,' came the reply.

'This is the Captain. We'll be dead in the water for a short while. Stay sharp.'

'Aye aye, sir.'

He replaced the handset and moved back to the compass platform, gauging their approach. 'Stop engines.'

The Cox'n acknowledged and *Brackendale* drifted to a standstill.

Armstrong took charge of the men at the quarterdeck rail and two lines snaked out over the Arado's fuselage. Their weight was enough to steady the seaplane and as the ship closed in, a seaman grabbed the port wing.

Someone pushed a small torch into Armstrong's hand and he wedged it in a pocket. Seeing his opportunity, he took hold of a strut and swung himself onto a float. Reaching up he hoisted himself onto the wing and crawled to the cockpit. With the aid of the shaded torch beam he peered inside and found himself staring at a bleak scene. The pilot had died at the controls, slumped back in his seat, a rivulet of congealed blood staining the front of his flying jacket. Behind him the observer lay sprawled across the twin machine-guns. His right arm had been severed at the elbow and the Perspex canopy ran red with blood. The man's leather helmet had a bloodied hole in the side.

Armstrong swallowed hard and shifted position, checking the interior. The radio was a wreck, smashed to pieces. A folded map had slipped to one side and he took it and tucked it away. Might be useful. But then, caught by the beam of light, a small piece of metal glinted off the central console between pilot and observer. He shifted his body to the rear of the cockpit, where the canopy opened up for the guns. There was Gothic lettering on a brass plaque and he strained to read it. His lips moved to each letter, and finally he had it.

"A.l.d.e.n.b.u.r.g".

He frowned with the effort of recalling the name. It rang a bell but he couldn't place it.

He pulled away, decided there was nothing else worth while, and scrambled his way back onto the quarterdeck.

'Keep it alongside while I speak to the captain,' he said, and headed for the bridge.

Thorburn swung round to meet his First Lieutenant. 'Anything?' he asked, not really knowing what to expect.

'Pilot and observer both dead. Radio's smashed, but I found this in the cockpit.'

Thorburn took the map and gave it a cursory glance. 'We'll have the crew bring those German bodies aboard. Check for identification and we'll bury them at sea.'

'Yes, sir,' Armstrong said. 'There's one other thing, sir. That seaplane's got a brass plate with an inscription, one word.'

Thorburn waited before giving him a prompt. 'Well, Number One, are you going to enlighten me?'

'Aldenburg, sir.'

With a low whistle Thorburn said, 'Really . . . , you know what that is don't you?'

'It's familiar, but I can't say for certain.'

'Then let me acquaint you,' Thorburn smiled.

'If my memory serves me correctly, the *Aldenburg* is a nine-thousand ton light-cruiser, and it mounts nine six-inch guns, twelve torpedo tubes, and a lot more besides.'

Armstrong's face spoke volumes and Thorburn grinned. 'Exactly,' he said. 'And that seaplane belongs to that ship, and we've found it floating about all on it's own out here. I don't like the idea of a German cruiser swanning about willy-nilly.' He thought for a moment. 'Ask Guns if he knows the range of an Arado.'

Armstrong nodded and turned away.

Thorburn buried his chin on his chest in thought. The discovery of a reconnaissance aircraft this far out from Norway left a lot of unanswered questions. The fact that it had been shot up, albeit the pilot had survived long enough to make a controlled landing, was not in itself a surprise. Beaufighters made regular day and night patrols, both east and west of the Faroes. It would have been a minor diversion for a Beaufighter's pilot, and in all probability, had been convinced of a kill. And of course, McGregor had to be informed. It would have been easier if radio silence had not been in place . . . , to relay the information via *Rosefinch* would make for unnecessary complications. As he wrestled with alternatives, Armstrong returned.

'Seven-hundred miles, sir, and that would be in ideal conditions.'

Thorburn nodded and made some quick calculations. Maximum flight out would be three-hundred and fifty miles, but if you were shot up? Maybe the pilot had tried to reach the Faroes.

'What do we do with the seaplane, sir?'

Thorburn didn't hesitate. 'Sink the bloody thing.'

Armstrong raised an eyebrow.

'Let Guns deal with it as we pull away,' Thorburn said, in no mood for finesse.

The First Lieutenant grinned. 'I'll pass the word.'

It took only a few minutes for the bodies of the Arado's pilot and observer to be brought aboard. There were mixed feelings amongst the crew, but most accepted the need to respect the dead and give them a proper send off. And as *Brackendale* gained momentum and pulled away, Lieutenant 'Guns' McDonald ordered one gun from each turret to obliterate the seaplane.

Thorburn nodded his approval, put the ship back on her original search pattern, and then returned to his cabin. It was there he remembered the map and pulled it from his pocket. He smoothed the folded paper on his desk and raised an eyebrow in surprise. A dozen or so pencil lines criss-crossed a map of the Norwegian coast, the majority plotted west across the sea. Many of them formed triangles and squares, but one, a straight line, led directly towards the Faroe Islands. It ended short, highlighted by a small circle, and Thorburn put two and two together, guessing the mark indicated a point of safe return. What struck him the most was that all of the lines, without exception, emanated from the fjords north of Bergen. He leaned both hands on the desk and stared hard at the map. If what he was looking at could be believed, a man might well conclude that a German cruiser lay hidden within that rugged coastline. And just possibly, the *Aldenburg* was not out on the high seas, but tethered peacefully inside a fjord.

Off the northwest coast of Scotland, the convoy had made steady progress. John Hennessey kept a close watch on the plot, pleased to note that two-hundred miles had passed by under his keel.

Still a long way to go, he thought, standing in the darkness of the bridge, but it was a promising start.

In a fjord in Norway, a grey dawn heralded the start of Friday September the 15th, and Admiral Krause sat in his cabin absentmindedly tapping a pen on the desk. Dönitz had given his orders and the U-boats were redeploying to their new stations. Luck would play its part, but with that many boats hunting for the convoy he felt sure that one of them would make contact. Unfortunately, a report from the Arado's hanger confirmed his suspicion that the floatplane had probably been lost. A valuable reconnaissance tool was no longer available.

But Krause was not a patient man, he did not like waiting for news which might not come. Not content with confining himself to the cabin, he made his way up to the bridge and stepped outside onto the port wing. It was cold behind the mottled shade of the camouflage nets and he paced forward rubbing his hands. He stopped and stamped his feet, staring down at the forward gun turret. The three big barrels pointed horizontally out towards the bows. Lifeless, an impotent monument to the Kriegsmarine's failure.

A gust of wind ruffled the netting, throwing shadows over the guns, and the flickering light giving an impression of movement. Krause stiffened, the faint stirrings of an idea percolating through his brain.

What if he, Admiral Mathias Johann Heinrich Krause, Knights Cross, put to sea in the *Aldenburg*? Hitler demanded the seemingly impossible. Dönitz wanted maximum effort. A cruiser might make the task a lot more feasible. If nothing else, the very threat of a major warship in northern waters must surely make the enemy think twice. At this stage of the war there was little to lose, much to be gained. He would need escorts for such an attack and he knew of at least another three destroyers hidden in the fjords.

He turned away and took a deep breath, full of doubts. Could he physically execute such a plan?

Was there enough time to intercept? And what about fuel? There had never been any intention of making any kind of sortie into the Atlantic. He cursed himself for not knowing, for such a basic error, and wondered if Bergmann had the answers? Krause drew himself up to his full height. It was time to find out. First things first, he must consult the charts. He left the bridge for his cabin, determined to turn the idea into reality.

By now a few of the wolves had begun to gather, arriving at their stations to form a tenuous line running north to south, hunting slowly towards the west in search of prey. The first to reach the designated area was U-395, a type VII-C under the command of Kapitänleutnant Heinz Müller, newly promoted from First Officer after his commander had been appointed to a brand new 'Electric' boat.

The next to arrive, the U-474, came on station five-hundred kilometres northeast of Iceland. Its deployment followed a two month repair and refit in the pens of Bergen. Only eight of its forty-two man crew had previously completed war patrols, and crucially, the commander, Günter Lehmann, had taken charge just two days before the boat departed the fjords. It had left little time for him to evaluate his inexperienced crew and even less time to trial the boat prior to operations.

U-824 came late to the party, hurrying south from northeast Greenland where it had been lying in wait for the next Russian bound convoy. Korvettenkapitän Rudolph Reinhart, a highly experienced submariner, had survived twenty-one months in the same boat. The crew thought he was invulnerable. Reinhart himself was more pragmatic, a realist in that he was convinced luck had played a large part in their fortunes. He didn't expect that luck to hold forever.

12 .. Signal

Captain John Hennessey swallowed the last of his toast and washed it down with the remainder of a tepid cup of tea. He leaned back and reached for a cigarette. The match flared and he drew smoke, mulling over the convoy's progress. So far, so good, he thought. They were ahead of schedule, and thus far without any mishaps. He stood and balanced himself against the ship's pitch and roll, the short seas making for a lively corkscrew. He was about to pour another cup, when the bulkhead voice-tube squawked.

'Captain to the bridge. Captain to the bridge.' He thought he heard tension behind the call, or was it excitement?

Hennessey snatched up his binoculars and raced for the ladder. One rung from the top he paused, steadied himself, and then stepped calmly onto the bridge.

'What is it?' he asked.

The Officer-of-the-Watch, Lieutenant Mike Harman, reported. 'It's the *Bannion*, sir. Falling out of line.' He pointed astern across the starboard side.

Hennessey lifted his binoculars, focussing on the right column, and immediately found the ship veering off course. He lowered the glasses and made a quick check of nearby vessels. It was imperative he find out first hand what she was struggling with. Decision made, he snapped off a command.

'Starboard twenty, thirty knots.'

'Aye aye, sir,' Harman said, and the destroyer kicked over, accelerating to sweep round in a wide arc. She cut through two of the columns before Hennessey realised a large freighter stood in his way. He reacted.

'Hard-a-port!'

The destroyer rocked upright and heeled to starboard, clawing her way clear of the other ship. Her bows cleared the tanker with yards to spare, and a seaman in the bows stared, mouth open.

'Starboard ten,' he said, and the ship turned, heading down to where *Bannion* was wallowing away from the convoy. He swept past, brought the destroyer hard round on a reverse course, and then slowed until the two vessels were bridge to bridge alongside one another. With twenty feet of water between hulls, Hennessey stepped over to the bridge-wing and cupped his hands.

'What's the problem?' he yelled.

A man wearing a captain's headgear appeared and shouted in answer.

'Starboard shaft has an overheating bearing. My Chief's on it but it'll take a couple of hours, maybe three.'

Hennessey thought rapidly. Half speed at best and two or three hours, then hours to regain station, maybe a day or more. He couldn't afford to leave them unprotected. At the same time it would mean a gap in the screen.

'I'll detach one of the escorts to keep an eye out,' he called.

'Thank you,' came the reply, and the man stuck a thumb up.

Hennessey grinned and raised a hand in salute. 'Good luck,' he added, then turned away and stepped back to the fore-bridge.

'Mister Harman. Signal the *Franklin George* to shepherd *Bannion* until she can return to station.'

'Aye aye, sir.'

Hennessey heard the order passed to the signalman and gave the next command.

'Half ahead together. Port ten.'

'*Franklin George* acknowledges, sir.'

'Very well,' he said. 'Mister Harman, you have the bridge. Put us back on the left flank.'

'Aye aye, sir.'

Hennessey stepped away from the voice-tubes and wondered if he should redeploy his escorts to fill the gap in the screen, but then thought better of it. *Franklin George* had been tail-end-charlie, and her primary tasks were stragglers and rescuing survivors. The convoy would have to take a chance for a few hours.

'Mister Harman.'

'Sir?'

'I'll be in my cabin if you need me.'

Aye aye, sir.'

Hennessey nodded and made for the ladder, trusting he'd made a correct decision. His earlier self congratulations about no mishaps and being ahead of schedule, had been a bit premature. He hoped to God nothing happened between now and when *Bannion* resumed station. The trouble with fast convoys was exactly that, they were fast. It took a good deal of time for a straggler to catch up. And stragglers were always vulnerable.

It was mid-morning on that Friday, and in the waters southwest of Iceland, a periscope emerged from the depths, rotated once, and came to rest pointing south of east. Peering through the lens Kapitänleutnant Helmut Eckermann scoured the sea for any signs of life. Earlier, before the break of day, and following a perilous night on the surface charging U-699's batteries, he'd ordered the boat to submerge. What followed was the automatic commencement of an underwater hydrophone search for the distinctive sound of propellers. Fifty minutes later his caution was rewarded by the operator's whispered report of a contact.

Eckermann scanned the horizon for more than a minute, carefully traversing the waves ahead. And then he hesitated, reversed his sweep and settled on a solitary, vague wisp of smoke. He rattled off the initial findings and lowered the periscope. He turned to address the chart. Co-ordinates were entered, range guessed at, speed and direction estimated. He gave it five minutes and then the periscope again broke the surface. He focussed the lens.

This time he found three columns of smoke, and established a direction of travel, from right to left across the bows.

He called out the bearing, verified the range and speed, snapped up the handles and lowered the periscope. More plotting, a line traced, calculations made. Minutes passed as U-699 pushed on, holding course, and then up went the periscope. He steadied on the smoke, twisted a handle to increase magnification, and found what he wanted to see. A ship's mast ..., and another. And the speed with which he had to turn the periscope to hold them in view confirmed his suspicions. This was a fairly fast convoy. But how many ships? What was the escort, and how many? And all convoys zigzagged to make it harder for U-boats to attack. What leg were they on? It would be better if he could establish a mean course.

He watched as long as he dared, three minutes, and ended the observation with another set of readings. This time he decided not to linger and took the boat down a little deeper.

At the plot, he and his First Officer assessed the results. Their conclusions reinforced the obvious. A fast convoy heading three-one-five degrees, with a speed of twenty kilometres. But unfortunately, with U-699 approaching from the convoy's left quarter, Eckermann knew he was in no position to mount any kind of attack. Neither would they be able to overhaul the enemy to obtain a firing position, not in daylight. He rubbed the stubble on his jaw and saw Kurt eyeing him closely. He gave him a grin and tilted his head in thought. U-boat Command would want all the information he could give. If he could get a little closer . . . . He glanced down at the chart and acted on impulse.

'Surface the boat!' he ordered, and moved to the base of the conning tower. The loud hiss of compressed air echoed into the buoyancy tanks and the needle in the depth gauge swung upwards. Lookouts and anti-aircraft gunners gathered round him and he planted a foot on the first rung. He watched Kurt, waiting for the nod, and when it came he lunged up the ladder. He slammed open the hatch and hauled himself out into teeming spray. He braced against the bridge steel, binoculars up for a fast search round the boat. The lookouts scrambled to their places, the gunners to the bandstand.

'Ahead full!' he called, and U-699 surged forward. Teeth gritted he glanced at the grey sky. It only took one attack from an aircraft, and if that led to damage…? But if he stayed on the surface, full power from the diesels, a few minutes might make all the difference. Stinging droplets lifted from the bow, and foaming seas rushed back along the casing. The conning tower lurched and swayed as the hull raced onwards. In normal circumstances Eckermann might have appreciated the exhilarating ride, but his thoughts were elsewhere, his whole being concentrated on making the gamble pay off. Minutes passed with the boat careering across the waves. He altered course towards where he thought the tail of the convoy might be, and gave a sharp reminder to the lookouts. Not that they needed reminding, their lives depended on vigilance. The same went for the gunners, alert at their station.

He brought up the heavy binoculars and settled his eyes into the rubber sockets. Sweeping methodically across the bows, port to starboard, he again picked up the telltale sign of smoke. This time he found another two fine traces and he steadied on the nearest. Masts became evident, several, enough for seven vessels, and merchantmen's masts were easily distinguished from the cluttered aerials and paraphernalia carried by warships. He passed his new findings down to the control room, and then focussed on trying to find escorts. If the escort was made up of destroyers and minesweepers then he knew how hard they would be to find, always relatively low in the water, and much smaller than the vessels under their protection.

The binoculars weighed heavily on his fingertips and he let them rest, squinting at the seascape.

'Ship!' called a lookout from the right of the bridge. 'Fifty degrees.'

Eckermann swung his glasses across the starboard side, caught the darker shape of a small vessel and held it in focus. A stubby, round nosed tug came into view, an ocean going workhorse that gave towing capability to any ship needing assistance. Likewise she would be first on hand to rescue survivors. And usually, such ships were stationed toward the rear of convoys, leaving them well placed to carry out their role. But with the tug clearly visible through the binoculars, the danger for he and the crew was self evident.

'Lookouts below! he roared. 'Gunners below!' and within a minute they were down the hatch to the Control Room.

'Hard left!' he shouted down, and listened for the acknowledgement. U-699 swept away in a tight circle until the boat's stern formed a right angle with the convoy's course.

'Hold..., steer two-zero-five.'

'Two-zero-five degrees, Jawohl Kapitän.'

Alone on the bridge, Eckermann checked the sky through all points north, east, south and west. No aircraft in sight. He stepped to the periscope and studied the waves beyond the stern. No sign of warships, no destroyers accelerating in his direction. A faint smile creased his face. He had ridden his luck, once again it was time to hide beneath the waves.

'Kurt!' he shouted to the Control Room, 'take us down.'

Eckermann dropped into the tower, secured the hatch, and dropped to the deck. He moved to the chart table and studied the plot. The initial reckonings had been correct from the very first calculation made, and his only possible course of action would be to send a signal reporting the sighting. But even so, it would not do to signal U-boat Command until the convoy was over the horizon. These days the enemy had high frequency direction finding apparatus, and a single radio transmission could bring lethal retaliation.

Three hours after Eckermann spotted the first wisp of smoke, U-699 flashed off a coded signal and then recommenced the hunt for another target.

A short time later, U-boat Command received his signal and Dönitz ordered the speed, location, and course of the convoy sent out to every boat in the vicinity. A copy was also passed to the wireless room aboard the *Aldenburg*.

Friday the 15th and the convoy had logged four-hundred and fifty miles since leaving Loch Ewe. Captain John Hennessey made a note to that effect and then made his way to the chart room. He carefully studied the area that lay ahead, the now familiar southwest coast of Iceland where waters of the North Atlantic made landfall, and which included his next major point of reference, Reykjavik. Then there was Greenland north of Iceland and that treacherous passage east-northeast to Jan Mayan Island, of recent times the latest area targeted by the U-boats. There'd been a number of sinkings, mainly of merchantmen unable to keep up with their convoys, picked off as they struggled to keep up. He smiled grimly, a bit like the *Bannion*. It was disconcerting and not to be ignored.

The convoy sailed on, oblivious to what had been the close proximity of Eckermann's U-boat. They relied on speed for safety, and only the unluckiest of situations would enable a torpedo strike. And with every mile covered the eighteen ships improved their chances of avoiding enemy action. But, as John Hennessey well knew, for S.S. *Bannion*, five miles astern and with only the *Franklin George* for company, it would be a few hours yet before she rejoined the convoy and the relative safety of numbers.

Acting on intelligence relayed from the "code breakers" of Bletchley Park, a Catalina flying boat based at R.A.F. Sullom Voe in the Shetland Isles, was diverted from its routine patrol of Icelandic waters and headed for the last reported co-ordinates of a U-boat in the North Atlantic. At the end of two hours flying time, twenty-one year old Flight Lieutenant David Croft heard his port blister gunner report what appeared to be a small wake moving west.

The pilot sheered away north and came about in a wide circle from the east. He brought the aircraft down to an altitude of a thousand feet, slowed to an air speed of two-hundred and allowed his crew to 'home' him in on the tiny speck of foam. At a range of twelve-hundred yards, the nose gunner, who doubled up as bomb aimer, called a warning.

'I see it, Skipper! Eleven o'clock!'

The co-pilot lifted his binoculars. 'I've got it. Schnorkel!'

'Sure?' Croft checked.

'Definitely.'

David Croft asserted his authority. 'Alright everybody, stand by, we're attacking,' He corrected the Catalina's bearing to bring her on the same course as the target, altered height and speed for the run in, and handed control to the bomb aimer.

'All yours, make it count.'

The flying boat went in unopposed and the entire crew knew they'd never have a better chance of a 'kill' than the target that now presented itself. The bomb aimer steadied them for the final moments and released four shallow set depth charges, two from either wing.

The straddle was perfection, and with the sea erupting beneath them, Croft hauled the Catalina away to starboard and swept round to see the result. For an instant the crew were dumbfounded. In the time it had taken to make the turn, a U-boat had been blown to the surface and lay port side up in the foaming sea. Clearly visible on the conning tower were the identifying letter and numerals of U-699. But the surprise quickly changed to a job not yet finished, and the port blister gunner opened up with his machine-gun, joined by the tail gunner as they flew over. A hail of bullets and tracer slammed into the hull, a trail of water spouts marking their path.

Flight Lieutenant Croft banked hard to port, keeping the U-boat under his wing, and the co-pilot grabbed for his camera. The shutter clicked rapidly, proof of their success, capturing the final moments of the U-boat's demise.

The boat floundered there, on its side, for a while longer, and every gun aboard the Catalina took a turn to inflict more damage, the conning tower in particular taking savage punishment.

Inside the U-boat, Eckermann and his crew

were thrown bodily through the internal spaces. The tumultuous explosions shattered the starboard pressure hull and cracked the tempered steel tube at the forward torpedo compartment. The bow tube outer doors tore open and two of the inner doors burst their catches. The sea rushed in unhindered. The boat lurched to starboard, and a torpedo broke free from its securing. It slammed into a crewman and flattened him against the opposing racks, his body pulped. A man landed hard and broke his back. He screamed. Throughout the boat eardrums shattered and men tumbled upside down. The engine room sprang a dozen leaks as seals failed, and the diesels, starved of external air from the Schnorkel, sucked oxygen from within the boat. No one had the strength to shut off the engines. Sea water surged through the open gash adding weight and U-699 leaned further until the starboard side became the deck.

Eckermann lay sprawled inside the base of the conning tower, and guessed what had happened. They'd been caught unawares, and now they would pay the price. A bulkhead light still glowed casting an eerie light over the interior. His right arm lay at an odd angle, broken, bone protruding through the skin of his elbow. He could see a man shouting, but couldn't hear the words. Oil spurted from a pipe and flames flickered through the insulation of an electric cable. Acrid fumes filled the control room. And then came more punishment and he felt the hammer blows of machine-gun bullets blasting at the conning tower, roving along the casing, dozens of rounds punching and probing.

In the dim light he saw a man struggling to regain his feet and was surprised that it was his First officer. Kurt made it upright, swayed and staggered. In that moment their eyes met, and the man shook his head, no words, just an expressive gesture that spoke volumes. He slipped sideways, fell and lay still, mouth open.

Eckermann felt the boat angle down bow first, wallowing uneasily with the movement of the sea. Battery fumes misted over him, as sea water swamped the terminals. The angle increased and he rolled with it, unable to support himself or stop it happening. From the corner of his eye he saw arms and legs slithering past, but he remained firmly wedged in the conning tower. He knew the boat was dying, beginning the long dive to the seabed. How long he might survive the pressure could only be guessed at. When would the hull implode? Four-hundred metres?

Within his pain wracked brain, he suddenly remembered that new phrase the press used to describe U-boats. 'Iron coffins', and Grand Admiral Dönitz had never disputed it. Eckermann closed his eyes, knowing now there was nothing he could do to prevent U-699 from sinking.

Inexorably, the boat began to drift down beneath the surface, the commencement of a final journey to join the long list of those who had gone before.

In the Catalina flying boat, Flight Lieutenant Croft watched with narrowed eyes. Slowly, nose first, the U-boat began to slip beneath the waves. Finally, after what seemed an interminable amount of time, the hated sight of an enemy submarine slid from sight. It was followed by a great bubble of air bursting from the depths and a spreading stain of iridescent oil. A last photograph and a jubilant crew bid the scene farewell.

After eight monotonous patrols over northern seas, it was their first confirmed sinking.

13 . . Heavy Going

Dusk came to Norway's west coast and marked the moment for *Aldenburg* to depart for the open sea. Krause watched from the bridge as the huge camouflage nets were hauled clear, the last remnants stowed below. The boilers had been fired up three hours previously and the propellers allowed to slowly rotate. By the time darkness settled over the black waters, all was ready, and the ship slipped its moorings.

Krause waited as the cruiser swung to port and steadied up facing the exit channel. He peered into the darkness ahead and frowned.

'Where are the destroyers?' he demanded.

Bergmann came forward to stand at his shoulder.

'In the narrow channel, they wait for us there.'

Krause let his irritation dissipate and gave a thin smile. 'That is good,' he conceded, and rubbed his hands in approval.

Helm orders passed round the bridge, small alterations of bearing acknowledged and obeyed. *Aldenburg* entered the narrow channel, the Navigating Officer attentive, alert to the encroaching cliffs. Minutes passed as they squeezed through successive rock strewn miniature headlands, and then Krause caught the flicker of a shaded signal lamp.

Bergmann pre-empted the signalman's call.

'That is Richter, Herr Admiral.'

Krause felt the tension evaporate. 'So,' he nodded, 'a new beginning. I feel it will be a time of great exploits, Bergmann. Do you not agree?'

'I will be happier when we are clear of this coast.'

'Ja, I too,' Krause said. 'But first we must go north, hug this shore. Then we turn west at Lofoten and take the north passage down to Iceland. You will make sure the Navigator has the correct charts.'

'I am confident he has, Herr Admiral.'

At that moment *Aldenburg* lifted to the open sea, twisted majestically across a long roller and dipped into the following trough. Krause relished the movement, allowing his body to sway in time. A broad smile came and went and he pondered on his decision. Many years back he had sailed these northern waters as a junior officer. He had learnt many things, and most importantly he had been instructed to study the weather patterns of the region. It was something he'd never forgotten and over the last day or so he'd made a point of compiling a stack of recent weather reports to see if, maybe, he could put that knowledge to good use. After much thought, he gambled that the Gods might be with him, and although it was risky, he decided to chance his arm.

The Navigator spoke quietly. 'Make your heading north-northwest.'

The helmsman acknowledged and applied a turn to the wheel, and the light cruiser began a swing to the right, the waves catching the ship on the port quarter, inducing a long corkscrew. Minutes passed while the warship came round to the new bearing, and finally the helmsman confirmed their heading.

The Navigator glanced round at Bergmann. 'We run parallel with the coast, Herr Kapitän.'

'Then all is well,' Bergmann said. He turned to Krause. 'Do you have any further orders, Herr Admiral?'

'Not at this time. You will inform me when we are due to turn west,' Krause said, and turned away. Heels clicked as officers stiffened to attention and he waved a dismissive hand. About to leave the bridge, he paused and looked over his shoulder. 'Make sure Richter remains on station, I want no deviation from the escorts.'

'Of course,' Bergmann reassured him, and Krause finally left the bridge.

In the darkness of a night made darker by heavy cloud, five German warships pushed north, only the pale light of an intermittent moon marking their passage.

Daylight on Saturday the 16th found the Northern Patrol pushing on through deteriorating weather. H.M.S. *Brackendale* lifted and dipped to a lively sea. The wind had increased to force five and with it came a fine rain driving in from the west. And the further north the ship pushed the colder it became, a noticeable drop in temperature.

Thorburn came to his feet out of the bridge-chair and banged his hands together. Bodily he was warm enough inside the duffle coat, it was the extremities that suffered first. During the night he'd passed the information regarding the Arado to McGregor via signal lamp through *Rosefinch*. Other than the customary acknowledgement there'd been no further comment. At the break of dawn half the crew had assembled port side and the two dead Germans had been committed to the deep. It had been a solemn service, and he hoped the sincerity he felt when reading the last rites had been fully accepted by the ship's company.

He crossed to the port wing and looked south. In the far distance he could just make out the ghostly shape of *Rosefinch* ploughing her way west, and already the bow wave was throwing spray over the fo'c'sle to envelope the bridge.

'Mr Martin?' he called.

'Sir.'

'What was the last weather log?'

'At 08.00 hours, sir. Barometric pressure dropping, wind force four, visibility nine miles, state of the sea . . . ,' he paused and Thorburn glanced at him. 'It's going to get a lot rougher, sir, bit of a hooligan coming in from the Atlantic.' He said it with a wry smile.

Thorburn nodded. 'Very well,' he said, and continued to watch *Rosefinch* punching the waves. The flotilla had altered course at dawn, changing from a northerly heading in line astern, to west in line abreast. It put the five ships head on into the weather, giving all of them the advantage of riding the waves bow first. A small mercy for those resting below decks. And the other factor coming into play was the disadvantage to the U-boats. Rough seas limited their operational capabilities, and Thorburn guessed their arc of visibility would be well reduced, even more so if heavy rain swept in. *Brackendale* thumped the next wave and buried her bows in a green sea, shuddering as she rose through the weight of water.

Richard Thorburn grimaced and moved back

to the bridge-chair. There was a long day ahead.

Thirty kilometres south of the Lofoten Islands, the *Aldenburg's* battle group turned west and increased revolutions. Krause was in no mood to dawdle. The ship could swallow almost sixty kilometres an hour at full speed but with the weather closing in he accepted the need for a prudent approach, reluctantly holding the ship at three-quarter speed. Briefly, he thought the destroyers might have trouble handling the conditions, and he smiled thinly. They would have to find ways to cope.

The convoy had slipped behind schedule. Leaden grey skies had warned of a coming storm and although it came from the west, the heavy following seas played havoc with station keeping. Driving rain blotted out entire columns from those in close company and the escorts found themselves under constant pressure to shepherd straying vessels back into some semblance of order. Inevitably there was a reduction in speed, some of the ships unable, or their captains unwilling, to risk their machinery in gale force conditions.

For Captain John Hennessey, watch keeping over the entire convoy had become a sleepless exercise in willpower and the ever present need to answer yet one more 'situation' as it arose. It became a different sort of war, a war against the elements, and after twenty-four hours of relentless buffeting, any thoughts of meeting the enemy understandably took second place. At the mercy of the seas the convoy pushed on, no longer the disciplined three columns, now it was more a group of individuals intent on their own survival.

On the bridge of H.M.S. *Rosefinch*, Lieutenant-Commander Peter Willoughby was just managing to hold *Brackendale* in sight to the north. To the south *Zeus* appeared and disappeared depending on whether *Rosefinch* hit a trough or crested a roller. In these conditions, he thought, visual watch keeping in accordance with McGregor's instructions was reaching the limit. If the weather deteriorated any further, and he reckoned that was definitely on the cards, the flotilla would be forced to reduce the gap between vessels.

'*Zeus* calling us up, sir,' came a warning from the signaller.

Willoughby turned with his binoculars, focussing south over the port wing. Through a haze of spray he caught the pinprick of light. 'Go on,' he ordered.

'Reads . . . , "*Seaham* in contact with U-boat," and then I think it was, "*Pegwell* assisting. *Rosefinch* and *Brackendale* to hold station." End of message, sir.'

Willoughby lowered his glasses. He couldn't blame the signaller; *Zeus* was all over the place in the waves. Even so, he was surprised McGregor had not ordered them to close in. 'Acknowledge,' he said.

The signal lamp clattered, answered with a brief flash from *Zeus*.

He turned away and looked north to where *Brackendale* twisted her way through the waves.

'Pass that to *Brackendale*,' he said.

'Aye aye, sir,' said the signaller, and the starboard Aldis lamp flashed.

As he watched the message being transmitted, Willoughby wondered whether Thorburn was on the bridge. If not, he soon would be. And like himself, he'd think it odd that McGregor had not stuck to his own orders.

'*Zeus* turning south, sir.'

'What?' Willoughby snapped, and raised his binoculars over the port wing. In utter disbelief he watched *Zeus* swing away beam on to the waves and corkscrew her way south, getting smaller by the minute.

'*Brackendale* acknowledges, sir.'

'Very well,' he said sharply, and lowered his glasses. McGregor had decided to leave *Brackendale* and *Rosefinch* isolated from the flotilla. With the weather thickening he thought it was a bad decision, no telling where they might end up while they rode out a storm.

He cursed quietly and leaned against the screen. Time to concentrate on conning the ship.

Kapitänleutnant Heinz Müller, in command of U-395, had been first U-boat to arrive on station in search of the convoy. But from the moment of departure from the fjords the boat had suffered intermittent failure of its diesel engines. Although Müller's Chief Engineer originally thought the jets may have had blockages, a simple repair for an engineer, on closer inspection the nozzles all proved to be functioning correctly. What was originally presumed to be no more than an inconvenience, turned out to be anything but. On further investigation, the reason for their irregular performance turned out to be contaminated diesel fuel. Sea water had entered the tanks. Whether it was a seal overlooked during the refit, or some kind of sabotage in the repair yards, only a thorough investigation would resolve the mystery.

In the meantime, with a boat unable to maintain any sort of guaranteed propulsion on the surface, and therefore reducing the capacity to fully charge batteries for submersible operations, Heinz Müller felt there was no alternative but to return to base for repairs.

First to come on station, U-395 turned away from the hunt and became the first to limp home for the sanctuary of the fjords.

In the outer harbour of Reykjavik's relatively sheltered waters, H.M.S. *Stirling* was making final preparations before putting to sea. But with only an hour remaining to the weighing of the anchor, Captain Taylor-Mitchell answered a call from the Chief Engineer who, full of apologies, reported a malfunction with the steering gear. He accepted the news with quiet stoicism, and wishing to see for himself, donned a pair of coveralls.

In the tiller flat at the stern of the cruiser, he was shown a cracked cast-iron bracket that enclosed the main bearing. That breakage would severely restrict the cruiser's ability to manoeuvre. Taylor-Mitchell's inevitable question was answered with an assurance that it could be repaired but might well delay their departure by as much as twelve hours. He ordered his engineers to start work immediately, and sent off a signal to Admiralty informing them of the unavoidable delay.

Three hours later, Captain John Hennessey, having intercepted the signal from Taylor-Mitchell, and well aware of the implications behind that terse message, steamed north past Reykjavik's safe anchorage. He hoped that *Stirling's* delay in taking station alongside the convoy would not translate into anything too serious. The consequences of her absence might prove the difference between success and failure.

Not that he dwelt on the issue for very long, he had enough on his plate trying to shepherd the convoy safely through a North Atlantic storm. Sitting in the bridge-chair and nursing a steaming mug of strong sweet tea, he mused over the fluctuating fortunes of war. One minute all had been well, how quickly the tide could turn.

It was midday when the leading edge of the predicted storm descended on the Northern Patrol. And *Brackendale's* navigator had it right, it threatened to be a full blown 'hooligan'.

Thorburn stood behind the raised bridge-screen and watched the storm front churning the waves into flying spume. He turned and found Armstrong in the starboard wing.

'Life-lines, Number One. Have the bosun rig them now. More if you think they're needed.'

'Aye aye, sir,' Armstrong nodded, and moved for the port ladder.

Thorburn's mind was still partly grappling with *Rosefinch's* message, which had been followed by Guns informing him of *Zeus* turning south. Strange, he thought, but McGregor obviously had good reason.

A powerful gust of wind rattled the halyards and *Brackendale* slewed off course before being caught by the helmsman. She clawed her way to port, riding the waves, twisting to the troughs. A belt of rain slashed in from ahead, stinging the face, bouncing off steel panels. The lookouts came out of their eye sockets, shook themselves, and wiped lenses. And then they were again searching through the murk, visibility severely curtailed. But most of them had lived through similar conditions and stuck with it, knowing how vital they were to the ship's safety.

Thorburn wondered if *Seaham* and *Pegwell* were having any luck with their U-boat? That of course depended on whether the 'contact' had been true. Many oddities could produce a spurious echo on an asdic reading.

Four-hundred kilometres out from Iceland's north-east coast, *Aldenburg* met the first of the rising seas. Krause had personally come to the bridge to oversee the next phase of operations and smirked with satisfaction as the initial squalls made their presence felt. The horizon ahead had darkened with heavy cloud and it was obvious there was worse to come. It was as he'd predicted and he took great pleasure in reminding Bergmann of his forecast.

'Is this not what I said would happen, Bergmann? Do you not see how important this could be? The British will not be able to fly in this weather. If this holds for another day we should have the convoy at our mercy. What have you to say now, eh?' His laugh was scornful, a sardonic curl to his lips, and he gave no time for a reply. 'When you sail these waters remember what I tell you, it is always wise to know your weather. It is the difference between success and failure.'

'As you say, Herr Admiral. I will take note for the future.'

'Good ..., good. You are well advised,' Krause said, and stepped forward to the bridge-screen. Beneath his feet the warship butted into the rising waves, thumping through the sea.

'Should we not reduce speed, Herr Admiral?' Bergmann asked in response, a worried tone to his query.

'No,' Krause retorted. 'We must maintain speed. I want to turn south.'

'But, Herr Admiral, these waves could damage our hull,' Bergmann pleaded.

Krause snorted his derision. 'These waves? Ha ..., I think not. This is a German ship, German engineering. Do not presume to tell me what this ship cannot do, Kapitän.'

'Of course, Herr Admiral, I was only thinking of our mission.'

'Let me worry about such things, Bergmann, you just carry out my orders.'

Kapitän-zur-Sea Bergmann nodded and clicked his heels. 'As you wish, Herr Admiral.'

'Good. Where is Richter?'

'Four kilometres ahead.'

'Inform him of what the new bearing will be and order him to move out to ten kilometres. Only when we are nearing Iceland will we turn north to find the convoy.'

Krause stuck out his chin, fumbled inside a breast pocket for a cigar and jammed it between his teeth. He wished he felt as confident as he sounded, but this was no time for showing indecision. The distinctive aroma of cigar smoke wafted round the bridge space and he strode purposefully across to the commanders swivel chair.

Soon, he thought, another few short hours and he would have the enemy within his grasp.

14 . . A Distant Shadow

Thorburn had been on the bridge two hours. In that time a new day had dawned and the ship's company had gone through the pre-dawn routine of Action Stations, and then, when no danger appeared, he'd relaxed the crew to Defence Stations. The reason for his prolonged stay on the bridge was simply the ferocity of the storm. Building from the north-west, the clouds had darkened into a dense forbidding swirl, it was not something to be taken lightly. And although fluctuating in strength, the rain drove in sideways.

'Ship! Bearing green nine-oh!'

Thorburn stepped briskly across to the starboard wing and raised his binoculars, Armstrong quick to join him. A distant shape caught his attention and he sharpened the focus. It was a vague smudge in the rain and he struggled to hold the image. Whatever it was, it steamed from east to west across their own course, broadside on, and the superstructure gave the appearance of a warship. But it had been a brief glimpse, a solitary moment before it disappeared and he was left watching waves.

'Number One?'

'Too quick for me. Caught something but I'm not sure.'

Thorburn bent to a pipe.

'Guns! Green nine-oh. What can you tell me?'

Powerful binoculars in the Control Tower ranged across the sea, and then McDonald's voice came back via the pipe.

'Enemy destroyer, sir.'

'Sure?

'More or less . . . , yes. Can't be certain but the upperworks looked like a Zerstorer class, two heavily raked funnels.'

'Not a friendly then?'

'Definitely not, sir.'

Thorburn pursed his lips and then took a deep breath. 'Very well,' he said, and looked at Armstrong. 'We'll take a closer look. Action Stations, Number One.'

The First Lieutenant straightened away and hit the button, and the shrill alarm echoed out along the decks. The now off duty watch, enjoying the relative comfort of at least being sheltered from the gales, scrambled for their posts.

Thorburn bent to the wheelhouse pipe. 'Starboard ten.'

It was Falconer who answered. 'Starboard ten,

aye aye, sir.'

The ship began her turn, a little to the northeast, and swayed to port. The waves caught her broadside on, and the strength of the wind tossed white water across the boat deck. But before the wind pushed *Brackendale* too far round, Thorburn corrected the bearing.

'Midships,' he said.

'Midships, aye, sir.'

'Steady . . . ,' Thorburn warned, one eye on the compass. 'Steer three-five-oh degrees.'

'Three-five-oh degrees, aye aye, sir.'

Brackendale twisted into a heavy corkscrew, buried her bows into a solid wall of water, and staggered under the weight. Men braced themselves with whatever came to hand. Foaming sea surged aft from the fo'c'sle, swilling down the quarterdeck, tugging at sea boots, seeking the unwary. Two men at their stations on the port depth charge throwers clung on to the safety line strung between the afterdeck housing and the stern rail. They emerged from the deluge sodden but unharmed, sheepish grins hiding their misfortune.

In the wheelhouse the Cox'n fought to hold the ship on course, applying more to the wheel than normally needed. Her head insisted on coming to starboard and it was all he could do to hold her steady.

'Guns-bridge?'

Thorburn bent low to the pipe. 'Captain

speaking.'

'Target confirmed as enemy destroyer, sir,' McDonald said.

'Range?'

'Sorry, sir, no time, but beyond our guns.'

'Heading?'

'Due west.'

'Very well, thank you Guns,' Thorburn said, and frowned in thought. What was a German destroyer doing out here? On a specific mission, or escorting something..., if so, what? Maybe it was time to inform McGregor, let him decide the next move. He glanced to the back of the bridge.

'Yeoman,' he called.

'Sir,' said the man, scribble pad in hand.

'Signal for *Zeus*. "Suspected enemy destroyer to north, moving west." Got that?'

'Yes, sir.'

'Who's on the wireless?'

'Leading Telegraphist Hardcastle, sir.' The man hesitated, nervous.

'What is it?' Thorburn prompted.

'I thought we were under radio silence, sir,' he said awkwardly.

Thorburn knew what it had taken for the man to openly remind his Captain of current orders, it wasn't an easy thing to do. He grinned. 'Not to worry, my decision. Get that off now.'

'Aye aye, sir,' the man said, visibly relieved, and moved off.

Brackendale slewed to port, sliding unevenly

across a larger wave, and Thorburn bent a knee to maintain balance. He glanced round for Armstrong.

'Who's on radar, Number One?'

'Leading Radar Mechanic Bellingham.'

Thorburn thought for a second before making up his mind.

'I'm going to have a word. Hold course and let me know when we make contact . . . , if we do.'

Armstrong ducked from a sheet of spray before nodding. 'Aye aye, sir.'

Thorburn dropped down the starboard ladder and then clambered down to the boat deck. He slithered as his boots hit an inch of sea water, and he grabbed for the safety line. A wave curled high over the side and plucked at his legs, and for a moment he could do no more than hold on. It receded and he cautiously took another step through the swirling foam. A minute later and he'd reached the midships housing with its radar 'lantern' mounted overhead. Grunting with the effort he unlatched the door, swung inside, and slammed it closed behind him.

The two operators looked round in surprise. It was unusual for the Captain to visit.

'Relax,' he said to put them at ease, then shook water off his cap. He recognised both men. One was fair haired with ruddy cheeks, very young, and for the moment his name escaped Thorburn's memory. But the other, stocky and much older, sat squarely in front of the radar screen, easily identifiable.

'Bellingham, isn't it?' Thorburn prompted.

'Yes, sir,' he answered with assured confidence.

'Any problems?'

The man frowned, on the defensive. 'No, sir, don't believe there is.'

Thorburn smiled. 'Good, pleased to hear it,' he said encouragingly. 'You'll be wondering why I'm here, so I won't keep you in suspense.' He leaned forward, enough to show he was taking them into his confidence.

'Just to put you in the picture, we spotted a German destroyer to the north, but the weather closed in and we lost it.'

Bellingham made as if to interrupt, and Thorburn raised a hand.

'You wouldn't have had it on screen, outside radar range. But,' he went on, 'and you can call it an educated guess, I think there might be something bigger up there. It's only a hunch, but you two need to be one-hundred percent on the ball. The lookouts are struggling to see much of anything in this weather so don't take your eyes off the screen. You might be our only warning of some big artillery. Understood?'

The youngster nodded, eyes wide. 'Yes, sir.'

Bellingham looked at his Captain square on. 'You can rely on us, sir.'

'Never doubted it,' Thorburn grinned. 'Alright then, carry on.' About to reach for the door, he turned back to the youngster. 'Remiss of me, but I can't remember your name?'

'Potter, sir.'

Thorburn studied him for a moment, an eager young man willing to please. How reliable in the middle of a battle, time would tell. Not much more than a boy, thrust into God knows what. 'Where are you from, Potter?'

'Hastings, sir.'

Thorburn nodded, smiled. 'Well, Potter from Hastings, keep an eye on Bellingham and you won't go far wrong.'

The young man grinned. 'Aye aye, sir.'

Thorburn opened the door and a gust of wind howled through the gap. He prepared to step outside and glanced back at Bellingham.

'You better shut this for me.'

He put his shoulder to the door, lurched into the open and reached for the safety line. He heard the door slam and then, hand over hand, hauled himself along the deck. The only saving grace, he thought, as he squinted through the rain and spray, was that he was better off here on the leeward side than if he'd been on the port deck. It took longer than expected but he finally made the sanctuary of the fo'c'sle.

When he eventually emerged off the ladder onto the bridge he was breathing hard and paused to take stock. The scar on his temple throbbed from the exertion and he found he was feeling light headed. He saw Armstrong looking concerned and waved him away.

'Signal from *Zeus*, sir.' The Yeoman had returned.

Thorburn took the message slip and glanced at the brief reply. "Investigate your contact. Will join you"

'Well done, Yeo. Let me know if there's anything else.'

'Aye aye, sir,' he said, and turned away.

Thorburn stepped forward to the compass platform and winced at the flying spray.

'Number One,' he said, voice raised against the wind. 'I don't want anyone moving on deck without good reason. Check on all the gun mounts and make sure the depth charge crews are properly tied off. I'll relax Action Stations if I can, but in the meantime they'll just have to make the best of it.'

'Aye aye, sir,' Armstrong acknowledged above the wind, and made for the ladder.

'Watch yourself down there,' Thorburn called, 'it's not good.'

Armstrong nodded and disappeared from sight. *Brackendale* ploughed on, pitching and rolling as the weather closed in, and Thorburn gritted his teeth, anxious.

When the full force of the storm finally struck, it was with a fury they could not have predicted. Wild seas and gale force winds lashed the ship, driving rain sheeting in sideways. He narrowed his eyes against the salt laden spray, knowing this would be a test of seamanship. Storms of this ferocity could capsize a ship. A momentary lapse of concentration, a rogue wave, and there'd be no coming back.

And as for the enemy, there'd be time enough for that later. Right now it was more important to ride this storm front. Sometimes the fury of a leading edge was a lot worse than the main depression.

'Port five,' he called down the pipe, needing to bring her head into the wind.

'Port five, aye aye, sir,' Falconer acknowledged.

Brackendale came left into the wind and rode high, cresting the next wave and diving down the trough.

'Midships!' Thorburn ordered.

'Wheel's amidships. Steering three-four-five, sir.'

'Steady on that, Cox'n,' Thorburn said, and settled himself at the screen. This might well be a taxing few hours.

At the stern rail Lieutenant George Labatt and his depth charge crew could only turn their backs to the driving rain and endure. They clung to precarious handholds and swayed with the undulating deck, ankle deep in foaming surf. It took all of their accumulated experience to withstand the furious onslaught and they suffered it with a stoic resilience. Two of those men, Higgins and Reid, the 'old salts', had experienced much the same on more than one occasion, and across the loaded racks they grimaced at one another and shook heads in unison. A small enough gesture, but it reinforced their long standing friendship.

Forward of the depth charge racks, a few feet away, eight men crouched behind the shield of the after gun mount in a vain attempt to ward off the worst of the weather. Ahead of them, the quarterdeck galley housing offered some protection, but the swirling wind brought rain from every angle, a penetrating swathe of cold water.

One of the gunners, Daniel Miller, sat with his back to the shield, water pouring from his steel helmet, and cursed. He cursed the wind and he cursed the cold, but most of all he cursed the rain. It was just his rotten luck to have been chosen to man the quarterdeck guns. If he'd been on the fo'c'sle he'd have had more protection, but no, he was here on the stern most pair of guns with nowhere to hide, and he wanted to make his feelings clear.

But the majority of gunners kept their thoughts to themselves. It was bad enough not knowing what action lay ahead. They could put up with a storm any day of the week.

15 .. Small Echo

Lieutenant-Commander Peter Willoughby

had his own problems. *Rosefinch* was proving to be a handful, bucking and twisting to every thumping wave. Like *Brackendale,* he'd brought the ship's head to the wind in an effort to reduce the worst of her unpredictable behaviour, but the storm front was proving to be a tough proposition. He had concerns for the safety of the crew and although only half of them, Blue Watch, were on duty, those on the weather decks could ill afford to relax their vigilance. He'd passed the word for all hands to limit their time in the open and hoped no one would be foolhardy enough to ignore the advice.

A violent pitch into the next wave had him grabbing for the rail and he swore softly. *Rosefinch* swayed to starboard, leaning at a dangerous angle before hauling herself upright.

Willoughby blew out his cheeks in response and grinned at his Number One, who nodded and raised a doubtful eyebrow. 'Don't want too many of those, sir.'

'All under control, Number One, she's had worse.'

His First Officer rubbed his nose and shook his head. 'If you say so, sir,' he said uneasily, and made a concerted effort to concentrate on the compass.

Willoughby turned back to the screen, the smile fading, and tried to envisage the current position of the flotilla. The three ships to the south had parted company, out of radar range and with no chance of being seen through the driving rain. And once or twice now, even *Brackendale* had slipped from view.

'Sir!'

He turned to find his Leading Telegraphist squinting into the rain.

'What is it?'

'*Brackendale* broke radio silence, sir.'

'Go on.'

'It was a signal to *Zeus* reporting possible enemy destroyer to the north. *Zeus* ordered *Brackendale* to investigate and added he'll join her.'

Willoughby stuck his chin out. 'Did he, by God? Nothing for us?'

'No, sir, that was all.'

'Alright, carry on,' he said, and jammed his hands into the duffle coat pockets. He was not impressed. McGregor's three ships were gone to hell hunting a U-boat, and now Richard was swanning off in search of a German destroyer.

Rosefinch squirmed awkwardly to a breaking wave and he braced his legs. But his mind still played with McGregor's orders. What about *Rosefinch*? Was he supposed to just carry on patrolling or do something meaningful? If there was a chance of combat then surely he should be following *Brackendale*? And then it dawned on him. McGregor's orders were clear. If one ship closed a target the next must go to her assistance, and despite the driving rain he grinned.

Action at last . . . , now it was just a matter of beating this weather and finding a way to bring *Rosefinch* round to the north. He could but try.

He raised his voice to the wheelhouse pipe. 'Starboard five.'

'Starboard five, aye aye, sir.'

Willoughby waited, watchful, feeling the ship's response through his toes. She came round, a little, the wind and waves off the port bow.

'Midships!'

'Wheel's amidships, sir.'

'Steer two-nine-oh degrees.'

'Two-nine-oh degrees, aye aye, sir.'

Willoughby straightened from the pipe, eyes narrowed. It wasn't much of a turn, but anything was better than doing nothing. At least they would be closer if called on.

Two hours into the storm and with the worst of the weather easing, *Brackendale* no longer thumped into heavy seas. 'Radar-bridge!'

'Bridge,' Thorburn snapped.

The voice belonged to Bellingham. 'I had a small echo at nine miles, sir. Bearing Green nine-five.'

'And you've lost it?'

'Yes, sir, just a couple of intermittent flashes.'

'Very well,' Thorburn said, and glanced right across the starboard side. It was no more than an instinctive reaction, as if by looking that way he might somehow see through the murk and identify the target for himself. He stepped down to the screen thinking rapidly. An echo at nine miles meant something large because the Type 271 radar had a limited capacity, and at that range only a big vessel would produce a response. He tried to recall a piece of simple rhyming verse designed to help memorise the range in miles. How did it go . . . ?

"Nine for a cruiser, submarine three,

The 'big one' ten, and six for me".

That was the theory, and the 'big one', the battleship, could even be seen at eleven miles. So the echo was probably a cruiser, but if so, where was the 'me' from the poem, the destroyer? If it had returned as close escort it wouldn't necessarily show up on the radar at that distance.

He winced at the ache in his left temple, and frowned in concentration. If only he had the benefit of a clear horizon. He rubbed the scar and made up his mind. To hell with caution he thought, storm or no, he must close the target. A tight smile replaced the frown. It was time to act. He bent to the wheelhouse voice-pipe.

'Starboard thirty.'

The Cox'n acknowledged and *Brackendale* heeled to port, leaning hard over. He watched the bows come north and then settled on a bearing of three-five-oh. Standing at the screen he stared ahead at the rolling seas, letting the cold rain wash his face. It was strangely refreshing and he lifted his chin, let it happen. The ship corkscrewed across the waves, clawing her way towards the unknown target, and he gripped the rail.

In compliance with the orders of Admiral Mathias Krause, *Aldenburg* had pushed ever westward and as the two hour mark approached he warned Richter to make ready for the turn south. The storm had not developed into the wild tumult he had hoped for and in the last thirty minutes the winds had backed off to leave the sea rough but no longer threatening. But the one thing still very much in their favour was the constant curtain of rain blotting out the seascape.

'Bergmann, it is time. You will come left and set a course south-southwest.'

'Jawohl, Herr Admiral.'

Krause nodded. 'And more speed. We have little time to spare.'

Bergmann gave his orders and nine-thousand tons of Kiel built cruiser swung ponderously across the turbulent waves. As the warship completed its turn and settled to the new course, the engine room connected all three shafts of the propulsion system, and with the combined drive of those big bronze screws, *Aldenburg* ploughed headlong into the heavy seas.

Krause felt the thump of waves, watched the

bow wave surge skyward, and held his nerve. This, he thought, was the moment to make best use of the poor conditions. They must drive on, use the power unleashed by the engines and pounce on their unsuspecting prey. As the *Aldenburg* pushed ahead, twenty-five officers and six-hundred crewmen braced themselves against the violent motion.

Out in the North Atlantic, the twenty-eight ships under Hennessey's protection were nearing the point at which he would order their next alteration of course. It would take them north and east parallel with Greenland's coast and west of Jan Mayan Island. Beyond that lay Bear Island to the south of Spitzbergen, followed by the final leg taking them into the Barents Sea and into the final approaches to the mouth of the Kola inlet.

For Captain John Hennessey, the gales of the past long hours, although causing some discrepancy with station keeping amongst the convoy, presented him with one over-riding concern..., the lack of air cover. Hundreds of miles from safety and with the confirmed threat of U-boats in the near vicinity, he knew that the ships still offered a prime target for any audacious German attack. And the persistent driving rain served only to add another layer of uncertainty to their progress. At times visibility would open up to five or six miles, and then without warning, the fo'c'sle would disappear in front of their eyes. Yes, he had radar, as did all the escorts, but that didn't apply to many of the merchantmen. For them, bad weather and no discernible horizon made for a dangerous passage through the waves.

He crossed the bridge to the radar repeater and studied the pattern of blips at the rear of the convoy. He found what he thought must be the S.S. *Bannion* still holding station at the stern of the right column. It had taken her hours to make up the lost time and eventually rejoin the line of ships, and in all that while the *Franklin George* had shepherded her patiently through

'Signal, sir. We intercepted it on short wave.' The man looked anxious.

Hennessey took the slip, shielding it from the rain, and read through. He returned the slip and pondered its meaning. An enemy warship of sorts . . . , yes. How much of a concern to the convoy? Something to bear in mind. He sat back.

The convoy and her escorts ploughed on through the heavy seas. For now their only worry was nature itself.

At Reykjavik, Captain R. J. Taylor-Mitchell answered a knock on his door. *Stirling's* Chief Engineer stepped in and made his report. The repairs were complete, the rudder tested, and he was happy with the results.

'Good as new, sir.'

The Captain looked at his watch, smiled and nodded, relieved. Eight hours, less than predicted.

'Well done, Chief, time we were under way.'

'Ready when you are, sir. Boilers are on line and pressure's up.'

'Very well, thank you,' Taylor-Mitchell said. 'I must see to the ship.'

Thirty-seven minutes after the Chief Engineer's report, a twelve-gun Royal Navy cruiser turned north in storm ravaged waters and picked up speed. On the bridge, Captain Taylor-Mitchell had the Plot firmly fixed in his mind, and made a further calculation. He estimated the convoy would be well into the Denmark Strait, around one-hundred miles ahead. It would be the best part of five or six hours steaming before *Stirling* could make contact. Add to that the imposition of strict radio silence, and the proverbial 'needle in a haystack' came to mind. And as always, in bad weather, there were no guarantees.

In *Brackendale's* Control Tower, Lieutenant 'Guns' McDonald stood head and shoulders above the 'tub' and focussed the ship's most powerful pair of binoculars on the northern horizon. His range of visibility was dictated by the ever changing frequency of rain squalls, one minute restricted to a few hundred yards at best, the next, opening out to many miles before rapidly deteriorating under sheets of rain. But he was nothing if not persistent, and he again swept the glasses steadily from left to right, eyes straining to catch that first, faint hint of trouble.

And in one of those rare moments when the rain unexpectedly cleared his field of vision, McDonald caught the ghostly shape of a distant enemy destroyer. He determined to hold it in focus and spoke from the corner of his mouth.

'There's a target at Green one-oh. Give me the range.'

The tub of the Control Tower traversed a little to the right, enabling the stereoscopic sights of the extended Range-Finder to home in on the target.

'Twelve-thousand yards, sir.'

'Stay with it,' McDonald ordered, and turned to the voice-pipe. 'Guns-Bridge!' he called.

'Bridge?' came the reply. It was the Captain.

'Enemy destroyer,' he reported, 'bearing Green one-oh, range twelve-thousand.'

'Course?' the Captain demanded.

'Coming straight for us, sir.'

There was a clear hesitation before the Captain answered. 'Very well, keep me informed.'

'Aye aye, sir,' McDonald said, and prepared his team for action.

Thorburn straightened from the voice-pipe and rubbed his forehead, giving himself a moment to consider this latest turn of events. He had a radar contact northeast of *Brackendale's* position, probably something major. From the same direction a destroyer was bearing down on them and it didn't take a genius to conclude it was one of the escorts. But how many in total? Surely there were more. He couldn't believe the Kriegsmarine would risk one of their few remaining principal warships without the protection of two or three outriders.

And what about German radar? Was *Brackendale* already on their plot and being sized up for targeting? If he'd been right about the possibility it was *Aldenburg*, those guns had a range of close on sixteen miles. At the same time, he couldn't remember if German radar had that kind of range. If not, the enemy would be restricted to visual range-finding equipment, and in this weather? Not ideal, but good for *Brackendale*.

He turned to look ahead across the starboard bow and made a decision. McGregor had ordered him to investigate, and to that end his duty was clear, he had to identify the threat. But it would be more prudent to skirt any immediate confrontation and tack westwards, dodge the enemy destroyer. He could then turn east and approach the larger more important target from the flank.

Fleetingly, Jennifer's parting words came to the fore, tugging at his conscience. He guessed she'd think he was at it again, throwing caution to the wind and diving in at the deep end. But he knew that wasn't the case. He had the ship's company to think of, *Brackendale* herself, but, and more importantly, there were eighteen ships, their crews, and their valuable cargoes relying on the Royal Navy to see them safe through the voyage. As for himself, having come this far, with the promise of the war being over in the not too distant future, it wasn't part of his plans to die early.

He shrugged off the doubts and leaned to the wheelhouse pipe. 'Port five.'

'Port five, aye, sir.'

Brackendale answered the helm, easing left, swaying with the waves. He waited until the ship's head pointed north-north-west and steadied the bearing.

'Midships..., steer three-three-eight degrees.'

The Cox'n acknowledged. 'Wheel's amidships, sir, steering three-three-eight degrees.'

'Very well,' Thorburn said, and *Brackendale* ran on. He wanted two or three miles under her keel before swinging right to intercept. And once again the rain lashed the bridge, hard, unrelenting, and opaque.

Thorburn wiped his face and smiled grimly. It was a timely intrusion, almost as good as fog. He might not be able to hide from enemy radar, but at least *Brackendale* could take advantage of not being in visual contact. Whatever happened, he had the plot in his head, with a rough estimate of the enemy dispositions. As Captain of a warship in action it was his primary function, to gather the information and harness the power of a human's brain to overcome the odds. All the electro-mechanical wizardry in the world couldn't replace a man's natural ability to understand what was going on around him.

He turned his face from the stinging rain and hunched his shoulders. A few more minutes on this bearing and then bring her east and trust his instincts.

'Herr Admiral, a signal from Richter.'

Krause turned his head slowly, deliberately giving the impression of not being overly concerned.

'Tell me,' he said softly.

'He reports a British destroyer coming north. It was lost in the rain.'

Krause lowered his eyes to hide a sudden sense of unease. He felt danger. The Royal Navy did not send lone destroyers to patrol this far north, and the convoy would still be well to the west or northwest of Iceland. What, he wondered, did this one warship signify? A battle group with outlying escorts? Heavy cruisers?

'Bergman,' he said, eyes narrowed, 'you will tell Richter to hold course. He is to report immediately any further contact but must not engage the enemy. You understand, Kapitän? Have I made myself clear?'

'Of course, Herr Admiral. I will signal the *Bruno Keplar*.'

Peter Willoughby squinted into the rain and cursed. *Rosefinch* was struggling and his lookouts had lost sight of *Brackendale*. The radar room had held her for a while but even that contact had evaporated and he was feeling irritated. The last report showed Richard pushing north, before altering a few points to the west. Willoughby's intuition reasoned that changing course to the west had to be justified by something other than the weather, a sighting maybe, or a radar contact.

Rosefinch pitched and swayed, behaving more like a porpoise than a modern built warship of His Majesty's Navy, and he nibbled at his bottom lip. Should he follow *Brackendale* to the west or hold to the north? It had taken a long time to bring *Rosefinch's* bows around from the west, but with a reduction in the intensity of the wind and waves he felt it was better to maintain their current heading. Again he cursed under his breath and wondered if he could squeeze a few more knots out of the engines?

He thought it was probably better not to try, but it was galling to be out of the picture . . . , near to the action, but not close enough. Still, he grinned, he might be lucky.

Korvettenkapitän Rudolph Reinhart in U-824, the late arrival from its hunting ground, had been forced to go deep and make repairs to the starboard bank of diesel engines. It had taken fourteen hours of slow underwater passage, but with the diesels now theoretically repaired, Reinhart headed for the surface to prove their performance and at the same time, recharge the batteries. It was not something he looked forward to. Their last fixed position had placed them three-hundred kilometres southwest of Jan Mayen Island, but since diving to carry out the repairs, navigation had become more of a guess than confirmed reality.

The boat rose effortlessly until it came to within fourteen metres of the surface. It was at that moment U-824 encountered unexpected turbulence and Reinhart had the periscope raised early. What he found through the lens looked not so bad, and he ordered his first officer to complete the manoeuvre. He opened the hatch and proceeded to carry out a thorough search of the rolling seas, but then waited until all the lookouts had reported it was clear. He gave the order to start main engines, and after a series of loud cracks and bangs, followed by a plume of heavy black smoke, the diesels finally belched into life

On the conning tower's platform, Reinhart ducked away from a sudden squall, visibility falling to below a hundred metres. Bad weather worked both ways, he thought. A blanket of cloud helped hide the boat from enemy aircraft, should they even choose to fly in such conditions, but the downside was meeting a Royal Navy warship with no warning. He squinted at his wrist watch and let the boat push on; they were well behind schedule.

16 . . In for a Penny

In *Aldenburg's* radar room, the Senior Operator and two of his underlings had become immersed in a heated argument over what might happen at the end of the war. Inevitably, their attention to duty slipped, became less focussed. Unfortunately, their briefing on taking over the watch had been to expect enemy formations beyond the Faroe Islands, and certainly not here in these stormy conditions. Therefore, as the disagreement intensified, the Senior Operator momentarily turned his back on the display and missed the first crucial echo pulsing on screen. And it wasn't until well after the argument had fragmented into a disgruntled stalemate that the man in charge caught sight of a flickering dot, followed by a second echo to the south-west.

But for all his faults the man was experienced enough to watch and wait, and to gather enough information before making a concise report to the bridge. His patience was soon rewarded.

Krause heard the insistent buzz of a telephone

and watched Bergmann answer.

'Ja, what is it?'

Silence followed, Bergmann head down and listening, and then, very deliberately, he replaced the hand-piece until it clicked into place on the forked cradle.

'That was radar,' he said, turning until Krause could see his face. 'Two enemy destroyers to the west, heading north. Range ten-thousand metres, speed twenty-five.'

Krause fingered his chin, and then nodded.

'Get me the Gunnery Officer,' he ordered, came to his feet and walked across to where Bergmann held out the handset.

Krause cleared his throat. 'There are destroyers to our right, can you see them?' There was a pause and he guessed that the armoured tower was traversing round for a line of sight.

'Nothing, Herr Admiral, the rain is too much. But I too have them now on radar.'

Krause considered his position. He felt certain the British had not identified *Aldenburg*, in which case, why advertise his presence by opening fire. At this stage, avoidance must surely be the better option. Whatever those enemy vessels were up to he had his own mission to accomplish.

'Then all is in order,' he said, 'but wait for my command.'

He heard the acknowledgement and swung round to Bergmann. 'Where is the remainder of our escort?'

'Three kilometres northeast. They cannot manage this weather,' Bergman said by way of explanation.

'Signal them to close up. We may need their torpedoes.'

'They do their best, Herr Admiral.'

'Then get them to try harder. In the meantime Kapitän, we go to Battle Stations,' and he managed a thin smile. 'I wish not to fight if it can be avoided, but prepare we must.'

'Jawohl, Herr Admiral,' Bergmann nodded, and sounded the alarm.

It took a full four minutes for the ship to come to readiness and Krause scowled in disgust. The men were sloppy, too many months sitting on their arses. Later, he thought, I will see to their training.

In the radar room the Senior Operator watched his targets fade and strengthen, and fade again. He had experienced conditions like this before, the storm was leaving its mark.

Thorburn braced himself as *Brackendale* thumped into the waves. The time was fast approaching to make the turn and he moved to the compass platform, He stepped up and stood for a moment, head and shoulders clear above the others on the bridge. He checked the ship's bearing and glanced at his wristwatch. If his calculations were correct the enemy should now be somewhere off *Brackendale's* starboard beam.

A bulkhead telephone clamoured for attention and Armstrong answered. He gave a curt, 'Carry on', and reported. 'Strong echo, bearing Green oh-eight-five degrees, range ten miles, sir.'

'Very well,' Thorburn said, and conjured up a mental picture of the situation. The German warship was more or less where he hoped it would be, almost due east off *Brackendale's* right flank. To the south, if it had not changed course, lay the enemy destroyer . . . , and then there was *Rosefinch*, seven or eight miles astern of Brackendale's starboard quarter, doing her best to give support.

'Number One, a minute if you please.'

Armstrong nodded and came to his side. 'Sir?'

Thorburn leaned both hands on the compass binnacle. 'I think,' he said slowly, 'our only course of action is to verify the target by getting into visual range. If it is the *Aldenburg*, and that is my gut instinct, things could get pretty lively. I don't have to tell you that our chances of getting away in one piece are pretty slim. But I'm convinced it's the right thing to do. I wanted you to know, see what you think.'

Armstrong stared at him. 'You want my opinion, sir?'

'We've come a long way together, Number One, you know I value your thoughts.'

There was a pause as Armstrong lowered his chin, followed by a slight shake of his head. He looked up with a glint in his eye. 'Permission to speak freely, sir?' he asked, lowering his voice.

Thorburn glanced round, not wanting their discussion overheard. He held up a hand and gestured at the bridge-screen, and they moved forward out of earshot.

'Go on,' he said.

'Well, sir,' Armstrong began, tentative, and Thorburn thought he showed signs of embarrassment. 'You've captained us from the beginning, and good or bad, *Brackendale* has always come through. Some of it might be down to luck, but mostly we . . . , that is the officers and crew, well they all believe that your decisions have carried us through.' He looked down and shifted his weight from one foot to the other. When he looked up, it was with a steely determination.

'If you want to hunt down this German ship, I can speak for the entire ship's company when I say we're with you. Good or bad, right now we're the only ship in a position to get some answers. It's more than the Admiralty bargained for, but you have to protect that convoy.'

Thorburn swallowed, struck by Armstrong's utter candour. Just for once he felt lost for words. Not knowing quite what to say, he simply reached out and squeezed his shoulder.

'Thank you, Number One. I'll not forget that.' He straightened up, and again checked the time. 'Another couple of minutes and we'll make the turn.' He grinned despite the stinging rain. 'In for a penny, eh?' He chuckled and turned back to the compass platform.

Behind his back, Armstrong muttered something.

'Sorry, what was that?' Thorburn asked.

'Just hoping we're not in for a 'pounding', sir.'

Thorburn laughed, the noise whipped away by the wind. Best not to dwell on that.

Leading Seaman Allun Jones, with his binoculars raised over the port wing, found that he'd heard the two officers talking. It wasn't that he'd been deliberately eavesdropping, but their voices had carried. A faint smile played across his lined face and he thought Armstrong had called it exactly right. Jones had joined ship before she was commissioned and he had first hand experience of how their 'maverick' Captain had earned his reputation. Above all, the man had courage, a devotion to duty that couldn't be questioned, a fighting spirit that was second to none.

He finished his sweep from bow to beam, wiped the lens and began again, from port beam to the bows. He remembered how many times the Captain had gone against tradition, ignored protocol, and triumphed by employing an apparently reckless rule of his own. The smile lingered as he eyed the visible horizon. This time it seemed as if the skipper was taking them into some serious trouble. He hoped their luck would hold.

Thorburn took a deep breath and bent to the wheelhouse voice-pipe. 'Starboard fifteen.'

The Cox'n's firm acknowledgement echoed in return. 'Starboard fifteen, aye aye, sir.'

And *Brackendale* swayed to port, her bows swinging east, and Thorburn waited, judging the moment. 'Midships!' he snapped.

'Wheel's amidships, sir.'

'Steady . . . , steer oh-nine-five degrees.'

'Oh-nine-five degrees, aye aye, sir.'

Thorburn stared ahead. They had a following sea now, no longer buffeting the bows but rolling with the ship's forward momentum.

'Radar-Bridge,' came from a voice-pipe.

'Bridge,' Armstrong said.

'Target bearing Green one-oh, sir. Range nine and a half miles. Course two-one-oh degrees.'

Thorburn nodded that he'd heard. The enemy had slipped past and ended up fine on the starboard bow, exactly as he'd hoped. But unless he altered course, came round to the south, he'd never get *Brackendale* on the German's stern.

'Starboard twenty!'

Falconer repeated. 'Starboard twenty, aye aye, sir.'

And the small destroyer responded to the Cox'n's hand, clawing her way round from east to south, punching through the waves. Spray lifted from her sharp stem, over the fo'c'sle and spattered the bridge.

Thorburn steadied the turn and *Brackendale* corkscrewed, the waves hitting the starboard beam. She rocked wickedly to port, and those on the bridge, unprepared for the violence of the lean, slithered on the gratings. Men grasped for a hand hold, cursed, and waited for the correction. The ship hung over for what seemed an age, but could be measured in seconds, before she abruptly righted herself.

'What's our speed, Pilot?'

'Eighteen knots by the log, sir,' Martin said.

'Very well,' he nodded, and then to Armstrong, 'Number One, ask radar if they can give me the target's speed.'

And then the fine rain turned to icy pellets, blowing in hard off the starboard beam, lashing the bridge and obscuring the bows. Men winced at the stinging fury, exposed faces made raw in the cold. Lookouts straightened out of their binoculars, met by a white sheet of driven ice.

'Twenty knots, sir,' Armstrong called.

Thorburn, his face half turned away from the hail, nodded. Twenty knots . . . , that meant *Brackendale* needed to be near her maximum to stand any chance of catching. And twenty-six knots in these seas was pushing it. He wracked his brain in an attempt to remember a light cruiser's top speed. Thirty or so knots? But that was unlikely. Unless the captain was desperate, economy dictated a more circumspect twenty or twenty-two knots, exactly what radar had confirmed. He bent to the pipe.

'Wheelhouse?'

'Wheelhouse, sir,' Falconer said.

'Ring up twenty-five knots, Cox'n.'

'Twenty-five knots, aye aye, sir.'

And in moments, even though the ship trembled to the thumping seas, a stronger pulse vibrated through the deck as the steam driven turbines imparted more power to the spinning shafts. *Brackendale* surged forward, leaping into the waves, her bows hammering at solid walls of water.

Thorburn gritted his teeth, forcing himself to face the biting needles. A thin layer of slush began to form on the ship's upperworks, accumulating in odd corners. He turned his gaze across the starboard side and all he found was more of the same, an unrelenting torment of hailstones bouncing off steel panels. Beneath his feet the small destroyer pitched and rolled, yawing off course, only to have her head coaxed back by Falconer's constant vigilance. But Thorburn felt that *Brackendale* had what it took to withstand this kind of turbulence, and he let the ship run on. It dawned on him that the German warship, moving southeast, was heading more-or-less towards where *Zeus* was hurrying to join them. It was a small comfort, something positive to lift a man's spirits.

The ferocity of the hailstones began to ease.

Aboard the German cruiser, Admiral Mathias Krause pushed himself out of the commander's chair and walked forward to the screen. Not without difficulty. The cruiser lurched and swayed in the heavy seas, battering through the waves. He reached for the mahogany rail that ran across the forebridge and stared ahead beyond the guns. He wondered about the enemy destroyers. Was this the convoy escort or a hunting group? If they were the outlying escort of such hunters there might well be cruisers involved, heavy cruisers. He rubbed his forehead. Surely the convoy would not be so far south? The normal route would have them much further north where he could approach from behind.

'Herr Admiral!' Bergmann called, an urgency in his voice. 'Radar reports one of the British destroyers alters course for us.'

Krause grunted in annoyance. 'Range?'

'Nine-thousand metres.'

'What?' he barked. 'We cannot be so close. Why was I not informed earlier?'

'The radar has been sporadic, the weather is not kind to the signal.'

Krause shook his head, frowning in thought. If these wintry squalls cleared, the *Aldenburg* would be in full view of the enemy. His position would be flashed to the British Admiralty and they would do everything in their power to sink him. He closed his eyes, evaluating tactics.

He could increase speed and possibly outrun the destroyer, although not so if it was Tribal class. And he must approach any enemy ships with much caution. He opened his eyes and thrust out his bottom lip. There was a further possibility. He could turn on this destroyer and attack from out of the poor visibility, have all *Aldenburg's* guns aim for the enemy's bridge and mast, take out their means of signalling. Even this poorly trained crew could not miss at such close range . . . , could they?

Lieutenant-Commander Peter Willoughby shook ice crystals from the peak of his cap and prayed for an end to the hailstorm, *Rosefinch* swayed under his feet, ploughing on through heavy seas, and he glanced at the compass to check their bearing. They were holding course a few points east of north, with only the radar able to penetrate their immediate surroundings. But a few minutes later, his prayers were answered and he breathed a sigh of relief as the icy downpour dissolved into rain. And the wind slackened, leading to a subtle improvement in visibility. He raised his glasses over the screen and swept the seas ahead . . . , and drew a blank. Only green-grey rolling waves met his gaze, topped by foaming crests, and he turned away in disgust. Whatever *Brackendale* was after and exactly where she was, remained a mystery.

To the south, *Zeus* had broken off her hunt for

the elusive U-boat and headed north. McGregor ordered *Seaham* and *Pegwell* to break off from the search and follow *Zeus* on a heading of three-five-five. Between the three ships, twelve patterns of depth charges had been dropped on their elusive prey. There was no doubting that they'd cornered a U-boat but all their efforts had seemingly come to nought. Probably shook up, and possibly damaged. If nothing else it had been forced to go on the defensive, and for now, given the circumstances, that was enough. Underwater it would be too slow to threaten the convoy.

Nothing more had been heard from *Brackendale,* and McGregor had a hunch he might be needed. Although Thorburn had broken radio silence, his reason for doing so couldn't be faulted. Admiral Collingwood had made no mention of possible interference from surface ships and it was imperative that such a sighting be investigated. And during the time he'd been conning *Zeus* in search of the U-boat, it had dawned on McGregor that Thorburn's discovery of the Arado seaplane might well indicate the presence of a major German warship on a sortie into the Norwegian Sea. He thought it was doubtful, but couldn't discount the possibility. What concerned him most was the now inevitable wide flung dispersal of his forces. And the severe conditions under which they'd been operating.

McGregor balanced himself at the forebridge

and peered into the rain, all the while reflecting on the current situation. For *Zeus*, with a displacement of two-thousand tons and a high freeboard, the storm left them relatively unaffected. But he knew from past experience, that smaller warships navigating heavy seas, with less power at their disposal, could tax a captain's seamanship beyond his reserves.

Not that a Flotilla Leader could do much about it, certain things were beyond a man's control. All he could do right now was to follow his hunch and move north. It might have been remiss of him to spread his forces so thinly, but at least he could help alleviate the error.

Zeus pushed on, bow wave flying.

The U-boat they'd left astern was in fact the U-474, and Günter Lehmann was astonished that his largely untrained crew had managed to survive a punishing few hours under attack from the Royal Navy. Nonetheless, U-474 could no longer continue with the mission. The bow door of torpedo tube No-3 had been damaged enough that water flooded into the chamber and spilled through the inner hatch. An extra turn to the clips stopped the flow, but the outer door had become non operational.

Also, a seal on the port propeller shaft must have taken a pounding. Seawater inundated the stern air compressor room and his engineer found a cracked casing. He thought it would hold for now, but buoyancy might end up being severely compromised. Numerous leaks within the electric motor room had eased as Lehmann reduced pressure on the hull by bringing the boat up towards the surface.

In the end, two hours after the last depth charge attack, he made the decision to surface, use the storm for cover, and head for the fjords. They'd survived . . . , just. It was time to withdraw.

17 . . Heavy Artillery

On *Aldenburg's* bridge Krause reached for the handset and called Fregattenkapitän Wilhelm Weiss.

The response was brief. 'Gun Tower.'

'Weiss, this is your Admiral. I am turning to attack. There will be little time to asses your target. Have all the gun crews ready for short range action. You must have them aim for the mast and bridge, cut the British communications. It is vital they send no signals. You understand me, Weiss? There can be no excuses.'

'Jawohl, Herr Admiral, I understand perfectly.'

'Good,' Krause grunted, and replaced the handset. He turned, raising his voice.

'Bergmann, if we cannot shake off this miserable dog then we attack. Time we taught the mongrel a lesson. Take us north.'

Bergmann bowed stiffly from the waist, and

passed the order.

And the large cruiser heeled over, high bows cutting left, the length of the armoured hull swinging wide. Krause let his body sway to the motion, willing the ship to obey. The turn became more pronounced, the rudder finding purchase. He watched the three guns of the forward turret move in unison, Weiss testing the controls. The bow wave curled high above the sharp stem, crashing onto the foredeck, wild water sluicing down the gunwales.

And *Aldenburg* came out of the turn, straightened, and steadied.

'On course at three-five-eight degrees,' Bergmann reported, and Krause nodded. He stepped up to the screen and noted the rain had eased, although the visible horizon stretched to no more than a thousand metres. The darkness had lifted, giving way to a pale-grey overcast, ragged wisps of whiter cloud chasing through.

Krause tensed. Was this the eye of the storm or had it run its course? If the weather cleared he would be vulnerable to aerial attack. He squared his shoulders. First things first, he must eliminate this threat and avoid *Aldenburg* being detected. He compressed his lips into a thin line. Any moment now he thought, and he would bring much destruction to the enemy.

The cruiser forged ahead, and the crew waited, fully prepared for action.

Richard Thorburn had a premonition that all was not well. That sixth sense that had served him so well in the past was once again niggling away at his innermost being. He'd had the same feeling back in Scapa Flow, and now here it was again . . . , persistent, invidious. He knew he was courting danger. Shadowing what might prove to be a heavily armed German cruiser was stating the obvious, but that was a deliberate decision on his part. No . . . , this was something more, a deep-seated feeling of real jeopardy that he couldn't shake. He glanced round the bridge, taking comfort from seeing all the watchkeepers focussed on their respective jobs.

'Radar-Bridge?'

He bent to the pipe. 'Captain.'

'Target has come north to three-five-eight degrees, sir. Range eight miles, speed twenty knots.'

'Very well,' Thorburn said calmly, but cursed under his breath. He mouth tightened with the realisation he'd been caught napping. He changed voice-pipes.

'Guns?'

'Sir?'

'Make ready. Target closing rapidly, dead ahead.'

'Aye aye, sir.'

Thorburn stood back and stared out beyond the bows, wracking his brain as to his next move. The weather had definitely moderated, improving by the minute. If he held course they'd meet the enemy with only minimal protection from the elements. Bow to bow, that meant facing a forward turret of three 6-inch guns, and although that was a damn sight better than a nine gun broadside, it was still nowhere near favourable odds. On top of that, the two ships were closing at a combined speed of nearly fifty miles an hour. Whenever that German popped out of the murk, there'd be little time to react. He leaned to the wheelhouse pipe.

'Reduce speed, Cox'n. Eighteen knots.'

'Eighteen knots, aye aye, sir.'

He heard the faint ring of the telegraph and moments later *Brackendale* slowed.

'Radar-Bridge,' came from a pipe, 'range to target twelve-thousand nine-hundred yards.'

'Very well,' Thorburn said, and in a split second made a snap decision to change course. Better to go about, zigzag, and let the enemy close from astern. That way he had a chance of ducking back into the worst of the weather. His objective was to identify the target, not get involved in a gun battle.

'Hard-a-starboard!'

'Hard-a-starboard, aye, sir.'

Thorburn braced as *Brackendale* flung herself into the turn, half submerging the port guard rail, and he smiled. This was where the ship excelled, her capacity to make the tightest of turns, an agility that the big Fleet destroyers could only admire. She dipped and banged her way round to the north, white water in her wake, and Thorburn waited. Finally the compass gave him what he wanted.

'Midships!'

'Wheel amidships, aye aye, sir.'

'Steady..., steer oh-one-oh degrees.'

'Oh-one-oh degrees, sir.'

Thorburn relaxed away from the pipe and walked to the port wing. He raised his binoculars astern, focussing beyond the blurred image of the four barrelled pom-pom and the closed up gun crew. A grey mist of distant rain filled the lens, shutting out whatever might be there, a curtain drawn to hide their foe. He moved back to the compass platform.

'Radar..., target at twelve-thousand yards. Course three-five-eight, sir.'

'Very well,' he said, and wiped spray from his face. Then to the wheelhouse, 'Steer three-five-five.'

'Three-five-five, aye aye, sir.'

Brackendale heeled a fraction and picked up the port leg of the zigzag. He glanced up at the Control Tower and noted it had traversed round to point astern. McDonald would be ready when the enemy was sighted.

Thorburn took a deep breath and stepped down to the bridge-screen. He looked at the lookouts keyed up at Action Stations. They'd been on the alert for some hours now, it might be better to shorten their watch periods. It didn't do to keep them searching the sea for longer than absolutely necessary. There would be strained eyes, fatigue. And with that thought it dawned on him that the feeling of imminent danger had eased from his consciousness, that he'd acted in a timely manner, averting what might have been a catastrophe. Not that he could be complacent, just that *Brackendale* was better off than she had been.

He bent to the wheelhouse pipe and ordered the next leg of the zigzag, and as he straightened he caught the welcome sight of heavier weather ahead. The storm was not done with them yet. He moved a few paces to the port wing, again raised his glasses, and steadied himself in the corner. All he needed was confirmation, and in his heart of hearts he was convinced that the *Aldenburg* lay hidden behind that veil of rain.

'Signal from Richter, Herr Admiral.'

'And?' Krause snapped.

'He reports the presence of a British Fleet destroyer coming north at high speed.'

Krause rubbed his jaw and took a deep breath. 'Range?' he asked.

'No more than fifteen-thousand metres.'

The Admiral flicked a tongue across his lips and turned back to the screen. Things were conspiring against him. From a single destroyer to three, and all in close proximity. And a Royal Navy Fleet destroyer was not to be taken lightly. There would probably be a main armament of 4.7-inch guns and two banks of 21inch torpedo tubes. The fact that the *Aldenburg* outgunned them all was no real comfort, not in this weather, and for the first time Krause began to doubt the wisdom of using the storm as cover.

He heard Bergmann answering the telephone. 'Ja? At what speed?' the Kapitän barked into the mouthpiece, then replaced the handset.

'The ship to the north has reversed course. It goes away at reduced speed, Herr Admiral.'

'So,' Krause said softly, 'maybe our little friend has a problem, no?'

'Possibly,' Bergmann agreed, 'but should we not first deal with the Fleet destroyer?'

Krause gave a subdued laugh and shook his head. 'No, not yet, he does not know we exist. His radar, if he has one, will not have picked us up, we are too far away. No . . . , recall Richter, and have all our escorts prepare to engage the enemy.'

Bergmann seemed to hesitate.

'Now, Kapitän!' Krause remonstrated, 'see to it!'

Bergmann straightened to attention and clicked his heels. 'Jawohl, Herr Admiral,' he said, and turned away, beckoning to the waiting radio messenger.

Krause watched the man write down the

order, salute and leave the bridge. As for Richter he thought grimly, he would be useful in causing confusion to the enemy.

Brackendale heeled to starboard as a wave caught her port beam, then twisted as she rode the flank. Salt laden spray encompassed the bridge, a drift of rain masking the fo'c'sle. The ship rose and fell, and pressed on through the rain, and then into relative calm.

'Ship! Bearing Green one-eighty!' and Cockcroft's hand jabbed astern.

Thorburn lunged for the starboard wing and there, not more than three miles astern, the enormous bulk of an enemy cruiser surged out from the grey bank of rain.

He spun back for the voice-pipes.

'Open fire!' he called, and then to the wheelhouse. 'Port twenty, full ahead both!'

The bellow of the quarterdeck guns drowned out Falconer's confirmation, but *Brackendale* swept to port, bows rising to the increased power of her engines.

'Midships,' he corrected, 'steer three-five-oh.'

This time he heard the Cox'n's reassuring acknowledgement. 'Three-five-oh, aye aye, sir,' he intoned, as if it were just another exercise out in the Solent.

And then came the formidable roar of the enemy's first salvo, which even at that distance made a man take notice.

Thorburn glanced round for Armstrong and found him braced in the starboard corner, glasses locked on to the enemy.

'Well?' he insisted.

The sea erupted astern, the enemy shells bursting into rising columns of wild water.

'That's the *Aldenburg* alright,' Armstrong called over the din, and let the binoculars drop to hang from the strap.

Thorburn grimaced to the constant reverberation of gunfire, and nodded to Armstrong. 'Get the sighting signal off to Z*eus*, copied to the Admiralty.'

His words were lost as the guns crashed a salvo of shells away towards the cruiser. He saw Armstrong nod and head for the wireless room.

'Hard-a-starboard,' Thorburn shouted at the voice-pipe. 'Make smoke!'

He caught a glimpse of the *Aldenburg* throwing up a huge bow wave, intent on running them down, its after guns still unable to target *Brackendale*, only the forward turret able to bracket the twisting destroyer.

But that range was rapidly reducing and Thorburn wasn't about to argue with the weight of a cruiser's broadside. It would only be a matter of minutes before the German captain turned and brought all guns into play.

At that moment a pall of thick black smoke began to billow from *Brackendale's* funnel.

'Midships..., steer oh-oh-five degrees.'

'Oh-oh-five, aye aye, sir.'

An enemy shell on a low trajectory whined over the bridge, and another in quick succession. A third skimmed by the main mast, hit one of the bracing stays and sliced it in two.

Thorburn instinctively hunched his shoulders and peered ahead in search of sanctuary from the weather, the darker rain front ever nearer.

Someone called from the back of the bridge.

'Signal form *Zeus*, sir. "Closing you from the south." That's all I got, sir.'

Thorburn turned his head and nodded at the Leading Telegraphist.

'Good man, carry on,' he said with a grin, and took a quick step across to the starboard wing. Looking aft through the coiling smoke he caught the fiery glow of *Aldenburg's* guns. *Brackendale* had not yet escaped this beast, but at least it was duty done. He'd answered McGregor's order to investigate, and the Admiralty now knew a German cruiser was 'out' on the high seas. In a moment of sheer childishness he felt like thumbing his nose at the German ship. Instead, he settled for a softly spoken, 'bloody marvellous.' He wondered if the approach of *Zeus* meant *Seaham* and *Pegwell Bay* in support?

In Scapa Flow, at the shore based Communications Centre of H.M.S. *Proserpine*, the duty Telegraphist jotted down a signal and passed it to his

Petty Officer. The man took one look at the message, banged down his mug of tea, and hurried off to find the Duty Officer.

Eight minutes later, at a meeting of senior officers in Rear-Admiral Collingwood's briefing room, there was an interruption by a young Officer-of-the-Day. He marched in to where the Admiral was seated and thrust a signal slip in front of his eyes. Collingwood studied it briefly and jerked to his feet.

'Good God Almighty! They've run into the bloody *Aldenburg*.'

A stunned silence settled over the room, eventually broken by a hesitant question.

'Who, sir?'

Collingwood stared at the speaker before replying. 'McGregor's patrol, *Brackendale* to be precise.

A subdued murmur went round the assembled officers, and someone could be heard explaining that *Brackendale* was a small 'Hunt' class destroyer.

The young officer then spoke quietly to the Admiral who shook his head.

'The news is not good, gentlemen. There's a storm crossing Iceland, and right now the R.A.F. are unable to assist.' He thought for a moment. The nearest meaningful support were *Stirling* and the convoy's escorting destroyers, and they could be anywhere from two to three-hundred miles from *Brackendale*. Eight hours steaming at best, more like fourteen. He turned to the young officer.

'Get a signal off to Captain McGregor and tell him he's on his own. Tell him to maintain contact if possible and report *Aldenburg's* movements. Make sure the Admiralty received *Brackendale's* signal, the C-in-C will have to respond. And you'd better contact Western Approaches. They might want to re-route the convoy.'

The officer finished making notes and left, leaving behind a room that had suddenly turned sombre.

Collingwood cleared his throat. 'Back to business, gentlemen, where were we?' He glanced at the oversize chart hanging behind his desk, but his thoughts centred on what must be a fierce engagement in stormy seas.

He turned back to the roomful of expectant faces. It was the next Russian bound convoy that was under discussion.

Captain McGregor stood braced against the Fleet destroyer's screen and tried to envisage the forthcoming engagement. He was no stranger to battle. He'd participated in the bitter battle to evacuate the Australian and New Zealanders from Crete in '41, and had later run the gauntlet acting as a convoy escort on the Gibraltar to Malta sailings. *Zeus* was in fact his third command and he'd been with her for the last eleven months, which included the D-Day landings. His officers made for a very experienced wardroom, cheerful, efficient and professional. The ship's company were well trained and the majority had seen action. He had no qualms about the ship's ability to engage the enemy. And the signal from Collingwood only reinforced his decision to attack.

He turned from the forebridge and spoke to his Second-in-Command.

Lieutenant-Commander Ian Hudson had served as his 'Number One' in their previous ship and McGregor was delighted when Hudson had accepted his offer of 'First Lieutenant', albeit a very senior one.

'If we can regroup quickly enough, we've a chance to make the *Aldenburg's* captain think twice about going after the convoy.'

'Yes, sir' Hudson said. 'I'm wondering what escort he has?'

'Two or three at the very least I should think. We'll cross that bridge when we come to it.'

Hudson nodded, reflective. 'Pity we don't have more destroyers.'

McGregor chuckled. 'We use the hand we're dealt. Not perfect, but things seldom are.'

Zeus powered ahead, hammering on through the choppy seas.

Commodore James Pendleton sat at his desk and signed yet one more order directing a resupply convoy to depart Harwich for the coast of Normandy. It was timed for 05.00 hours the next morning. He placed the message into the tray marked 'Priority' and leaned back with a sigh. Sometimes, he thought, fingering the length of his beard, there were moments when he longed for the feeling of a deck beneath his feet. He shook his head and reached for a pack of cigarettes. He lit one and drew smoke, exhaled slowly and watched the blue tendrils drift towards the window.

There was a sharp rap on the office door and before he could answer a flustered Jennifer Farbrace hurried in. She held out a signal slip.

'You ought to see this, sir, it's an intercepted signal. To *Zeus* copied to the Admiralty.'

Pendleton's eyes twinkled with amusement, although he made certain the smile didn't surface. It was highly unusual for his normally unflappable First Officer to be fazed by anything. He leaned forward, took the slip and glanced at the wording. He stiffened in the chair. What had seemed slightly amusing a moment before, now became deadly serious. He looked again at the latitude and longitude, and closed his eyes. *Brackendale* had reported engaging the German light-cruiser *Aldenburg* in a position roughly northeast of Iceland.

'My God,' he said softly, 'Richard's got himself into trouble this time. That's a nine-thousand ton cruiser he's tangling with.' He met her eyes as he spoke, there was no point hiding the truth.

Jennifer nodded, composed now, holding her head high. 'Yes,' she said, 'I thought it was something like that, but I didn't take the time to check.'

Pendleton slumped back in his seat. 'Let's hope *Zeus* isn't far away. The weather report predicted storm force conditions up there. Won't be much in the way of air cover.' He smoothed his beard. 'I'm sorry, young lady, there's not much we can do to help. It's in the lap of the Gods.'

A taut smile flicked across her face. 'In that case, sir, there's nothing to worry about. The Gods have always been on his side.'

Pendleton inclined his head, tending to agree. Thorburn did seem to have some kind of guardian angel looking out for him. 'You could be right,' he said, and then a thought struck him.

'Do we know if it's only *Zeus* he has for company?'

Jennifer frowned, the elegant eyebrows wrinkling in thought. 'I'm not sure, sir.'

He ran a hand through his greying head of hair. He could give her something positive to help alleviate the anxiety 'We must find out. See what you can do.'

'Yes, sir,' she said, visibly brightening, and strode out.

Momentarily, Pendleton's eyes followed her, then he stood and walked over to the wall chart. He pinpointed *Brackendale's* location and stood back. Seeing the distances involved, he couldn't help but wonder if Lieutenant-Commander Richard Thorburn hadn't bitten off more than he could chew.

First Officer Jennifer Farbrace sat down at her desk, determined to find out exactly what was happening in the far flung waters off Iceland's northeast coast. She knew of a Wren officer now stationed in the Orkneys who'd become a good friend during their time together at Chatham dockyard. Then in '43 she'd been posted to Scotland and now served at the main Base HQ and Communications Centre for Scapa Flow. In typical Navy fashion the building, a square, uninspiring concrete block had been awarded the rather grand title of, H.M.S. *Proserpine*.

Using the authority of Pendleton's office, but knowing full well she might be overstepping the mark, Jennifer picked up the telephone.

'Put me through to *Proserpine*. And it needs to be a secure line.'

'Yes, ma'am,' said the girl on the switchboard, and the line hummed as she moved the plugs.

'Connecting you now.' There followed an audible click and a male voice answered.

'*Proserpine* . . . , how can I help?'

'This is First Officer Farbrace, Combined Operations at Portsmouth. I believe you have a Second Officer Mary Thomson on your staff and wondered if she was on duty?'

'Yes, ma'am, she is. I'll put you through.'

'Thank you,' Jennifer said, and waited, briefly.

'Hello, Jenny, what a nice surprise.'

'Hi, Mary, how are you?'

'Getting webbed feet up here, never seems to stop raining. You?'

'Engaged, Richard finally proposed.'

'Lucky you, nice ring?

For all her misgivings, Jennifer recognised the need to satisfy the small talk. 'Lovely,' she said, but then decided to grab the moment. 'And it's Richard I'm calling about. We intercepted an urgent signal. Commodore Pendleton needs to know if there were others involved.'

Silence greeted the query and she held her breath.

Mary spoke quietly. 'All I can say is that he's one of five.'

Jennifer breathed again, feeling a little more optimistic. 'Convoy escort?'

'No ..., not exactly. Northern Patrol.'

'I see, so he's not playing Arctic Circles?' She deliberately used that phrase rather than the more specific 'Russian convoy' or 'Murmansk'. Mary would understand.

'No,' came the answer, followed with studied emphasis, '*no* icebergs.'

Jennifer stared at her desk, half relieved, half afraid. What she'd feared most wasn't part of the equation, and yet somehow Richard had still managed to find trouble, and by all accounts, serious trouble.

'Okay . . . ,' she said slowly, 'thanks very much, Mary. I'll let the Commodore know. He'll be very grateful.'

There was a small chuckle on the other end of the line. 'I'm sure he will. And don't forget where I am, Jenny. Stay in touch.'

'Yes,' she said, 'I'll do that. Thanks again.'

'One more thing,' Mary said. 'I assume I'll be invited to the wedding?'

It was Jennifer's turn to laugh. 'Of course, you'll be first on the list. You'll need a new hat.'

'That'll be nice, if I can find one. Bye, Jenny.'

'Goodbye, Mary. God bless.' She replaced the receiver and sat back in the chair. She didn't have the full picture but at least *Brackendale* had more than just *Zeus* in support. She came out of the chair and smoothed her skirt. Better let the Old Man know.

18 . . Senior Officer

Krause had his binoculars glued to the twisting, half obscured destroyer. The smoke screen, buffeted by the wind, was largely ineffective, but although that gave him some satisfaction, he was fuming in disbelief. *Aldenburg's* gunnery had proved to be abysmal. Even through the dense black smoke he could see the enemy's White Ensign flying proudly from the mast, and that should not be. The mast and wireless antenna should no longer exist. He cursed and turned on Bergmann.

'Kapitän. Come hard right for bombardment.'

Bergmann called out the order, the wheel came over, and the cruiser's vast bulk heeled into a lengthy turn from north to east. The main armament traversed, nine guns, three to each turret, located the target. The long barrels elevated and an officer in each turret pressed the 'ready' indicator.

Fregattenkapitän Wilhelm Weiss made sure the Attack Table had made all relevant calculations. Satisfied, he nodded to his subordinate.

'Feuer!'

The guns bellowed in unison, spitting flame, and nine high explosive shells arced out towards the British destroyer.

Thorburn had seen *Aldenburg's* guns lift and steady, and reacted to the thunder of a full broadside.

'Hard-a-port!'

Falconer spun the wheel, *Brackendale* heeled over, and the small destroyer turned sharply from north to west. And in turning she ploughed into the sanctuary of driving rain, so dense the bows became momentarily lost to view. On the quarterdeck, the pair of 4-inch guns blasted off a last salvo.

'Midships!'

In *Brackendale's* wake, seven of the enemy

shells erupted into foaming columns of wild water. The eighth shell exploded off the port quarter and Thorburn felt splinters lacerate the hull. The ninth detonated amidships and *Brackendale* shuddered to the explosion. It struck the deck between radar housing and galley, ripping a six foot hole in the steel plating and spraying the immediate surroundings with splinters. The gear room below was left exposed to the elements and a stray splinter severed an electric cable. The bare wiring sparked and started a small fire.

On the pom-pom, Taff Williams heard an agonised scream and glanced round to find one of the gun crew slumped against the screen. Blood pumped from a shattered leg. Two loaders went to his aid.

Krause, watching through his binoculars, caught the flash of a shell exploding on the enemy destroyer. It appeared to strike the main deck. As the British ship then melted into a bank of rain, her after guns fired a final salvo. A twisted smile distorted the hard mouth. Those 4-inch shells were but pebbles thrown at a castle's walls, a wasted gesture.

But both projectiles found their target. One hit the curved armoured shield of the forward turret and ricocheted into the sea. The second, crucially, failed to explode. It punched a hole in the cruiser's side above the armoured belt. And deflected down to embed itself in a diesel supply pipe. Thirty-six seconds later the big engine spluttered and died.

On the bridge, the telephone buzzed.

Bergmann answered. 'Ja?' He listened before cradling the handset and turning to face Krause.

'We have lost power, Herr Admiral. The diesel is kaput.'

Krause took a deep breath, and in a voice rasping with suppressed anger asked, 'What speed *can* they give me?'

Bergmann dropped his gaze. 'Three-quarter speed only.'

Krause cursed and paced the bridge. Not long since, all had been well, and now, because of one small destroyer, his calculations for intercepting the convoy . . . ? It might be a lot harder. But in the meantime he did have enemy warships in close proximity. *Aldenburg* had not lost the capacity to fight and powerful weaponry was his to command. If nothing else he could teach this pack of dogs not to tempt fate. He would hold on this bearing and draw them in.

To Bergmann he said, 'We will maintain course, Kapitän . . . , for a while.'

Thorburn swore quietly and eased the cap from his aching temple. That broadside had been too accurate, a lot better than their first efforts. But he wasn't about to let up. It was important the German commander recognised

Brackendale as a threat. He half smiled at the thought. Not much of a threat, granted, but if he could just keep the cruiser in range, who knows what might happen.

'Radar-Bridge. Enemy bearing Green two-oh, range five miles, course oh-nine-oh, speed twenty-four knots.'

'Very well,' Thorburn said, and glanced at the compass. *Brackendale* held course towards the east and *Aldenburg* to the west. If he altered course to follow and then moved southeast from behind the rain front and into the open, he could give 'Guns' a few salvos before he switched back into cover. Mind made up he bent to the pipe.

'Guns?'

'Sir.'

'I'm going after the enemy, let them know we're still here. It'll be a quick out and back in again. Feel free to open fire.'

McDonald's response was enthusiastic. 'Aye aye, sir!'

Thorburn switched pipes. 'Starboard twenty.'

Falconer, eyes fixed on the Lubber-line, lifted his head to the tube. 'Starboard twenty, aye aye, sir.'

Thorburn waited until they were heading broadly east.

'Midships..., steady.'

'Course oh-nine-two, sir.'

'Very well. Half ahead together, make revs for twenty-five knots.'

'Half ahead both, speed twenty-five knots, aye aye, sir.'

And either side of the wheel, the Telegraphists rang up revolutions for the port and starboard engines.

Brackendale lifted her nose and powered on, bow wave flying, thumping and banging through the waves. Thorburn, with one eye on the compass, delayed the next turn until he was sure the ship had picked up enough speed. He saw Armstrong look round from the port wing and gave him a warning. 'Stand by.'

Another thirty seconds and Thorburn made his move.

'Starboard twenty!'

Falconer called an acknowledgement. 'Starboard twenty, aye sir!'

And Thorburn braced to the turn, feeling the ship beneath his hands.

'Midships . . . , steer one-one-oh.'

'Wheel's amidships, steering one-one-oh, sir.'

Brackendale swept out from the bank of rain, and Thorburn tensed. There in the distance was the *Aldenburg*, stern on and going away. He estimated the range as six miles.

From below the bridge the 4-inch guns blasted into action, acrid smoke billowing back across the screen.

Thorburn coughed, eyes stinging, straining to follow the enemy's silhouette. He saw *Aldenburg's* rear turrets shift and steady. The barrels flamed.

'Hard-a-port!'

Brackendale's guns thumped again, another pair of shells on their way. The ship heeled over, fighting her way round.

He leaned to the pipe. 'Meet her .... Steady!'

Two hundred yards out on the starboard beam, six columns of water shot skywards, spray drifting in the wind. Again *Brackendale's* guns fired, and the shells splashed wide.

Thorburn lifted the binoculars and steadied on the cruiser's turrets. As he did so, the two after mounts began swinging south, away from *Brackendale*. The German commander was disengaging. Why? He had the opportunity to make mince-meat of a small destroyer and yet he'd chosen not to.

'Guns-Bridge?'

Thorburn answered. 'Captain.'

'*Zeus* is closing the enemy, sir.'

Brackendale ploughed headlong into the obscurity of the rain front.

Thorburn ignored the sheets of rain. 'From where?' he demanded.

'She's off the enemy's starboard quarter.' And then they all heard the roar of enemy guns.

Richard Thorburn grimaced, he had to act. This wasn't the moment to play hide and seek. McGregor needed all the help he could get, and right now that help could only come from *Brackendale*. He glanced at the compass.

'Starboard thirty!' The ship swayed into the turn, coming round to the south-east. 'Midships, steer oh-four-oh!'

'Oh-four-oh, aye aye, sir.'

Driving spray hit the bridge, ice cold, but a minor irritant set against what might happen next.

And *Brackendale* burst into the open. The *Aldenburg's* guns all pointed to the south and Thorburn focussed his glasses. He found *Zeus* racing towards the enemy warship, her torpedo tubes deployed in readiness.

'Open fire!' he snapped, and the forward turret slammed a pair of shells at the target. Seconds later another pair, this time rewarded by hits on the cruiser's afterdeck.

Thorburn grinned through the smoke. 'Bloody marvellous,' he said over the din, then realised he needed to give the quarterdeck guns a chance to join in.

'Port ten.'

Brackendale yawed left, bringing her starboard side to the enemy, and the after guns thumped into action.

'Midships . . . , steer oh-three-oh.' He glanced over the starboard wing. *Zeus* was charging on, her Battle Ensigns flying, manoeuvring to optimise a firing position. The sea around her was alive with jumping geysers, and multicoloured tracer flashed across her decks.

Aldenburg's main armament cracked out another salvo, and McGregor's 'A' and 'B' guns barked in reply.

Thorburn found himself mesmerised, willing McGregor to launch his torpedoes. An explosion erupted below her bridge, a blinding flash, and 'B' gun fell silent.

Brackendale's guns added to the mayhem, firing steadily, wreathed in smoke. They scored another hit, this time forward of the cruiser's main funnel, a red glow glinting from steel upperworks. Thorburn moved his binoculars, concentrating on *Zeus*.

Jones yelled a warning. 'Enemy turning, sir!'

Through the lens, Thorburn again picked out the cruiser. 'I have it,' he acknowledged. *Aldenburg* was indeed swinging north across *Brackendale's* path and away from the threat of *Zeus*, presenting the least possible target against a torpedo strike. He watched the big guns traversing round to realign on *Zeus*. An instant later the cruiser's after guns thundered simultaneously.

Commencing her own turn in the chase, *Zeus* was neatly straddled. Three of the six shells found their target. The first exploded on the foredeck. The second hit the navigating bridge and blew it apart, killing all those at their stations. McGregor and his First Lieutenant died instantly, blasted to a pulp.

The third and last projectile to make contact struck a warhead on the central array of torpedoes. Semi-Armour piercing, the shell penetrated the outer casing and a millisecond later seven-hundred pounds of TNT detonated. In a terrible moment of catastrophic chain reaction, the adjacent warheads exploded and added their ferocity to the fireball. An enormous explosion ripped through the Fleet destroyer and *Zeus* broke apart.

Stunned by the sight of such devastation, Thorburn whipped up his glasses. As the smoke cleared he focused in on the remnants of a once proud warship. The after section had already begun to settle beneath the waves. 'X' gun was trained hard round over the starboard side, and from behind the shield two men staggered out and collapsed. 'Y' gun's position was all but swallowed by the water, only the tip of the barrel showing. Fifty yards ahead, the separated fo'c'sle had lifted to an odd angle, the blackened bridge a mess of twisted steel, along with the shrapnel scarred Control Tower. The angle of the deck became more apparent, quickly lifting to the vertical. It hung there momentarily, smoke pouring from 'B' gun's mounting. Three or four crewmen slithered down the flag deck, flailing arms and legs. The bows twisted above them, as if surveying the carnage, and then with a final lurch it gave up the unequal struggle and plunged to the depths.

Thorburn lowered the glasses and took a deep breath. He felt a helpless anger surge through his body and the scar throbbed beneath his cap band. It had happened so fast, so brutally effective. How many of her crew were still alive, or half drowned and injured, desperately clinging to life? And right now, under the threat of the enemy's guns, he could do little to help. It was a hard to ignore.

Shrapnel lashed the bridge, hammering at the steel panels. Brought back to the moment he looked ahead and saw the German's guns swinging towards *Brackendale*. The range had closed swiftly and he gauged it at seven thousand yards, a meagre four miles.

'Hard-a-port!' he shouted, and braced against the compass housing. And once more the little ship swayed to starboard, grappling with the heavy seas, heeling hard over. He hunched his shoulders to the bellow of six-inch guns, involuntarily reacting to the lethal threat. *Brackendale* swung through north and came round to the west, and he winced as shells whined overhead. A shell hit the sea off the port bow and a column of water jumped high, cascading across the fo'c'sle. But somehow they'd avoided the broadside and he steadied her to the southwest.

'Make smoke!' he ordered, and then stepped quickly to the port wing. The quarterdeck guns were still fully engaged, keeping to a steady rate of fire, salvo after salvo ripping out at the enemy. He guessed the gunners would be tiring, and at the same time wondered how many rounds had been expended? He reached for the bulkhead handset.

McDonald came on.

'Cease fire, Guns. We must conserve ammunition.'

'Aye aye, sir,' came the reply, and before Thorburn replaced the handset he heard McDonald giving the order. 'Check, check, check.'

Armstrong, who'd left the bridge just prior to *Zeus* being annihilated, suddenly reappeared from the starboard ladder.

'Number One?'

'I was checking for damage, sir. There's a hole in the deck portside. Fires are out, but the Gear room is exposed to the elements. Chief's got it in hand. Some splinter holes above the waterline.'

'Casualties?'

'Two dead, five wounded.'

Thorburn nodded, glancing across the sea to where *Zeus* had been cut in half. It could have been a lot worse.

'Enemy turning away, sir,' Jones called.

Thorburn frowned and met Armstrong's gaze. 'Now what?'

The First Lieutenant shook his head. 'God knows, but with *Zeus* gone, it's your flotilla now.'

For a long moment, Thorburn stared at Armstrong. Busy with trying to keep *Brackendale* in one piece it hadn't occurred to him that he was now Senior Officer and in command of the Flotilla.

'Ship, bearing Red three-oh!'

Thorburn raised his binoculars to focus across the port bow. He found a distant, dark shadow shrouded in rain, and wondered if it was an enemy destroyer? He called to the signaller.

'Make the challenge.'

The lamp chattered as the shutter flashed a query and a pinprick of light flickered in reply.

'It's *Rosefinch*, sir.'

Thorburn rubbed his jaw, thankful it wasn't the enemy. 'Tell her to join me.'

'Radar-Bridge?'

Armstrong answered. 'Bridge.'

'Enemy heading oh-four-five degrees.'

Thorburn nodded. 'Very well,' he said, and frowned in thought. Northeast, on course for the Norwegian coast. Or was that too obvious? What if it chose to circle northwest? That would put it on a bearing to intercept the convoy.

'Range?' he called.

'Six miles, increasing rapidly.'

No surprise there, they were moving in opposite directions. He bent to the wheelhouse pipe.

'Half ahead, make revolutions for sixteen knots.'

He heard Falconer's acknowledgement and turned to look at Armstrong. 'I can't let that cruiser just take off, not with the convoy up there.'

'No, sir,' Armstrong agreed.

'We'll have to stay in touch, for as long as

we're able.'

'Yes, sir. But the others don't have our speed.'

Thorburn felt his temple throb, fought back the nausea that came with it. This was no time for weakness. He closed his eyes to let it pass. Spray from the bow wave hit the bridge, cold to the senses, and he licked his lips. The pain subsided and he opened his eyes.

'We'll go it alone. But first things first, I want a signal sent to Admiralty.'

Armstrong called to the back of the bridge and a Telegraphist came forward with his pad.

Thorburn gathered his thoughts and then said, 'Make to Admiralty, "Have engaged enemy cruiser. *Zeus* sunk. Enemy has disengaged at reduced speed, possible damage. Will attempt to shadow." Get our position from Pilot and send it immediately.'

'Aye aye, sir.'

'Good man, carry on.'

'Radar-Bridge?'

'Captain.'

'Target now at eight miles, sir.'

'Very well,' he said, and looked at the Aldis lamp. 'Call up *Rosefinch* and tell her to pick up survivors.'

The piercing whine of an enemy shell made them tense, and a column of water erupted two-hundred yards off the starboard quarter. They waited, but there was no repeat.

Thorburn met Armstrong's eyes and pursed

his lips. 'I think,' he said, emphasising the point, 'that means we're not invited to the party.'

Armstrong gave a lopsided grin. 'Not very friendly, is it?'

The signalman interrupted. '*Rosefinch* acknowledged, sir.'

Thorburn nodded. 'Number One, ask the Chief how much fuel we have left. We don't want to overdo the chase.'

'Sir,' Armstrong said, and moved off.

And just for a moment, Lieutenant-Commander Richard Thorburn found himself alone with his thoughts. He narrowed his eyes, straining to fill in the detail. He'd heard nothing from either *Seaham* or *Pegwell* and guessed they were still to the south. Willoughby had *Rosefinch* searching for survivors a mile or so to the southeast, and beneath his feet *Brackendale* moved west away from the enemy. And of course, *Zeus* was no more. The thing that irked the most was an unknown . . . , where were the German destroyers? He straightened up and settled his cap. No good worrying about what was out of his control. Keep it in mind, yes . . . , but don't allow it to dictate proceedings. It was time to become the tracker, to pursue as a huntsman shadows his prey, the outcome never certain. But it was his duty to do everything in his power to protect the convoy and he bent to the wheelhouse pipe.

'Port twenty, make revolutions for twenty-five knots.'

'Port twenty,' Falconer answered. 'Speed twenty-five knots. Aye aye, sir.'

Thorburn stepped down from the raised platform and moved to the bridge-screen, watching the bows sweep round to the east. He steadied her on a bearing of oh-eight-five and moved to the chair.

Armstrong came to his side. 'Chief reckons we're good for another eleven hundred miles if you don't ask for too much speed.'

Thorburn smiled. 'Sounds like he'd prefer fifteen knots rather then twenty-six.'

'Something along those lines, yes sir.'

'Well, I don't think he'll be too happy. We're already tracking that cruiser, and I'll stay with it as long as we can. If nothing else we can signal warnings of its intentions.' He had one eye on the compass and leaned to the pipe. 'Steer oh-nine-five.'

A bridge messenger reported. 'Captain sir, Admiralty acknowledges your signal.'

'Very well, carry on,' Thorburn said, and looked up at Armstrong. 'I have a feeling we're nearing a point of no return, Number One.'

The First Lieutenant stroked his chin and gave a faint smile. 'Lap of the Gods, then.'

'I'd like to think we might have a little to do with the result.'

Armstrong assumed his most attentive expression. 'Of course, sir, most definitely,' he said, and nodded vigorously.

Thorburn grinned. There were moments when Lieutenant Robert Armstrong made for a very likeable companion.

'What,' Armstrong asked suddenly, 'are your orders for the rest of the flotilla?'

Thorburn frowned, he'd clean forgotten his new responsibilities. He looked out over the starboard wing to where *Rosefinch* was combing the waves. Peter would have to continue the patrol. There was after all, still the threat of a German destroyer, whereabouts unknown. And it wouldn't harm to have *Pegwell* and *Seaham* come further north with *Rosefinch*, establish a fresh offensive line.

'Yeoman,' he called.

'Sir?'

'Make to *Rosefinch*. "*Brackendale* will shadow enemy cruiser. *Rosefinch*, *Pegwell* and *Seaham* to reform. Possible enemy escort group to north. My bearing north by east." Got that?'

The Yeoman finished scribbling. 'Aye aye, sir.'

'Very well, send it.'

The big signalling lamp began to clatter, and Thorburn peered through the rain for an answer. When none came he frowned, perplexed.

'Send it again,' he said, a note of annoyance in his voice. This time there was a brief flicker to show it had been read, but no acknowledgement. What, he wondered, was Willoughby playing at? He gave it a while longer, patience running thin. And then a beam of light sparkled through the rain.

'*Rosefinch* answering, sir. Message reads . . . , "Should I not assist *Brackendale*?" Message ends, sir.'

Thorburn held back a smile. Peter wanted more than the humdrum routine of anti-submarine work, he wanted in on the action.

'Make, "Kind offer, your top speed an issue," and give me the reply.'

'Aye aye, sir,' and the harsh light flashed across the waves.

This time the response was immediate. '*Rosefinch* acknowledges, sir.'

'Good,' Thorburn said, and turned back to the screen. *Brackendale* ploughed on, rising and falling to the angry waves.

19 . . Convoy

Captain Charles Taylor-Mitchell was asleep in his cabin when the bulkhead telephone buzzed. He fumbled for the receiver.

'Captain.'

'Bridge, sir. Convoy in sight.'

Taylor-Mitchell smothered a yawn. 'Very well, I'll come up.'

Three minutes later he emerged onto the navigating platform and stepped forward to the screen.

His Number One pointed ahead off the starboard bow, the incessant rain making visibility difficult. 'Green one-oh, sir, eight miles. Radar found them an hour ago, but I waited till I could at least see two of them.'

Taylor-Mitchell smiled into the wind. He looked around at the sky, still filled with clouds chasing through from astern, no less angry, a heavy overcast with no end in sight.

'Well done, Number One. Where's *Scitalis*?'

'On the convoy's starboard flank, sir.' He waved a hand at the line of merchantmen.

'Good. Tell her to hold station while we come up.'

'Aye aye, sir.'

A Petty Officer Yeoman answered the call and the big lamp beamed across the waves. Five miles away a gleaming light flickered in reply.

The Yeoman's lamp clattered once. '*Scitalis* acknowledges, sir,'

'Very well,' Taylor-Mitchell said, and followed up by addressing his Navigator. 'Pilot, put us south of the convoy. We'll join the escort Leader.'

'Aye aye, sir.'

Stirling swayed to port, eased away to starboard, and headed for the stern of the American flagged, *Franklin George.* In twenty minutes they swept past her taffrail, pushed on beyond the convoy's starboard column and slowed as she came astern of *Scitalis*. The Captain then ran the cruiser up alongside and with two-hundred yards separating the two warships, signalled across to the escort Leader.

"Admiralty report indicates enemy cruiser in vicinity. Take station five cables astern and conform to my movement. If attacked I expect convoy to turn away under smokescreen from escorts. *Stirling* and *Scitalis* will attack on sight."

A lamp on the destroyer's bridge sparkled in answer. 'Acknowledged, sir.'

Taylor-Mitchell ordered an increase in revolutions to sixteen-knots and a glance astern showed *Scitalis* swinging into his wake. The ever present threat of U-boats could not be ignored and maintaining speed was an imperative in disrupting any possible attack by torpedoes. He began a broad sweep along the length of the convoy and deliberated over exactly where *Aldenburg* might make a strike from. To the north and east the storm obscured the horizon and he was mindful to warn the radar operators of an obvious point of contact.

The cruiser settled on a bearing of oh-four-eight degrees and Taylor-Mitchell paced the bridge. Patience was a virtue.

John Hennessey, grateful for the late arrival of Taylor-Mitchell's well armed cruiser, sat in his bridge-chair and nursed another sweet mug of tea. All the escorts now knew of the probable threat and, more importantly, the tactics to employ in response to an attack. For Hennessey, it had eased the burden of fending off a powerful adversary with only destroyers as defence. And the signals his wireless office had intercepted hadn't made for good reading. With *Zeus* sunk, he marvelled at the tenacity shown by what he knew to be a small 'Hunt' class destroyer. It must have been a daunting prospect to tangle with the *Aldenburg* and then to commence shadowing in poor weather.

He looked up beyond the bridge-screen to study *Stirling's* quarterdeck array of 6-inch guns. They might soon be in action.

Admiral Mathias Krause stood staring at the turbulent seas and thought through his options. Other than one unlucky hit on the diesel supply pipe *Aldenburg* had survived the encounter with no serious damage. 'Superficial' was the Engineering Officer's assessment, only minor defects to the cruiser's fighting efficiency. And even now, the engineers were attempting to run a secondary diesel pipe to replace the original. Not that anyone believed they were immune from danger. Just because it hadn't exploded on impact didn't mean the shell was inert. The decision had been made to leave it as it lay, and only attempt removal by extracting an entire section of the supply line. For now, a new line was the priority, and that would have to suffice until a more appropriate time.

He turned away from the screen and looked down at the deck between his feet, trying to asses the whereabouts of the convoy. His best guess was north, possibly a few points west.

'Bergmann,' he called sharply.

'Herr Admiral?'

'Signal Richter and tell him to take command of our escorts. He is to attack the British destroyers and create a diversion. Then we will make a break for the north and find that convoy.'

Bergmann hesitated.

'What?' Krause demanded.

'But if the weather clears . . . , would it not be better to make for the fjords?'

Krause glared at him. 'You disappoint me, Bergmann. We have before us an opportunity for a great victory. Already one Royal Navy destroyer is kaput and another has fled, tail between its legs. And then you say we should run for home.' He shook his finger in admonishment. 'This is a great opportunity. I will not let that convoy pass without a shot being fired.' He drew himself up to his full height and stuck out his jaw. 'Have our escorts finish these enemy ships while you take us north.'

Bergmann clicked his heels, suitably chastised. 'As you wish, Herr Admiral.'

'Exactly so, Kapitän . . . , exactly so.'

And moments later *Aldenburg* swayed into the turn and commenced a searching run to the north.

First Officer Jennifer Farbrace looked up from

her desk and took a signal slip from the duty Telegraphist. She dismissed him and quickly scanned the message. Her heart sank. If Richard had not exactly been in the thick of things before, he certainly was now. He might have survived the opening encounter, but *Zeus* had been sunk, and that didn't sound encouraging. Now he was chasing an enemy cruiser, alone, and with no real hope of assistance. She slowly came to her feet and eased out from behind the desk. Patting her hair into place she walked methodically across to the Commodore's door. Desperate as the news was, she was determined not to show Pendleton any sign of weakness, not this time. She put on her most resolute face, knocked, and entered his office.

'Signal, sir,' she said, and handed it over.

He looked it over, nodded, and met her eyes. 'Sorry, young lady, but he'll do well to come out of this in one piece.'

Jennifer took the message slip and stepped backwards towards the door. She managed a forceful, 'yes, sir,' turned, and escaped to her office. Sinking into the comfort of her chair she rested her head in both hands and fought back the tears. All these years, she thought, and now he had to jump straight into the fire. She gathered herself, returned to the typewriter, but about to strike a key, hesitated.

'Richard Thorburn,' she whispered, 'if I'm forced to wear black I'll never forgive you.'

A trembling smile accompanied the words, but voicing her fears had helped, and she hit the first key.

At Scapa Flow, the signal from *Brackendale* had been passed to Collingwood. A Wren altered the plot, and the Admiral took careful note of each ship's last reported position. The marker for *Zeus* had been removed and he stared at the vacant spot. McGregor had been an outstanding destroyer man; it was a sad day. The Royal Navy had lost not only the man in command, but from the briefness of the signal, an entire ship's company may have perished. He shook his head and turned his focus to the convoy. His orders had instructed him to despatch an offensive patrol, but at this stage of the war, no one had envisaged enemy surface vessels coming to the fore. And a light cruiser was almost beyond comprehension. The patrol had been all about anti-submarine warfare, they were not equipped to tackle the *Aldenburg*. He reached for the telephone.

'Get me Western Approaches.'

'Yes, sir.'

Collingwood stared at the chart, lost in thought. There was a second cruiser at Reykjavik, just arrived to play her part in the next convoy. It might be worth putting her to sea, give the *Aldenburg* something more to think about. But realistically it might take her twenty hours or so to get involved, too long to be a serious threat. Still, he thought, it was an idea worth putting forward. And it would add weight to the convoy's escort.

'You're through now, sir.'

'Thank you . . . . Hello, Henry? I have a suggestion, wondered what you might think.' And with that he launched into his proposition, hoping all the while, he wasn't wasting his breath.

Down in *Aldenburg's* engineering compartment an auxiliary supply pipe had been loose laid in readiness. It measured a total of four metres in length, made up of three sections coupled together. On either end a flange plate waited to be married up with the existing plates. Before attempting to connect the new line, men were despatched to scour the ship for mattresses and blankets. They returned with an odd assortment of materials and dumped them in a heap.

Under the watchful eye of a senior engineering officer, the section of pipe from which the 4-inch shell projected was carefully supported and cocooned to prevent any sudden jolt detonating the explosive charge. Finally, with only those personnel absolutely necessary to complete the task, the bridge was informed and they braced themselves for the moment to proceed.

Krause gave the order to alter course and bring the cruiser west into the oncoming seas. He reduced speed in an attempt to smooth the ship's progress, and although not entirely successful, achieved a relatively stable passage. He had to balance the need for greater speed against the possible repercussions of the shell exploding, and in the end the decision had come down to fighting capability, to accelerate at will. He brought the ship to Battle Stations, every hatch, door and watertight compartment sealed, and only then did he give the order for the repair to proceed.

Below decks the engineers began the delicate task of uncoupling the damaged pipe. Originally 'made to measure' by the dockyard, the four bolts holding each of the end flanges in place were carefully unscrewed and extracted. Such was the exactness of fit, the mating faces remained locked together. Not wanting to take it apart by brute force and a hammer, two men began trying to wriggle it free. Shoving and pulling in equal measure they at last managed to free the feed end.

A dribble of diesel trickled to the deck and a man slipped in the oily pool. He lost his grip on the pipe and stumbled forward. Instinctively he reached out to support himself and his weight tore the pipe down. Men froze as it rocked on the pile of mattresses. The pipe twisted and the protruding shell swivelled to the horizontal, and stopped.

The men stared in horror, mesmerised by a dreadful expectation.

Moments passed while they hesitated, fearful. Slowly the tension eased, and the man who'd stumbled levered himself to his feet. His movement broke the spell and they found the original length of pipe now lay clear of the existing flanges. The men set to and removed the old gaskets, scraping clean the steel faces of any worn bits, and fitted new seals. Four men lifted the new piping and a flange was offered up to its mating component. Bolts were inserted and the nuts were threaded on and spun up finger tight.

Aldenburg lurched to the impact of a bigger wave, and as they fought to keep their balance, the pipe swayed awkwardly. The cruiser recovered and settled, allowing them to make the final connection. All eight nuts were tightened in sequence.

With the fresh pipework fully installed they slowly opened the diesel valve and checked the joints. No leaks were found. The senior engineer primed the engine and glanced at his team. There were faint nods, willing him to get on with it. He turned back to the machinery and hit the starter. The big diesel clattered and coughed, vibrated, and then caught. He threw a lever, and another. The needle of the pressure gauge swept round and the engine barked. It settled to a sustained roar, and through sweat grimed faces the men grinned.

A gut wrenching thirty-seven minutes was at an end.

'Radar-Bridge!'

Thorburn turned to the pipe. 'Captain.'

'Target turning north, sir.'

'Very well,' he said, and gave a rueful smile. As he'd guessed, the German was going after the convoy, and in all probability looking to intercept off the east coast of Greenland. For a moment he considered his options. The obvious course of action would be to turn north-east and cut the corner, which would shorten the range and give Dawkins the added advantage of saving fuel. Whether it made any difference to the German's plans was really neither here or there, at least *Brackendale* would remain in the picture. But he needed to update the Admiralty.

'Yeoman, signal the Admiralty. "*Aldenburg* has turned north." Get our position from Pilot and get it sent immediately.'

'Aye aye, sir,' the man said and left the bridge.

He leaned to the wheelhouse pipe.

'Port ten.'

'Port ten, aye aye, sir.'

Thorburn gave it time and then established their new course. 'Steer three-one-oh degrees.'

He noticed the wind had slackened, making for less disturbance, though the rain was just as heavy. The waves moving in from the west were a little less pronounced, but hitting the port quarter, still imparted enough power to make the ship corkscrew awkwardly. It made for a lively passage. It was now a matter of hanging on the best they could, for as long as the fuel oil allowed. But only five minutes later there came an unexpected interruption.

'*Rosefinch* signalling, sir.'

Thorburn moved to the starboard wing, curious. 'And?' he prompted.

'Reads, "Four enemy in sight . . . , bearing . . , oh-two-five, course one-nine-oh, speed thirty knots," end of message.'

'Acknowledge,' he answered, and shut his eyes. Four ships approaching from north-northeast. They must have been out to the east of *Aldenburg*. He raised his glasses. *Rosefinch* was a grey smudge against the backdrop of dirty clouds. She had already turned away from *Brackendale's* starboard quarter, heading to intercept. Willoughby had deliberately made himself a target and would certainly draw enemy fire.

He lowered the binoculars and swore. The Germans had to be manoeuvring under orders from the *Aldenburg*, and four enemy warships, one of which must be the Zerstorer, was an entirely different kettle of fish. Between them they could cause mayhem. The saving grace was that he now knew where they were. Conversely, what could he do about it? If the Germans made a move on *Rosefinch* there'd surely be only one outcome. She had neither the speed nor firepower to compete on her own.

'Admiralty acknowledges, sir.'

'Very well,' he said automatically, still battling his dilemma.

'Radar-Bridge!'

'Bridge!' he barked.

'I think we have *Pegwell* and *Seaham* bearing one-five-oh, course three-six-oh, range six miles.'

'Well done, Bellingham,' he said. That would go some way to evening the odds. So all he had to do was decide on whether to help Willoughby or continue the chase? And the longer he thought about it the less chance he had of achieving either one. He turned to face the bows, took off his cap and breathed in. The presumption had to be that *Aldenburg* had set course for the convoy. In that respect he'd done his duty, the Admiralty were abreast of the situation. Realistically *Brackendale* couldn't shadow for long, there wouldn't be enough fuel. He hesitated for moments longer, and then made up his mind. *Rosefinch*, *Pegwell* and *Seaham* were under his command, he must not leave them to face the enemy alone. He would fight . . . , as he always had. Battle the odds, and devil take the hindmost. Time to take action, and it boiled down to simplicity itself. Make the first move, use the element of surprise. Turn towards, and engage the enemy.

He jammed on his cap, winced where it

scraped his temple, and stepped onto the compass platform.

'Hard-a-starboard!' he snapped at the pipe.

It was Falconer in the wheelhouse. 'Hard-a-starboard. Aye aye, sir!'

And *Brackendale* swept into the turn, leaning hard, her port rail swamped by the sea. She tore through the water, careering round, pitching and rocking to the waves. He steadied the ship as she came northeast, determined to cross ahead of *Rosefinch* and attack on sight. Willoughby would have to play a diversionary role on the flank. It was possible, he thought, the Germans might choose not to engage and take off in a hurry, and the speed differential, thirty-six knots as opposed to *Brackendale's* twenty-six, would see them out of sight in minutes. But he had a hunch *Rosefinch* was too tempting a target to ignore.

He raised his glasses. *Rosefinch* steamed on, three miles out from *Brackendale's* beam. Somewhere off her starboard bow the Germans might be almost in view.

'Guns-Bridge!'

'Captain.'

'Enemy in sight! Four destroyers. Twelve thousand yards. Bearing Red one-five.'

'Well done, Guns. Fire when ready.' He turned his head. 'Yeoman, make to Admiralty, "Four enemy destroyers. Attacking." Pilot will give you our co-ordinates. Get that off sharpish.'

Thorburn raised his binoculars, and there, half hidden in the rain shrouded sea, were the enemy. *Brackendale* dipped to a trough, came out of it, and rode the crest. At exactly the same moment, her guns roared into action.

He dropped the glasses to his chest and glanced to his right across the starboard wing. Willoughby was turning away, going about to put distance between himself and *Brackendale*. It was a sensible ploy, and would cause the Germans to split their firepower. Thorburn returned to look beyond the bows. Waterspouts lifted, short, and the enemy altered course, towards *Rosefinch*. The leading German destroyer opened fire.

'Captain, sir, Admiralty acknowledges.'

'Very well,' he said, and set himself for the battle ahead.

Lieutenant-Commander Peter Willoughby hauled *Rosefinch* round to the east and then eased her a few points to starboard. It gave all his 4-inch guns a field of fire across the port side, but without exposing the ship's broad flank to the enemy. He estimated the range to the German destroyers as six miles, and they were strung out in line abreast. The nearest, the Zerstorer, chose that moment to commence firing.

Willoughby reacted. 'Open fire!'

The main armament blasted out an opening salvo. Off to port he saw *Brackendale's* guns smoke, caught sight of the recoil.

Ahead of *Rosefinch*, enemy high explosive shells hit the sea and detonated, columns of writhing water jumping high. In the distance, a second German warship rippled with gunfire.

'Starboard ten!' he snapped.

An erratic line of shells whined overhead, falling long.

'Port twenty!'

Rosefinch heeled, gun muzzles swinging to compensate. A shell exploded off the port bow, shrapnel lashing the hull.

Willoughby bared his teeth and gripped the handrail. The range rapidly decreased.

20 . . Engage at Will

Thorburn had his eye fixed on the leading destroyer. 'Guns' had identified the other three as Elbing and Narvik types, smaller, with less firepower. The main danger facing him was a torpedo strike; the enemy were all equipped with torpedoes, unlike his own flotilla.

He glanced at *Rosefinch*. She was wreathed in smoke from the guns, maintaining a steady rate of fire. The ship had initially swept wide, but now she was jinking left and right, zigzagging to upset the enemy gunners.

The sting of cordite enveloped *Brackendale's* bridge, and he choked, coughing on the dense fumes. His temple throbbed with the effort and he forced himself to control the cough, eyes watering. It eased, and he gulped air. He reached to the compass binnacle for support, weak at the knees. It passed and he stood upright.

'Guns-Bridge!'

'Captain,' he managed.

'*Pegwell* and *Seaham* to the south, twelve-thousand yards,' McDonald reported.

Thorburn's head cleared. 'Very well,' he said, and raised his binoculars. He searched through the smoke and rain beyond the German ships. Twelve-thousand yards, roughly seven miles, and all he could see was grey on grey, no horizon. And then . . . , a smudge of something darker and he focussed on it. The Frigate hove into view, bow wave churning, head on. He moved the glasses left, and there, not more than two-hundred yards off *Pegwell's* starboard beam, *Seaham* ploughed north in close company.

'Yeoman!' he shouted above the din. 'Make to *Pegwell Bay*, "Engage at will," the same to *Seaham*.' He didn't want them to be in any doubt.

The big Aldis lamp clattered under the Yeoman's hands.

The Gunnery Officers on both ships must have been waiting for that exact order, for their fo'c'sle guns exploded into life, hammering shells at the enemy.

In the Radar Room, Bellingham struggled to detect friend from foe. Seven echoes intermingled on the cathode display. Telling them apart was becoming more like guesswork. He decided to leave it all to 'Guns' and the lookouts. No point in giving the bridge a confused report. He concentrated instead on watching for anything new.

Richter felt he had the upper hand over the British sloop. His guns were accurate, bracketing the ship, shells bursting all around. It could only be a matter of time before she was hit.

Five-hundred metres to his right the nearest Elbing turned away and he saw the torpedo tubes arrayed over the port side. The intention was clear, but Richter thought the range too great for a successful outcome.

'Herr Kapitän, a British destroyer!' The lookout stretched a finger across the starboard side.

Richter turned. Beyond the Elbing the enemy ship came on at speed, bow on, firing as she did so. The Elbing seemed unaware, its guns trained on the sloop.

'Signalman!' he called, and ordered the man to warn them. The big signal lamp flashed and Richter noted the "received" glinting through the rain. The Elbing turned to intercept, guns swinging to the new target. It opened fire at long range.

Richter turned back to the screen, concentrating on the sloop. She had altered course again, attempting to dodge the shells.

'Take us left,' he ordered, and watched the

compass swing round.

'Hold,' he said, and satisfied that the ship had steadied, gave the new bearing. 'Course one-seven-zero.'

He straightened and trained his binoculars over the starboard bow. The sloop's guns fired rapidly. A spread of four hit the water dead ahead, the nearest at only fifty-metres.

His own guns roared again.

Willoughby caught an orange flash lancing out from the enemy muzzles.

'Starboard ten,' he called, and *Rosefinch* edged away, her guns swinging to compensate. Waterspouts erupted in a line heading straight for the bows. The last shell reached her and detonated on the forepeak. Packed with high explosive it hurled shrapnel in every direction. A fire flared up in the paint locker.

In the Control Tower, the spotting team again zeroed in on the target.

'Shoot!'

The guns bellowed in unison, shells whipping away at their foe. A lurid flash lit up the German's bridge housing and a seaman shouted.

'A hit! We've hit it.'

Willoughby allowed himself a small smile. Tit-for-tat went through his mind.

The guns barked again.

Richter had seen the hit on the sloop's foredeck. A few more like that and the enemy would be in trouble.

The British guns retaliated and seconds later one of their shells ripped into his bridge upperworks. It exploded on the starboard side in a brilliant flash. An instantaneous fireball swept the platform, the nearest men blasted of their feet. Skin shrivelled, burned, blackened, and men died. Those on the port side of the bridge, Richter included, escaped the worst. He coughed violently, his lungs seared by the intense heat. It took time to recover his wits, almost blinded by the explosion. He managed to drag in a lungful of cold air, gritting his teeth. His cap had gone, eyebrows singed. He coughed again, eyes watering.

And all the while, the two ships exchanged gunfire.

Richard Thorburn peered through the driving rain and held his breath. He could see Willoughby slugging it out with the leading destroyer and was willing *Brackendale* on to intercede. But now he had a more immediate concern. The Elbing had turned towards and there was no option but to take it on, three miles and closing. Visibility had deteriorated, from poor to abysmal. He must gain some kind of advantage, and quickly. He raised his glasses to study the Elbing's outline. It had deployed torpedo tubes to port, a significant risk.

A shell shrieked by the starboard wing, and a second thumped into the sea off the port beam.

'Port twenty!' he called.

Brackendale rocked to starboard and swung left of the Elbing's bow. The manoeuvre served both McDonald's need to fully engage over the starboard side, and also to avoid the enemy's port side tubes.

'Midships..., steady.'

'Steering two-oh-five, sir.'

Beneath his feet, Thorburn felt the ship heave to a large roller. The bow wave streamed in the wind, foaming water boiling over the fo'c'sle. He braced against the screen and squinted ahead. He guessed the range at no more than four-thousand yards, little more than two miles.

The Elbing changed course to remain bow on to *Brackendale*. Gunfire followed the move.

Thorburn glanced south and focussed the glasses. He could just make out the shape of *Pegwell Bay*, her guns flaming. She was swinging to a more broadside stance. He checked to the east and saw *Rosefinch* turning south, the Zerstorer chasing her down.

Brackendale's fo'c'sle guns cracked off a pair of shells. Both found a target. They struck the Elbing's Gun Tower abaft the bridge. The combined weight of explosive power blew the housing apart, killing all those inside. The ship's guns fell silent, and a moment later the destroyer veered away to the southeast. A thick smokescreen billowed out astern and the ship became lost behind it.

Thorburn switched his attention back to *Rosefinch*, almost invisible in the heavy rain. The Zerstorer, starboard side of the bridge glowing with dancing flames, had closed to within what looked like three-thousand yards. Gunnery at that range would be highly accurate. He had to do something to upset the German's determination. He bent to the wheelhouse pipe and raised his voice.

'Full ahead together.'

Falconer repeated, echoing up the tube. 'Full ahead both, aye aye, sir.'

Thorburn reached for the bulkhead handset.

'Guns?'

'Sir?'

'Shift target. The Zerstorer, we must help *Rosefinch*.'

'Change of target, aye aye, sir.'

Thorburn slapped the handset back on its bracket and looked up over the screen. He thought it was a long shot, best part of six miles, and in these conditions? But it was imperative he distract that destroyer. He pursed his lips. McDonald might actually do some damage.

Rosefinch began laying a smokescreen.

Willoughby had no intention of fleeing the battle. Damage Control had managed to douse the fire in the paint locker and had moved on to splinter holes. Astern, the German destroyer had seemed intent on closing to finish it, but Willoughby had other ideas. Turning stern on to the enemy and laying smoke had been a deliberate ruse. The westerly wind fanned the smoke east and created an impenetrable, swirling screen. He watched it hawk like as it rolled over the sea. The enemy were in for a surprise. He waited . . . , and the right moment arrived.

'Hard a-starboard!' he barked at the pipe.

Rosefinch swayed into the turn, leaning hard as she fought her way round. As the bearing came due west, he let her run parallel with the smoke, before finishing the turn by coming north. Hidden behind the smoke, he prepared to face the enemy.

Richter wiped his face and looked beyond the ship's bows. The sloop had turned to flee and a dense ribbon of coiling black smoke drifted in the wind. Her masthead showed briefly, and then she melted into the murk.

He shook his head. To enter the smokescreen would be foolhardy, and he ordered a reduction in speed. He coughed again, eyes streaming. An agonised scream made him glance across the bridge. Flames still flickered in the wrecked remains. A First Aid party arrived and began tending the wounded.

Then columns of wild spray lifted either side as an enemy salvo straddled the ship. He snatched a glance to starboard. The Royal Navy destroyer was attacking, and with no sign of the

Elbing.

'Hard right!' he shouted, and grabbed for a bridge-phone. 'Gun control? Make your target the British destroyer.'

'Jawohl, Herr Kapitän,' the officer said, and the barrels in the turrets lifted.

With his ship aligning head on to the small destroyer, Richter's guns thundered.

21 . . Call His Bluff

Thorburn watched the German turn into the attack and allowed himself a faint nod. He'd achieved one aim, *Rosefinch* was no longer alone. So far so good. Now it was a matter of outmanoeuvring the Zerstorer. He saw its forward guns spit smoke, and *Brackendale's* replied. Enemy shells plunged astern, two-hundred yards clear. His own shells looked to have fallen short. He balanced as the ship slammed through the waves, spray whipping over the bridge. He guessed that with the two warships both moving at high speed, they were closing at something near a mile a minute.

'Port twenty!' Thorburn called, and *Brackendale* ploughed into the turn, leaning way over to starboard.

And then, unexpectedly, enemy shells erupted off the port bow. He looked up over the port screen and spotted another ship attacking from *Brackendale's* port bow. It was coming to the aid of the Zerstorer. And that left Thorburn in a difficult position, enemy to the right, enemy ahead to port.

'Midships!'

Falconer calmly gave the repeat. 'Midships, aye aye, sir.'

Brackendale swung sharply upright as the helm came off.

'Steady . . . , steer two-six-five.'

'Course two-six-five, sir.'

Thorburn frowned. He had *Brackendale* pushing down to the southwest, which placed both enemy destroyers to his right, one off the starboard bow, and the Zerstorer off his starboard beam. It gave McDonald broadside capability but gave the German more length of ship to aim at. And all the time the range shortened.

In the Control Room of U-824, now on station three-hundred kilometres due north of Iceland, Korvettenkapitän Rudolph Reinhart gave orders to bring the U-boat up to periscope depth. The boat had headed slowly south under Reinhart's direction, intentionally traversing the most likely route of a Russian bound convoy. But this was a vast expanse of sea and there were no guarantees that a single U-boat would ever locate a few ships in such storm tossed waters. Reinhart's one advantage centred on a recent report by U-699 detailing the passage of a convoy heading north for the waters west of Reykjavik. He knew

Eckermann well enough to give credence to his report, and that the speed of travel appeared to indicate a fast convoy. Unfortunately, nothing had been heard of U-699 since the sending of that lone signal.

Using his experience, Reinhart had made a number of calculations and then made an educated guess on the convoy's probable whereabouts. There were many possible solutions to such hypothesis, and gambling was an inherent part of decision making.

At the click of his fingers the periscope came out of its well and he took hold of the handles. The grey-green world above threatened to make a nonsense of his diligent efforts to see much beyond the bows of the boat, but perseverance was all, and Rudolph Reinhart withdrew the periscope and dived to fifty metres. The hydrophone operator looked at his commander and Reinhart nodded. Sounds travelled great distances through water and, with a sizeable convoy, a listening watch often rewarded the hunter.

Rosefinch hit the smoke at maximum revolutions. Willoughby waited at the forebridge, tense with expectation. For what seemed long seconds the ship bored into the dark swirling mass. And then she punched into the open.

The enemy Zerstorer lay directly across his bows, broadside on and totally exposed. Its guns were ranged ahead firing at *Brackendale*.

Rosefinch let go with the twin 4-inch, blasting shells across the void. At less then two-thousand yards, it was effectively point blank range. A shell exploded in a flash of orange-red. It struck the base of the forward funnel and Willoughby grinned. The next shell hit a ship's boat ahead of the forward bank of torpedo tubes, turned it into matchwood. A second salvo whipped away. Both rounds hit the hull just abaft the fo'c'sle break, exploding on contact. Flames glowed red from the interior.

Green tracer fanned out from the Zerstorer's secondary armament and *Rosefinch* began taking hits, the forward gun shield rattling. His own Oerlikons banged into action, a twin mounting either side of the bridge. Scarlet tracer chased across the waves, flaying the enemy bridge, biting at steel plates, seeking a weakness.

But the speed of the Zerstorer began to tell and the German's three 5-inch quarterdeck guns crashed in reply.

'Port thirty!' Willoughby yelled, and *Rosefinch* swept round to run parallel with the enemy's bearing. The port Oerlikon fell silent, unsighted. In its place, the after 4-inch guns joined the fight. More enemy shells landed close, columns of water writhing off the starboard beam, and splinters rattled the hull.

Willoughby clamped his teeth in defiance, determined to play his part. No quarter given, none asked for.

Thorburn flinched at a near miss, the shell exploding off to port, a plume of water cascading onto the bridge. *Brackendale* juddered to a hit, a shell bursting on the starboard bow. A fire took hold between the lower decks.

He saw the moment *Rosefinch* come barrelling out from the smokescreen, her forward guns blasting at the enemy. Immediately the Zerstorer's quarterdeck guns swung away towards the sloop, and Thorburn gave a tight smile. He'd been going to Willoughby's aid, now it seemed to be the other way round.

Dead ahead he spotted *Pegwell Bay* letting loose at the Narvick, and far beyond her, almost lost in the rain, *Seaham* had engaged the tail-ender. From the amount of tracer involved it had to be at close range.

Richard Thorburn made a snap decision. He would turn straight for the Zerstorer and reduce *Brackendale's* profile.

'Starboard twenty!'

'Starboard twenty, aye, sir!'

Guns hammered, the bitter taste of smoke filling the bridge space. 4-inch shells winged north, enemy shells returning, columns of water jetting high. *Brackendale* clawed her way round, butting across the waves.

She was just coming out of the turn when Thorburn felt the shock of an explosion from somewhere astern.

The 5-inch round caught the radar housing mid-height, and in a violent, all encompassing fireball, obliterated the entire structure. Bellingham was alive one minute, gone the next, leaving no trace of his existence.

On the pom-pom platform, Taff Williams rocked to the blast of heat and cursed as the rim of his steel helmet struck the bridge of his nose. He shoved it back on his head and took a moment to glance towards the radar lantern. His eyes widened as he saw only the pathetic remains of smouldering wreckage. Flames flickered at deck level and oily smoke fanned astern. He shook his head and turned back to the gun sight. Bellingham had been a good shipmate, it was hard to take.

He focussed on his job. His guns would soon be in range, and now he had an added incentive to do some damage. He prayed for the chance.

In the rising heat of the engine room, Bryn Dawkins also felt the muffled shock of the explosion. He wiped his face with a dirty rag, oil and sweat smudging his cheek. He had his eye on the pressure gauges. No-1 boiler had lost pressure, not a huge amount . . . , yet. At this stage he could only guess at the cause. A fuel injector partially blocked? Splinter damage? Whatever it was, the super heated steam no longer gave maximum output.

He shouted above the mind numbing din.

Leading Stoker 'Ginger' Moore glanced up, and Dawkins waved him over. Pointing at the pressure gauge he yelled, 'losing steam!' and spread his hands in query. He pointed to the boiler room. 'See what you can find.'

Moore nodded through a mask of dripping sweat. He raised a greasy thumb.

'Right Chief.'

The Welshman nodded him away and took another look at the gauge. The ship rocked to a near miss, while overhead the guns roared. Dawkins took a deep breath of humid air and watched the bank of controls. Above the waterline a battle raged, and which way the fortunes swung were beyond his control. His sole purpose was to supply the Captain with working engines, and no matter what, his duty was clear.

Kapitänleutnant Richter raised his binoculars at the British destroyer and grunted in annoyance. His guns were inflicting damage, but not enough to make a difference. And his own situation was now less certain. A battle that had begun with four against four, and with the weight of firepower in his favour, had quickly deteriorated to leave him one down.

He lowered the glasses away from his bloodshot eyes, burnt lashes stuck together. Turning to the ship's left quarter he peered over the stern rail. The sloop clung on, firing rapidly. And like the destroyer, those guns pumped out shells at a formidable rate. They might only be 4-inch against the weight of his heavier calibre, but sheer numbers would take their toll. He wondered if it would be more prudent to use his greater speed and temporarily disengage? Unlike Krause, Richter worried about the Fuhrer's reaction to this battle. The Royal navy were tenacious. If his Flotilla suffered heavy damage his future prospects might well be short lived.

A shaft of sunlight broke through the wind blown clouds and shimmered on the dark waters. A brief splash of gold light, gone in seconds. He glanced astern at a brightening sky. Was the storm blowing through? He lowered his head in concentration. Torpedoes might be the answer. Krause wanted them for use against the convoy, but if the British could not be defeated here, then they might never be deployed at all. But a full spread of eight, that must produce a favourable result.

The ship took another hit astern and he lifted his head. It would be torpedoes.

'Full speed!' he grunted, his voice hoarse from the heat. He snatched the telephone from its cradle. 'Gun Tower?'

'Kapitän?'

'I am breaking contact to attack with torpedoes. Concentrate on the destroyer while we get clear.'

'Jawohl, Kapitän.'

The ship surged forward, all guns swinging to

target the small destroyer. A short pause, and the muzzles spat smoke and flame.

Brackendale quivered as she was hit. The shell exploded on the fo'c'sle deck, port side, level with the twin capstans. The blast tore open the thin plates and left a gaping hole. Splinters ripped through the capstan steam lines and a fire sprang up in the mess decks below. Another shell struck the starboard bridge ladder, detonated and wrecked the flag deck. The steel tubing of the mainmast took the brunt of flying shrapnel and the mast sagged to port. The wire stays held, aerials and halliards whipping taut. The White Ensign took hits, was holed and shredded, but continued to fly valiantly from the masthead. In the wireless room, splinters punched into the main transmitter and wrecked the electrical circuits.

On the bridge, Thorburn felt every blow, knew the ship was taking punishment. But he'd committed *Brackendale* to the attack and her guns were still in action, a steady stream of shells hitting back at the enemy.

A larger wave caught the ship's port bow. She twisted into a corkscrew, and as the wave moved under her length she dipped to starboard. At that exact moment the guns fired again.

At that angle of lean, the guns fired low. The 4-inch shells skimmed the wave tops, and the Zerstorer, bows lifting on a crest, took two hits below the waterline on the starboard bow. Two more exploded in a bright flash ahead of the forward gun shield, raking the housing with razor sharp splinters. Flames burst from the deck, black smoke billowing over the bridge. Inside the gun shield, three men were killed outright, two more suffered lethal wounds, and one man was thrown off his feet to land in a heap, concussed. A single large splinter ricocheted off a barrel and wedged itself in the training mechanism. Richter's Gun Control, quickly realised they'd lost the use of that turret.

Thorburn smiled grimly. *Brackendale* was dishing it out. Whether it was enough to make any difference, he could only hope. And now the two warships were rapidly coming together, opposing courses, starboard to starboard. Who would blink first? Thorburn set his jaw against the fury to come. This was not the time to turn away, not for the faint hearted. He steeled himself to call the German's bluff.

Taff Williams traversed the pom-pom round across the starboard side until it hit the fire stop. If he hit the trigger now, the fire stop prevented him from shooting up his own ship, but as he waited for the sights to pick up the enemy's bow, he assured himself that the target had closed to within four-thousand yards.

Stationed to his right, Seaman-Gunner Terry Kent, the 'Trainer', who elevated or depressed the guns as necessary, asked the question.

'What we aiming for, Taff?'

Close by, the quarterdeck guns blasted off a salvo, and Taff swallowed to clear his ears. 'Deck and bridge, any bloody thing that moves.'

'Right,' Kent said. 'Any minute now.'

Twenty-two seconds later the destroyer's bow came into view and Williams readied himself. The gun sight found the fo'c'sle, followed the upper deck, past the smoking wreck of the forward gun, and found the enemy's bridge. The four barrels jumped under his hands, thumping out the staccato beat, scarlet tracer winging towards the target. Sparks flew from steel panels and he swung the guns right as the two ships began to pass one another. Around him the loaders stretched to the feed rails and slammed home boxes of 2-lb ammunition. Empty shell cases ejected from the guns, clattering down over the thin shielding, and gathering in a heap.

Then, on the enemy ship, tracer flickered from three mountings, curving upwards in a lazy arc before raining down on *Brackendale*. 20mm cannon shells slammed into her upperworks, ricocheting in all directions, punching holes in steel panels.

Williams gritted his teeth, hunching his shoulders, an instinctive reaction as if to ward off the blows. He stuck with it, concentrating on the bridge, and the guns hammered on.

Signalman Nobby Clarke found himself flat on his back on what remained of the signal deck. Battered and dazed, ears pounding, he heard his name shouted.

'Clarke!'

It was the voice of Petty Officer Grant and he opened his eyes.

'You're okay, get up.'

He felt hands under his armpits and was dragged to a sitting position. His head swam, vision blurred. He blinked and rubbed his eyes. Grant's ruddy face appeared, close, out of focus.

'Come on, son, you can manage.'

Clarke shook his head and took a deep breath. He reached for support and Grant hauled him to his feet. Upright, he staggered with the ship's movement and then braced his legs. The outline of the bridge took shape, and in the far corner he could see Allun Jones with his binoculars. He took a tentative pace forward, found that his legs held his weight, and nodded at Grant.

'Okay,' he said.

'Right then, with me,' Grant said, and moved to the port ladder.

Clarke followed, holding on with a firm grasp. At the foot of the ladder thick smoke engulfed them. He choked, retching in the fumes, but stumbled on. Ahead, two ratings had a fire hose directed down through mangled deck plates. Steam and smoke vented in swirling clouds.

He stepped forward, closing up behind the two men, and found it was Alf Higgins and Sid Reid, temporary members of the Damage Control party. Higgins was having trouble with the hose and Clarke reached across him.

'Alright, Alf, I've got it.'

Higgins looked up through the billowing smoke, eyes narrowed. Blood ran down his forehead, face blackened. He managed a feeble smile.

'Go on then, I've about had me fill.' And he let go.

Clarke took the nozzle, holding it on the flames below, and Higgins staggered away.

Grant yelled. 'I'm going for the starboard hose!' He hurried off beyond the capstans, merging with the smoke.

Flames leaped from the hole, a fierce gust of heat licking high. Clarke felt the scorching heat, turned his face away. Behind him, Reid grimaced, straining to support the hose.

'Hot, innit? Good time for a pint.'

Clarke couldn't help but grin. Only Sid would think of that in this situation. He nodded and forced himself to confront the fire, aiming the jet down the hole.

Grant reappeared, hose thrust forward. He opened the nozzle and water gushed, a second powerful stream aimed below.

Between them they fought on, and the improvised fire party slowly began to douse the flames.

22 .. Damage

Richter ducked to avoid a stream of tracer. Dense smoke coiled over the bridge, burning paint, acrid and potent. The British destroyer's secondary armament had latched onto his bridge and through the smoke he could see tracer coming from the four-barrelled after mount, what the English called a pom-pom. It was normally an anti-aircraft weapon but he'd let the *Bruno Keplar* come within its range. And for the thin plating surrounding the bridge those two-pounder shells were making themselves felt. He saw the wireless aerials torn away, the masthead lookout station ripped apart. They slammed into the Gun Control tower behind him, and he heard men screaming. Shrapnel hissed and ricocheted, splinters gouging at soft flesh. Men died.

More than that, Richter had an impression the ship was listing to starboard. Speed could nullify the effects of damage by enemy gunfire, but he thought there was a sluggishness in how the bows cleaved the waves. Worse still, Richter knew he'd made a mistake, an unforgivable error. With all that had happened so quickly, he had forgotten to prepare the torpedo tubes. His plan had been to break free and only then, return with a torpedo attack. In his mind he'd criticised the Elbing for deploying too soon, and now he could only hang his head for not doing the same.

He turned to the back of the bridge, found a junior officer.

'Hauptman,' he snapped. 'Get me a damage report, the bows.'

'Jawohl, Herr Kapitän!' the man called in reply, and made for the undamaged port side ladder. He was five rungs down when a pom-pom shell struck a stanchion and glanced off. Cast iron fragments zipped through the air and sliced into the Hauptman's throat. He fell and lay still, blood spurting to the deck from his severed jugular, a red pool expanding with the final beats of his heart. He died alone, his mission incomplete.

And the *Bruno Keplar* took on yet more water. With every plunge into a trough the sea surged into the lower decks. The weight of water slopped heavily from port to starboard, and as the ship rose to the next crest the water swilled astern through the compartments, only a weakened bulkhead preventing serious flooding.

Richter steadied himself against the forebridge. He had a feeling the ship was beginning to slow.

The after guns crashed off another salvo.

Nobby Clarke shut off the nozzle and took a step back, hauling the heavy hose away from the charred hole in the deck. At that moment an enemy 5-inch shell came in on a flat trajectory. Travelling at 3,100 feet per second, it almost passed straight across the fo'c'sle and out to sea. But *Brackendale* lifted to a wave and the shell struck the starboard capstan. Fused for impact detonation, the violent explosion shattered the shell casing into countless steel fragments. The blast sent high velocity splinters scything across the deck, a deadly array of shrapnel. The anchor chain sheared in two and, without its lock mechanism to hold it, the weight of the anchor dragged the heavy length of cable rattling into the depths.

Higgins was hit in the head, right arm and thigh, hurling him to the deck. Petty Officer Grant took a half dozen hits to the face and chest, staggered and fell. His hose began to snake aimlessly over the deck.

Reid bore the brunt of the blast. The sheer force of the explosion blew him to port. He catapulted over the guard rail and hit the water face first. He was dead before being swept beyond the stern.

Clarke felt something slam into his left calf muscle, lost his footing and tripped with the hose. Two fingers of his left hand were slashed by a splinter, torn away. The back of his skull hit the deck, bounced once, and he groaned, eyes screwed tight shut. Pain came in waves, flooding his senses. The sound of gunfire faded, ears throbbing. He tried to move off his back, head ringing, limbs unresponsive. He tried again and managed to roll onto his right side. Eyes open, all he could see was a pink deck. It dawned on him it was blood mixed with water, shifting with the ship's movement. With his good hand he levered himself up on one knee, his left leg dragging, a mind of its own.

He looked up and found Higgins lying a few feet away. With an effort, Clarke crawled over and peered at the man's face. It was a bloodied mess, strewn with cuts, but he was breathing.

'Alf,' he prompted, not recognising the sound of his own voice. 'Alf.'

Higgins groaned softly, one eye opening.

'Is it night?' he asked. 'How long's it been dark?'

Clarke looked closer and saw that the eye didn't follow any movement, just stared blankly. The other eye had blood oozing from between the lids, and Clarke looked away. Higgins was blind. Shock or wounds, it didn't really matter, there wasn't much he could do to help.

'Lie still,' he said, and looked across at Grant. He lay chest down, face turned towards Clarke, lower jaw smashed, eyes open, sightless. There were rivulets of blood on the deck, more blood swelling from his back, too much to survive. Another glance around. No sign of Reid.

A stab of pain made him gasp, intense, agonising. He saw the two stumps where his fingers had been and dropped his head. God, but it hurt, and he screwed his eyes shut against the torment. Then he felt a burning sensation rising to his groin. Almost afraid to look, he turned to find a piece of shrapnel protruding from his calf muscle. He let himself down on his side, and with his right hand grabbed the shard. He took a breath, steeled himself, and wrenched it out. The worst of the pain subsided and he lay back, breathing hard.

The sound of guns penetrated through to his brain, his hearing recovering. He lay still, hurting from his wounds, but wanting to get help for Higgins. A little longer, he thought, then I'll move.

On the *Aldenburg's* bridge, Krause found himself caught in two minds about ordering Richter to engage the remaining British warships. If he was going to inflict maximum damage on the convoy, then he needed to call them off now and have them rejoin immediately. He scowled in thought, convincing himself of a new battle plan. He could throw them in at the convoy's escort while he held *Aldenburg* at long range and picked off the merchantmen. After all, destroyers were there to be sacrificed should the need arise, and there was no greater need than that of Admiral Mathias Krause.

'Bergman,' he called. 'Have the wireless office contact Richter. Order him to rejoin *Aldenburg*. Speed is essential.'

Bergmann clicked his heels and turned to the bridge messenger. 'Tell the wireless office the Admiral wishes to transmit a signal.'

'Jawohl, Herr Kapitän,' the man snapped, and moved off to call a Telegraphist. Three minutes later the air waves responded to the power of the cruiser's transmitter.

Drawn to the bridge screen by an explosion, Thorburn looked down on the smoking wreckage and found three casualties. One of them crawled over to another before collapsing on to his back. He lay without moving.

'Stretcher bearers to the fo'c'sle deck!' he called, and then ducked from probing tracer. A glance to starboard showed him the enemy's quarterdeck fast gliding by. Under McDonald's guidance the fo'c'sle guns traversed hard right pointing as far astern as the stops allowed. The barrels steadied and blasted a pair of shells.

Rosefinch caught his attention, still coming on, guns blazing. If anything she appeared to be gaining, and he tried to fathom why? Was the Zerstorer damaged in some way? An unseen failure?

More tracer hammered the bridge, whining and fizzing off steel panels. The bridge screen disintegrated, lethal fragments. Ignoring the tracer he levelled his glasses at the German's stern, focussed them along the ship's length, and steadied on the bows. The destroyer dipped and twisted to a wave, and he found two shell holes, so close together they almost merged as one. They looked to be below the waterline. Was there flooding? Could that be enough to slow it down? One way to find out.

'Hard a port!' he snapped at the voice-pipe.

Brackendale heeled over and once again the starboard rail immersed itself in writhing foam. On the fo'c'sle, the stretcher bearers tending to the casualties lost their footing, slipping over the slanting deck. They persevered, caring for the obvious wounds, kneeling to administer aid.

Thorburn braced against the tilt, eyes flicking between compass and enemy. A fountain of spray erupted from a near miss and splinters battered the hull. But *Brackendale* clawed her way round, rolling with the heavy seas.

Sunlight took him by surprise, the sea bathed in brilliance. He looked up over his shoulder. The weather had definitely cleared, a large swathe of blue replacing the scudding grey clouds. Still rain-dark in the east, but bright to the west.

Another glance at the enemy.

'Meet her, Cox'n!'

The little destroyer swayed up from the angle of lean, straightening from the turn.

'Midships..., steady.'

He checked the compass, almost due south, and at a guess the range had opened up to five miles. The guns in the forward turret traversed and lifted over the port bow. They fired simultaneously, smoke and flame, recoil. He stepped to the port wing and looked astern. *Pegwell Bay* had swung away north in pursuit of her adversary. The Narvik was laying a smoke screen and beginning to leave *Pegwell* floundering in its wake.

Heavy smoke in the distance resolved itself to be *Seaham,* on fire amidships, though there appeared to be no lessening of her salvos. Her opponent also looked to be breaking off the engagement and heading north.

He took a moment to study *Rosefinch* pressing on three miles off *Brackendale's* port quarter. Her fo'c'sle guns fired at regular intervals. Satisfied that she was still in reasonable condition, he turned his attention back to the Zerstorer and raised his binoculars. The German's gunfire had become more erratic, less co-ordinated. Somehow, by some quirk of fate, or just possibly the combined firepower of two Royal Navy warships, the enemy destroyer no longer held the upper hand. He very deliberately picked up a bulkhead handset.

'Guns?'

'Sir?'

'That German's in trouble. I'll come five points to starboard, then give it all you've got.'

'Aye aye, sir.'

Thorburn leaned to the bell mouthed pipe. 'Starboard five.'

'Starboard five, aye, sir.'

And the small, wounded destroyer, veered to the right.

In the Range Finder Director, 'Guns' McDonald, for the first time in the engagement, found himself presented with a clear, sunlit view of the enemy. His own Trainer and Layer settled their sights squarely on the base of the Zerstorer's mainmast.

'Broadside,' he warned the gun mounts. 'With semi-piercing.... Load.'

Behind the shields the gun crews followed the director's output, traversing and lifting onto the target.

McDonald allowed *Brackendale* to steady on her new bearing, waiting those few vital extra seconds.

'Shoot!'

The guns crashed in unison, and four 38 pound shells, accelerating at 2,660 feet per second, whipped across the sea. Three of the rounds found targets. One exploded exactly as prescribed, at the base of the forward funnel. The blast ruptured the main boiler room exhaust pipe and split the tube down to the drum. Superheated steam screamed from an ever widening vent. Another shell struck the midships housing and detonated in the 5-inch ammunition handling room. The fuse setter died instantly. A series of explosions marked the moment fused shells began erupting. The third 4-inch shell punched into the radio room abaft the bridge and exploded in a white hot ball. Shrapnel wrecked the adjoining wheelhouse ahead.

Two men in the boiler room died in scalding steam, three in the radio room were incinerated, and another two seamen flayed by shrapnel in the wheelhouse. *Bruno Keplar* lost steerage and veered to the right, out of control.

McDonald's jaw tightened with grim satisfaction. That had been an eight-thousand yard salvo, the best part of four and a half miles, and now he had the opportunity to really inflict some punishment. He held the enemy in his sights.

'Shoot!' he called, and the four guns barked again.

Willoughby caught the flashes of *Brackendale's* three hits and grinned.

'Tally Ho,' he mouthed, and touched the peak of his cap in salute. He saw the enemy destroyer veer right, slowing, and his eyes widened. Thick smoke billowed from the German's after housing, white steam adding another layer. He gripped the rail.

Now, he thought . . . , now was the time to make it count.

'Port five!' he snapped at the pipe, and still moving at top speed, *Rosefinch* presented her starboard side to the enemy. The main armament took full advantage, and a succession of 4-inch shells whipped away towards the target.

23 . . No Way Back

Kapitänleutnant Herman Richter stood in the wreckage of his bridge and swore. Half the platform was a smoking black ruin, and the remainder showed the holes and scars of multiple hits from secondary armament. And the ship had now swung off course. He shouted to the wheelhouse, but with no answer. He staggered as another hit juddered the deck, and cursed aloud, the sound of his voice lost in the deafening whistle of escaping steam. The reassuring thump of two guns firing from aft brought a glint of satisfaction to the bloodshot eyes. He still had a pair of main armament working, and all his torpedoes housed in their tubes.

But first he needed steering. Was it disabled from the wheelhouse, or had the rudder been damaged? He tried the wheelhouse again. This time he heard a response, faint, shaky.

'Kapitän?'

'Do you have movement in the wheel?

A pause. 'Ja, I feel pressure from the gear.'

'Middle it,' Richter urged, and looked up at the bows. They stopped swinging, steadied.

'Hold,' he said, and reached for a telephone.

The reply was instant. 'Torpedo platform.'

Richter recognised the voice of Lieutnant

Becker. 'Prepare all tubes to starboard. If you get a chance, fire by your own decision.'

'Jawohl, Herr Kapitän.'

'Good, you will see to it.' He slapped the phone back on its cradle and turned to look at the enemy. He found they had closed quickly, both firing broadsides, each ship turning away in opposite directions.

The screaming cacophony of escaping steam reached a crescendo, and then abruptly stopped. He swallowed hard and raised his binoculars at the British destroyer. He thought how small she looked in comparison to the *Bruno Keplar*. At the same time he knew her captain to be a worthy opponent. If he could just find a way to sink this Englander, then he might salvage some honour from this mess.

Beneath his feet, the deck took on a greater angle of lean. He corrected his stance to compensate, one knee slightly bent. Why, he wondered briefly, had the Hauptman not reported back on any damage to the bows? Through smoke and spray he stared despairingly at the British destroyer. If they held course how could he shorten the range for the torpedoes?

His guns thumped again.

A German shell plunged into *Brackendale's* galley housing amidships. The explosion ripped open the vulnerable thin steel and splinters raked the area. Perched over the galley, the pom-

pom lifted bodily to the detonation and then slewed down to collapse in the wreckage.

Taff Williams felt the shocking impact of the blast. A steel cross-member dislodged and splintered his right kneecap. He gasped at the excruciating pain. He fell and landed hard. An ammunition rack broke free of the gun mount and struck his chest. The weight crushed him, broke ribs, and pinned him where he lay. A sharp edge pierced his lungs and his next breath came in a rasping hiss.

'Taff..., Taff?'

He heard the call, recognised the voice, but couldn't summon the strength to answer. Flames sprang up from somewhere round his feet, hot on his legs. He began to slip into unconsciousness, knowing he was weakening, short of breath. A last wheezing intake, the pain left him, and with an involuntary shudder, Taff Williams breathed his last.

Thorburn trained his glasses on the enemy bridge. It looked to be in chaos but he found the vague shape of men still conning the ship. He let the binoculars drift down astern of the forward funnel. The smoke and steam had thinned, and then as he focussed amidships he tensed at the sight of torpedoes being brought to readiness. A thin smile creased his face. It was a forlorn gesture at this range and he had no intention of being drawn in. He could see McDonald was on target, hitting more frequently. *Rosefinch* too had the measure of the German, her salvos straddling the quarterdeck. Near misses exploded close to the hull, bright flashes bursting on deck. Flames sprang up abaft No2 funnel, grey-black smoke billowing astern.

He glanced at *Rosefinch*. She was moving out onto the enemy's opposite flank, holding her distance, all guns engaged.

But then Thorburn realised the German destroyer had lost a significant amount of speed, and that *Brackendale* would shortly overshoot and run ahead.

'Half ahead together, twelve knots,' he called to the pipe.

'Half ahead both, twelve knots, aye aye, sir.'

From the port bridge wing, Armstrong raised his voice over the sound of the guns. 'Listing to starboard by the look of it.'

Thorburn again raised his glasses. 'Yes . . . ,' he said slowly, 'I think you're right.' The Zerstorer's deck was becoming noticeably visible, angled down towards them.

Brackendale's guns crashed again, and across the waves, *Rosefinch* unleashed another salvo. Eight shells converged on the target, and five of the eight found their mark, slamming into the destroyer from opposite directions. Seconds later, two more separate broadsides were fired.

Those four consecutive salvos, a lethal combination of semi-armour piercing and high explosive, wreaked havoc above and below decks. From the German's forward gun mounting, a huge cauldron of red-black flame ridden smoke surged up and enveloped the bridge. Thorburn grimaced at the sight. The seething mass shredded in the wind and left the entire bridge structure a smoking ruin.

Fierce fires raged along the deck and burning men scrambled from below decks, to hurl themselves overboard. The aftermost gun housing exploded, twisted steel and broken bodies flung into the air.

And all the while, *Brackendale's* guns hammered salvo after salvo at the dying ship.

Thorburn lowered his binoculars. There was no longer any need for magnification, the naked eye revealed all. The Zerstorer's main deck heeled to forty-five degrees, far too great an angle from which to recover. The fo'c'sle dipped, succumbing to the waves. Slowly, inevitably, two-thousand tons of German destroyer began to slip away.

Brackendale's guns ceased their bombardment and a strange silence settled over the ship.

Armstrong finally broke the quiet. 'Finished,' he said in a hushed voice. 'No way back from that.'

Thorburn nodded, watching men desperately seeking to abandon ship. Some managed to jump clear, while others were swept from precarious perches before they were ready. A few attempted to release the motor-boat, but it jammed in the falls. Then they too were swallowed by the sea.

Brackendale's crew, those in a position to do so, stared in mute fascination at the dying moments of a powerful adversary. Finally, after what seemed an age, but could be measured in mere minutes, the battered, smoking ship sank from view. A great bubble of oil and trapped air heaved to the surface, boiled and frothed . . . , rippled away and subsided. Floating debris and oil blackened heads were all that remained on the surface.

From somewhere astern, Thorburn heard a half-hearted cheer. It dwindled quickly, faltering, as if those involved were somehow embarrassed to be the victors. It might well be their own shipmates struggling in the water, their own small destroyer headed for an ocean grave. 'Number One,' he said quietly. 'You'd better check on the damage. And I want a full list of casualties.'

'On my way,' Armstrong said, and made for the portside ladder.

Thorburn bent to the wheelhouse pipe. 'Port ten, slow ahead together.'

Falconer's steady acknowledgement echoed up the pipe. 'Port ten, slow ahead. Aye aye, sir.'

Brackendale came round towards the spreading pool, drifted closer and nosed gently in amongst the floating remnants. A few hands waved despairingly, not many. Two or three men attempted to swim. The viscous coating of fuel oil held others in choking spasms, lungs thick with black fluid. Others wasted valuable energy splashing and shouting while some swam towards *Brackendale* without sound, the waves threatening to overwhelm them. Many, numbed or shocked, or exhausted by the struggle, sank from view, lost in the swirling sea.

Lieutenant George Labatt ordered a rope net to be cast over the side along *Brackendale's* starboard quarterdeck. A flailing hand reached from the sea grasping for a secure hold. Sailors shouted encouragement but the man shook his head, lacking the energy to make the climb. Two of the crew swarmed over the side, legs in the water, and hauled him bodily up the net. More hands grabbed hold and dragged him onto the deck. He lay in a sodden, oily heap, groaning in pain. And then the crew saw why he'd struggled to help himself. The lower portion of one arm below the elbow had been totally severed and blood oozed from the ragged stump. Someone applied a makeshift tourniquet and a stretcher appeared to take him down to Doc Waverley. Labatt urged the men to hurry, knowing how vulnerable they were to a strike from a U-boat. It seemed as if everything conspired to slow the operation. Even those Germans who had strength enough to climb the net struggled to make it onto the deck.

Labatt saw one man slump across the gunwales, too exhausted to move, and he reached out to haul him inboard. A thick slime of oil covered the man's upper torso, and Labatt lost his grip. He leaned out over the side, found the man's belt, and unceremoniously dragged him to the deck. Another German made it to the net, and this time members of the crew were waiting, waist deep, to give him a hand up. Others reached down and pulled him aboard. It was rough and ready, and although their first instinct might be to show compassion, time and circumstances gave an urgency to their actions. Every man aboard felt the danger of being almost stopped in the water, and each man fought against the desire to curse these hateful figures, to show no kindness. And yet, there was that sailor's unwritten code, seldom spoken, but always adhered to. Never leave a man in peril of drowning, do whatever it took to make him a survivor, even when it involved the enemy.

George Labatt spoke quietly, fully involved, helping where needed, and they struggled on, doing all in their power to save lives. By the time they'd finished, seventeen had been rescued, four of them being tended by Doc Waverley. The remainder sat or lay sprawled on the quarterdeck, the cloying stench of oil strong in the air.

Labatt searched the sea once more, and for the first time realised that *Rosefinch* had also pushed into the mass of floating debris. But his search proved fruitless and he turned to look at the bridge. He waved an oil blackened hand.

'Clear!' he shouted, and he saw Thorburn lift a hand in response. The welcome tremor of the engines throbbed beneath his feet, and *Brackendale* gathered momentum, easing away from the squalid remains of battle.

Armstrong had toured the ship as best he could, deliberately avoiding the rescue efforts and concentrating his search below decks. The fo'c'sle flats were almost impenetrable and the fire had reduced the area to a smouldering mess. Gallons of water sluiced back and forth, the result of fighting the flames. To starboard he had seen that the bulkheads were starred by shrapnel, and scuttles lay open to the sea. There were no sign of casualties and he'd then made his way down to the Stokers Mess. Again no sign of casualties but a haphazard array of splinter holes was allowing sea water to enter the compartment. Brief but thorough inspections continued. Provision room, naval stores and cable locker, down another ladder to the Asdic compartment and the forward 4-inch magazine. Up a deck to the Low Power room and the Stewards Mess. Some puncture holes, nothing serious. Up another level to the wardroom, not yet being used for the wounded. A quick word with Doc Waverley. Twelve wounded, seven dead. The wardroom served as a secondary sick bay. On into the wireless room where two Telegraphists were trying to repair the main board. One gave a thumbs up and the other reported having already repaired the main aerials.

'Well done,' he said, nodding his approval. He left them to it and headed outside.

Now on the main deck abaft the funnel, he picked his way aft, gingerly stepping over twisted steel plates and trailing wires. He stopped short of where the Radar Housing had once stood. It had gone, wiped from the ship. And beyond that lay the pitiful remains of the Galley housing and the wreckage of the collapsed pom-pom lying at a crazy angle inside. The after 4-inch gun mount looked to be unharmed, the gunners busy clearing spent shell cases over the side. He took a quick glance at the German survivors before dropping down through the hatch to the Engine Room. Bryn Dawkins was in a shouted conversation with one of his Stokers but caught sight of Armstrong stepping off the bottom of the ladder.

Armstrong lifted a thumb, stuck it up in the air, and then dropped it to point down, and back up again, the easiest way of asking if everything was alright. Dawkins got the gist and grinned, gave a thumbs up.

The First Lieutenant nodded and took himself back up onto the deck. There was still the steering compartment, workshop and aft 4-inch magazines to check. All in all, he thought, as he entered the stern section, things could have been much worse. *Brackendale* was still very much in one piece. Her upperworks had taken the brunt of damage and other than the multi-barrelled pom-pom, her main armament remained in good order. He bent his head and slipped inside the engineering workshop.

Thorburn took the opportunity to make a thorough inspection of the flotilla. *Seaham* appeared to be in the worst shape, smoke blackened and listing to port. There was a lot of shrapnel damage to the hull and the Range Finder Director looked like a colander.

'Yeoman!' he called over his shoulder. 'Ask *Seaham* for a damage report.'

The shutter clattered and Thorburn switched focus to *Pegwell Bay*. She looked to be in reasonably good condition, a few holes here and there, but apparently relatively unscathed. Sighting on *Rosefinch*, he could detect a fair bit of damage to her bows, and the bridge housing had suffered from what he thought must be small arms fire. Of course, anything he could see on the surface didn't necessarily reflect reality. Internally there may well be some serious damage. Casualties would be verified later.

'Reply from *Seaham*, sir. "Have taken multiple hits. Engines good. Holed on waterline, pumps coping." End of message, sir.'

'Acknowledge,' Thorburn said. Few words by

way of explanation, and it spoke volumes for her captain's composure. She must be a mess. He tried to concentrate on his next move. The battle had been fierce while it lasted and the entire flotilla had suffered damage of one sort or another. They'd managed to sink the Zerstorer, but it hardly made amends for the loss of *Zeus*. Annoyingly, three of the enemy had managed to escape into the distance. There was no point in trying to catch them, their speed would have taken them well clear by now. Would they mount another attack? He doubted it, unless they launched torpedoes from range. No . . . , they would be licking their wounds and attempting to join forces with the *Aldenburg*. He wondered on the whereabouts of the convoy? Again he looked round his command. Their original objective had been to hunt for U-boats, disrupt the enemy threat. Drive them under or sink them, given the chance. But now he was faced with a difficult decision. Should he continue the patrol or call it a day and return to Scapa? Certainly *Seaham* needed to find a safe haven, and he suspected the number of casualties among the flotilla would be stretching the skills of the surgeons.

He sighed and rubbed his face. He was astonished to find blood on his fingers and tentatively rubbed again. He found a wetness on his cheekbone and touched his temple. The wound had opened up, blood trickling down his jaw.

He swore under his breath and hunted for something to clean the blood off. In the end he opted for a handkerchief. He perched on the bridge-chair and cleared his mind. First things first, inform the Admiralty, and he called for the Yeoman.

'Take this down . . . "Admiralty, repeated to *Stirling*. One enemy destroyer sunk. Three enemy disengaged. Moving north at high speed. *Seaham* afloat, listing to port. *Pegwell Bay*, *Rosefinch* and *Brackendale* damaged. Request orders." Code it up and get it off.'

'Aye aye, sir.'

He watched the man leave the bridge and turned to the screen. Right now he needed to restore order, get on with the patrol. But he decided to hold them in line astern with a mile between ships. He relayed that to the Signalman and the Aldis began to clatter.

Armstrong came up the port ladder and Thorburn looked round. 'Tell me,' he said.

The First Lieutenant gave him a full report; damage, state of repairs, and the list of casualties. When he finished, Thorburn rubbed his jaw. 'What have we done with the Germans?'

'Lieutenant Labatt has them under guard in the Petty Officers mess.'

'Good,' Thorburn said. 'I'm getting on with the patrol, but I've asked the Admiralty for orders. And we'd better arrange for someone to sort out a meal. The main galley might be gone but the wardroom stewards should be able to conjure up something.'

'I'll see to it,' Armstrong said, but stood without moving, concern in his eyes. 'Are you alright, sir? There's blood on your face.'

Thorburn grinned. 'I'm fine, just the scar weeping. I probably made it look worse when I wiped it.'

Armstrong pursed his lips and nodded. 'If you're sure?'

'I am, you can carry on.'

'Sir,' Armstrong said, and turned for the ladder.

Thorburn moved to the bridge chair and sat, thinking things through. The situation wasn't ideal, but the flotilla still had teeth. It would do for now.

24 . . Gunfire

In U-824 the hydrophone operator pressed the headphones to his ears, his face frowning in concentration. His fingers turned a knob, tuning the receptors for fine direction. He looked up, eyes narrowed, lips pursed in concentration. Reinhart watched him closely. The man whispered.

'Propellers, Kapitän . . . , many propellers. Bearing two-seven-zero.'

Reinhart pushed his cap back and rubbed his jaw. Coming from the west, exactly as expected.

'Sure?'

'Ja, there can be no mistake.'

'Can you give me the range?'

The man closed his eyes and turned the dial, clockwise, anticlockwise, and clockwise again.

'To say is difficult, Herr Kapitän. Eleven-thousand metres?'

Reinhart pulled down on the peak of his cap. He needed to see for himself. And the weather out there would help him avoid detection.

'Surface!' he snapped, and the boat headed for the waves.

U-824 emerged from the depths and Reinhart found himself encased in driving rain. Visibility was not the best, but it sufficed for what he had in mind. He altered course to the northwest, towards the coast of Greenland, intending to make an attack from the convoy's northern flank. Twice before he had attacked convoys from inshore and both times had taken advantage of a weakness in the cordon of escorting warships.

For thirty minutes he held that course, and then brought the U-boat round to the south. The prevailing wind churned the sea into a frenzy, but occasionally offered brief interludes where visibility might increase to almost three-thousand metres. In one such moment, a lookout called a warning.

'Ships, Herr Kapitän!'

At last, he thought, and swung his binoculars to follow the outstretched arm. But what loomed into view was the exact opposite of what he wanted. He found two British destroyers, one of which turned straight for U-824.

'Alarm!' he shouted. 'Dive the boat!' and the lookouts scrambled for the hatch.

Reinhart watched them down and snatched a final glance at the destroyer. It was attacking at speed, the sharp stem lost behind a welter of flying foam. A flash of gunfire came from the fo'c'sle, and then a second. He lunged for the hatch and threw himself inside. The sea ahead erupted to an explosion, another shell burst close alongside. He desperately secured the hatch, tumbled below, and rattled off fresh orders.

'Hard left! Depth one-hundred!'

The boat spiralled down, turning away at right angles to the enemy. Deeper they went, fifty, sixty . . . , seventy metres.

The sound of propellers drawing closer, eyes up following the thrashing cavitations of a warship's attack.

'Water bombs!' the operator called.

Still the boat dived deeper and someone said 'passing one-hundred.'

Reinhart nodded. 'Good,' he said, self assured, 'more yet.' And they waited for the inevitable. They weren't to be disappointed.

Two explosions battered the boat, and shock waves hammered the hull. Two more, louder, heavier, the pressure hull absorbing brutal blows. The fifth detonation rocked the boat violently. The depth charge must have burst level with the conning tower and a jet of water streamed from the periscope housing. An oil pipe let go from a flange and a gauge glass shattered. The lights flickered, faded, strengthened.

'Level!' Reinhart demanded. The depth gauge showed one-hundred and eighty metres. Two further explosions came from aft, more muffled. The boat levelled off at a depth of two-hundred metres. Men in the Control Room fought to smother the flow of water.

'Slow ahead.'

'It goes away, Kapitän,' said the hydrophone operator.

'Not, I think, for too long,' Reinhart said, and within minutes the sharp, penetrating chirp of Asdic pinged against the hull.

Korvettenkapitän Rudolph Reinhart jammed his cap down tight and grinned at the crew. 'Now we play cat and mouse with the British. Let the party begin.'

In the *Aldenburg*, Krause had purposely remained within the broad periphery of the storm. He paced the bridge, prowling restlessly from chair to screen, then across to either bridge wing, and back to his chair. If as he expected, the convoy was on one of the previously used routes, a course alteration taking *Aldenburg* northwest would allow him to intercept from the southern flank. Ideally he would have chosen to approach from astern but with little in the way of up to date U-boat sightings, anywhere along the southern flank would suffice. Having sat for a while, he at last gave the order.

'Bergman,' he said from the chair. 'Bring us round to the northwest, and you will remind all lookouts to be vigilant. The convoy's escort will react swiftly, and their Fleet destroyers will be a handful. But our advantage is the range of our guns. If we keep our distance then the merchant ships are kaput.'

Bergman nodded. 'Jawohl, Herr Admiral,' he said, and passed on the order. But he kept his thoughts to himself. In his opinion this whole operation had been badly planned and executed. Yes, they'd sunk a British Fleet destroyer, but the smaller destroyer, the 'Hunt' class, had escaped real damage, and had then, almost unbelievably, started shadowing *Aldenburg*. Details of their position, course and bearing would have been flashed to the Admiralty, and also to any lurking Royal Navy battle groups. Signals from the Kriegsmarine's Intelligence Service had not reported any such operation, but just because the U-boats had found nothing, did not mean that enemy forces were not in the vicinity.

Aldenburg turned through the wind and rain and came round to the northwest, and Bergman steadied the ship to the new bearing. He would never class himself as a defeatist, but there were surely better ways to achieve what Krause wanted.

He set his jaw and watched the sea. If they found the convoy, the Royal Navy would definitely make itself known.

H.M.S. *Stirling* thumped through heavy seas. A dense blanket of rain gave little comfort to the lookouts, and their ability to give any adequate warning was severely hampered by the conditions. Out on the convoy's port quarter, H.M.S. *Transient* was in contact with a U-boat and currently attacking with depth charges.

Taylor-Mitchell ordered a turn from southwest to northeast for another run alongside the convoy's right flank, and it had just been completed when radar picked up an echo that indicated a large surface vessel. The operator reported the range as sixteen miles and approaching from fifteen degrees off the starboard bow. Subsequent bearings were quickly entered into the Plot and the target's speed estimated as twenty-eight knots.

Captain Taylor-Mitchell, satisfied that all the information coincided with the expected attack from *Aldenburg,* acted accordingly. He looked round the bridge at his executive officers and gave a firm nod.

'Gentlemen.... Action Stations. And hoist the Battle Ensigns.'

Orders were passed, a bugler sounded the call,

and the cruiser came to life. Two large battle flags were run up, one on each mast, and all four gun turrets began to traverse left and right in anticipation.

Taylor-Mitchell checked on *Stirling's* speed. It wouldn't do to go charging ahead with no clear idea of what might emerge. But with the target coming in off the starboard bow he wanted to ensure that he had ample room to manoeuvre for a broadside.

'Number One,' he said, and turned to Lieutenant-Commander Tim Brockhurst. 'Warn *Scitalis* of possible enemy approach and tell her to take station off our port beam. If the enemy appears, attack on sight.' He looked to the sky and shook his head, if only they had better visibility. He glanced at his watch, but there wasn't much good news there. Another forty-minutes and they'd be in darkness, and darkness made for unexpected consequences.

'Radar-Bridge!'
'Forebridge.'
'Range to target fifteen-miles.'
'Very well.'

The rain abruptly stopped, the heavy cloud lifting, and the lookouts doubled their efforts. *Stirling* ploughed ahead, holding steady at fourteen knots, the crew tensed for action. Down in the sick bay, the Surgeon laid out the tools of his trade and sick berth attendants stacked sterile dressings for when quick application might be needed. In the Director Control Tower, the Gunnery Officer, Lieutenant-Commander Eric Dempster and his crew, diligently scanned the horizon for whatever might emerge. Their unswerving commitment in gathering information about the target was a vital component in bringing *Stirling's* guns to bear. Forewarned is forearmed, and the unflappable Dempster could be relied upon to have the range-finder brought into use at the earliest opportunity.

'Radar-Bridge!'

'Bridge?'

'Range twelve-miles, bearing one-one-oh degrees.'

'Very well.'

Taylor-Mitchell narrowed his eyes and clamped his teeth. That indicated a slight change of approach, the enemy now aligned off the starboard beam, but anticipated by *Stirling's* continued movement alongside the convoy. He thought of previous battles and how this same sense of expectation gripped every man aboard, and particularly these moments when you knew contact was inevitable, and yet there was an unreal sense of calm.

He grimaced, his mouth strangely dry. Waiting was always the worst.

'Herr Admiral, radar reports convoy off the starboard bow at nineteen kilometres.'

Krause rose from his chair. 'How many ships?'

'At least fifteen, maybe more.'

Krause rubbed his hands. 'Are they in sight?'

Bergman snatched up the telephone to Gun Control. 'Can you see the convoy from up there?'

'Ja, they are just in view. Smoke and mastheads.'

'Can you see any escorts?'

'Possibly, but at this range, hard to say.'

Bergman hesitated. 'Can your guns reach the target?'

'Ja, but the fall of shells would not be seen.'

'Mmm,' Bergman mouthed. 'Be ready.' He slapped the phone back onto its bracket, turned to the Admiral and repeated what he'd heard.

Krause thrust his hands behind his back and fixed Bergman with hard eyes. 'Then we attack. Bring us to full speed and prepare for the turn north to bombard. You will fire on my command.'

'Jawohl, Herr Admiral.'

Orders were given, and the ship lifted to the extra power, thumping through the waves.

Admiral Mathias Johann Heinrich Krause gave a tight smile of satisfaction. Battle was about to be joined.

On *Stirling's* bridge, Taylor-Mitchell waited, running his tongue over his teeth. This was truly the proverbial calm before the storm.

'Radar--Bridge!'

'Bridge?' he answered.

'Target has increased to thirty-two knots, sir.'

'Very well,' he said, and found Tim Brockhurst. 'Warn Guns to be ready.'

'Radar..., enemy turning north.'

And then far off in the distant murk they all saw the ominous flash of gunfire.

Taylor-Mitchell reacted. 'Full ahead. Starboard thirty. Tell Guns to open fire when ready.'

Brockhurst passed the orders and *Stirling* swung south away from the convoy, action imminent.

Twelve minutes had passed since radar first reported the target, and now, drawn by the flash of gunfire, Lieutenant-Commander Eric Dempster found *Aldenburg's* distant ghostly shape. He instantly trained the Range Finder onto the enemy and began the job of tracking. Three decks below, the Admiralty Fire Control Table received that information, and by use of clever analogue computation, converted the figures and calculated the correct deflection and elevation needed. That instruction was passed to the Transmitting Station and instantly relayed to the Control Tower where 'Guns' watched the 'Ready' lamps change, one by one, from red to green. The twelve 6-inch guns of the main armament traversed to port, lifted and paused.

Dempster gave the order. 'Shoot!'

Inside the four triple-mounted turrets, the Gun Captains heard the musical 'ting ting' and reacted.

The guns thundered, wreathed in smoke, and the first broadside winged towards the target. And while the first salvo was still in the air, a second broadside followed, and a third. The gunners worked on, unstinting in their efforts to feed the guns.

Aldenburg's opening salvos burst harmlessly between the merchantmen, all nine round plunging down to explode in fountains of drifting spray. And it wasn't until those shells had hit the sea that a second barrage roared from the muzzles. At that same moment a lookout stiffened in alarm and shouted a warning.

'British cruiser off the port side!'

Krause whipped up his binoculars in disbelief. It looked to be a Town class, and he cursed. Twelve guns to his nine and all ranged for a broadside. He saw them fire, stabs of orange flame, cordite smoke ballooning astern. The barrels lowered to reload. And seconds later the sea erupted in a frenzy of waterspouts. The fact they detonated short of *Aldenburg* gave him no comfort, it was very accurate for an initial salvo.

'Hard right!' he snapped in annoyance. They had said no Royal Navy cruisers, not true. The ship began to turn, but then a second broadside arrived and Krause winced as it straddled *Aldenburg*.

The deck shuddered to an explosion, and another. A shell smashed into the superstructure high on the bridge, exploded and showered the platform with splinters. The armoured glass had never been designed to withstand such force and shattered into fragments. Shrapnel hurtled through the air and a barbed segment hit Krause between the shoulder blades. It deflected off his spine, went deep, and penetrated a lung. He staggered, eyes wide, and dropped to his knees. His body convulsed as he desperately tried to draw breath, He coughed violently, and a trickle of blood dribbled from the corner of his mouth. It left a bright red stain on the white of his collar. Twitching in the throes of death, he crumpled to the deck. An agonised smile flicked across the bloodied lips. He knew it was the end. The twisted smile was in recognition of a simple truth, he would now never be part of a subjugated Germany. His brain, starved of blood, ceased to function. The officer dressed in the high ranking uniform of a Kriegsmarine Admiral, and wearing a Knights Cross at his throat, died where he'd fallen, just one of thirty-two casualties that had fallen in the salvo.

Over on the far side of the bridge, Bergman saw Krause go down, crunched his way through a carpet of glass, and knelt at his side. The eyes were vacant and he felt for a pulse. Nothing.

He levered himself to his feet, stunned by the turn of events. What now? Like it or not, he was in Command. A quick glance round the bridge and he could see the majority of men still at their posts. Another salvo of 6-inch shells hit the sea close astern, and he frowned. *Aldenburg* was still turning, obeying Krause's last command, and the British guns had not quite ranged correctly. He looked back at the man's body and grimaced. Krause had brought them to this, a futile gesture of arrogant pride. Bergman had advised against it, but the Admiral had chosen to disregard his caution.

Aldenburg jolted to another explosion as the ship was bracketed yet again. He crossed the bridge and stepped outside, staring at the enemy forces now converging on his stern in the form of two pincers. He raised his glasses. Northwest he counted three destroyers, and southwest lay the fearsome sight of that twelve gun cruiser. Were there more? None that he was aware of, but there might be.

Bergman hesitated for a second longer, and then made up his mind. The ship continued turning to the east where the weather lay thick and squally. He would use it to break off the engagement.

'Make your course east,' he demanded. 'Emergency full ahead.'

The ship steadied, swung upright, bow wave ploughing through heavier seas. The two aftermost gun turrets fired simultaneously, six shells arcing out at the British cruiser.

'Smoke!' Bergman called. 'Make black smoke!'

And before the next Royal Navy broadside splashed down the *Aldenburg* made a timely escape into a bank of rain, leaving astern a thick veil of black smoke.

Taylor-Mitchell turned the ship to follow the enemy and picked up a handset to the Range Finder Director Tower. 'Do you have him on radar?'

Dempster replied quickly. 'Yes, sir. Nine-miles.'

'Give him another three salvos and we'll rejoin the convoy.'

'Aye aye, sir.'

The Captain replaced the handset and the forward guns bellowed. Twenty-two seconds later, another salvo, and a third followed at twenty-one seconds. Dempster then called the ceasefire. 'Check, check, check.'

Taylor-Mitchell ordered a reduction in speed and altered course to take *Stirling* round towards the convoy. As ordered, the merchant ships had turned away from the German intruder and he now signalled for them to resume their original course. It had not escaped his mind that his over-riding priority was the convoy's safe and timely arrival in Murmansk. Chasing off after the *Aldenburg* in poor weather with the added risk of a possible destroyer presence, unnecessarily endangered both *Stirling* and the convoy's security. With a probable further ten to twelve days of steaming ahead, they were only part way through a long voyage. Let caution be the watchword and see what transpired. *Aldenburg* had seen what it was up against and without reinforcements it would be a brave man who returned to the fray.

With night falling, Taylor-Mitchell settled into the bridge chair and studied the sea ahead. The remnants of the storm had not finished with them yet.

H.M.S. *Standing*, after two hours of depth charging an unseen enemy, reluctantly broke off the battle, and adhering to escort instructions, rejoined the convoy.

25 . . Battle Weary

With the coming of darkness, Thorburn made his way back up to the bridge and slumped into the bridge chair. The small amount of effort required to clamber up the ladder brought a stinging ache to his forehead, and he eyes his closed, fighting the pulsating throb in his temple. It came in waves, unbidden, and he sat there waiting for the pain to subside.

'Captain, sir?'

He opened one eye and squinted at Leading Telegraphist Simmons. 'What is it?' he asked.

'Signal, sir,' he answered, and held out the pink slip.

'Read it for me.'

'From Scapa, "Return to base." That's all, sir.'

'Very well,' Thorburn said and digested the order. Three words, a decision made from far off, and the battle was over. He glanced at Armstrong.

'That's it then, time to go home.'

'And not a moment too soon, in my humble opinion.'

'I'm inclined to agree,' Thorburn said. 'I think we've had enough of this lot.'

Despite his aching head, he came to his feet and studied the other three Royal Navy warships. Scarred and battle weary, they'd performed magnificently. The thought struck him that in the convoluted, complex history of naval engagements, what had happened here in the past hours would probably end up as just a long forgotten footnote in some dusty Admiralty archive. As for his own part, he would leave that for others to rule on. In hindsight, his decision to stop tailing the *Aldenburg,* and instead go to the aid of *Rosefinch*, might well be construed as an error of judgement. But it was done in good faith, in the heat of battle, and he sighed. No use crying over spilt milk.

'Number One, have the flotilla take station line astern on *Brackendale*.'

'Sir,' Armstrong acknowledged, and moments later a shaded Aldis lamp began sending instructions.

Thorburn brought his small destroyer round

to the south, slowed until each ship took position, and then increased speed to an economical sixteen knots.

U-824 had waited for two hours after the last sound of propellers had receded into the distance. Now the boat rose from the depths and Reinhart ordered the periscope raised. A mechanical grinding screech came from the housing and the periscope remained stationary.

'Damaged, Herr Kapitän. No movement.'

Reinhart cursed and nodded to the attack periscope. 'We use that one.'

It rose smoothly and he gripped the handles. Bent to the eyepiece he could see only blackness, no sign of starlight, no breaking crests. Normally at night a periscope always revealed a little of the outside world, no matter how dark. The realisation came that this periscope had also succumbed to damage, the upper lens possibly destroyed. Maybe it was that first attack from the destroyer, a shell hitting the bridge. They had endured many depth charges since that opening salvo but he'd not thought any had come close enough to inflict serious harm. He stepped away.

'Periscope down,' he said, and for a minute or so wracked his brain as to his next move. Without 'eyes' he was at the mercy of the enemy, never able to check the seas before surfacing. The boat could not reach the fjords on what was left in the batteries, and yet to attempt reaching home on the surface . . . , it was not viable. Once the storm cleared he would be vulnerable to air attack and he would be throwing away the lives of his crew, for what? The Fatherland could not hold out for much longer, the world of Hitler's Thousand Year Reich was nearly over. He glanced round at the crew, at the men who obeyed his every order without hesitation. He said nothing but moved to the chart table. He studied it for a long time, many thoughts in his mind. Finally he straightened up, looked once more at his men, and made his decision.

'Surface the boat.'

He waited while the U-boat swam up the last few metres and prepared to climb the tower.

'No lookouts,' he said to the First Officer. 'I will have the bridge alone.'

His Second-in-Command shrugged his shoulders. 'I hear you, Kapitän.'

U-824 broke the surface and Reinhart clambered out from the conning tower. He made the mandatory sweep of the horizon and marvelled at how clear the night actually was. The storm had swept through to leave relatively calm seas and he turned his binoculars to the southwest. The snow capped mountains of northern Iceland glinted in the lens, and he gave a grunt of satisfaction.

'Start the diesels,' he called, and they coughed into life. 'Come to course two-one-zero, and half speed ahead both.'

He looked round at the periscopes and nodded at the damage. The one for normal observation had been sliced where it entered the housing, and the attack periscope's head had imploded, both types of damage irreparable at sea.

He turned to look ahead and a slow smile reached across his face. Soon they would be beached on the coast of Iceland, and only when it was too late for a change of heart would he let his men know. Korvettenkapitän Rudolph Reinhart, rode his luck again, and hopefully he thought, for the last time in this war.

Under Armstrong's guidance, *Brackendale's* crew set about making good the worst of the battle damage, and tired though they undoubtedly were, by dawn the next day, the ship had taken on a more aesthetically pleasing appearance. The obvious damage to the fo'c'sle and wrecked galley housing was nonetheless beyond their current capacity, and they could do little more than make superficial repairs. Where the radar lantern once searched for signs of the enemy, only the reinforced base plinth remained, and Armstrong made certain any debris was cleared overboard.

It was late in the afternoon when *Brackendale* swung round the southern headland of South Ronaldsay and led the way north to the entrance of Scapa Flow. A cutter opened the boom nets to allow access, and swiftly closed the nets behind them.

Thorburn took the ships west towards Hoy and a short while later they began to pick up their moorings. Two tugs came out to *Seaham* and began circling, waiting patiently for the moment her captain might reluctantly agree to their assistance.

Rear-Admiral Lawrence T. Collingwood, R.N., D.S.O., D.S.C., took himself down to the quayside and watched the ad hoc flotilla begin to pick up their moorings. *Rosefinch* was heading straight for the quayside, the first to land her extra passengers, the few men who had survived the destruction of *Zeus*. He could quite clearly see the results of battle, pock marked hulls bearing evidence of a hard fought engagement. He lifted his binoculars and picked out *Seaham*. She was listing far enough over that he had no problem in seeing the majority of her deck plates, and it was easy to distinguish heavy damage to her upperworks. Her gun barrels were blistered and blackened from the amount of salvos fired and he could only guess at the number of casualties. *Rosefinch* and *Pegwell Bay* both showed evidence of fire damage, and both had sustained significant shell damage to their hulls and superstructure.

Lastly he focussed on *Brackendale* and pursed his lips in wonder. The fo'c'sle looked badly holed and the forward gun shield had taken a beating. Rows of jagged bullet holes formed unsightly patterns in her wheelhouse plating and the forebridge was charred by fire. The mast leaned at a crazy angle, though the stays had obviously held. Abaft the funnel, amidships, there was a gap where he expected to find the radar housing, and he took a sharp intake of breath as he looked at the remnants of the galley housing and pom-pom.

He lowered the glasses, the shadow of a sad smile lingering round his mouth. He thought of how much he'd asked of these men, and in particular of *Brackendale* and her Ship's Company. Twice now he'd used his authority to order her into battle, primarily because he'd set so much store in the capabilities of Lieutenant-Commander Richard Thorburn. The first time, back in '42, it was Collingwood himself who'd ordered Thorburn to take command of other ships; this time command had come unasked for in the midst of battle. And the man's unstinting devotion to duty, his almost uncanny knack of leadership, they were qualities that couldn't be taught, an inherent part of the man's makeup, and thank God for that.

Collingwood turned away. There was no need of his presence at this particular time, the less pomp and ceremony the better. He walked quietly back up the slope and headed for his office.

Tomorrow, he thought, would be soon

enough for a debrief, let them first recover with a well earned rest.

In a fjord on Norway's west coast the *Aldenburg* once again lay hidden behind the protective screen of camouflage nets. Kapitän-zur-See Bergmann had issued instructions for the captains of the three surviving destroyers to report to him immediately on arrival. During *Aldenburg's* absence, a number of signals had arrived from the headquarters of Grand Admiral Dönitz, all demanding to know under whose authority the cruiser had put to sea. And now, in the last hour, a further, urgent message from Dönitz insisted on Admiral Krause sending a full report of actions taken.

Sitting in the commander's cabin, Bergmann looked at the three men opposite and gave a sad smile.

'Are we all set on how to proceed?' he asked.

The oldest of the three spoke up. 'Ja, our orders were clear and at least one of the British ships burned badly, it could not survive. Before we could do more, Krause sent a signal to join him.' The man shrugged his shoulders. 'Richter made a mistake, wrong tactics. We should have launched torpedoes, all of us. But no, we are ordered to save torpedoes for the convoy and to use our guns. Gott in Himmel! We were fighting the Royal Navy, not some untrained navy with hardly a ship to their name.'

Bergmann nodded and held up a hand. 'I hear you, Franz. We were all under orders, and like you, I too could see the mistakes Krause was making. That he is dead does not serve us well. All I can do is submit my report and hope the Fuhrer is pleased with my decisions. The ship is saved, better to have it fight again than to have it lost for no good reason.'

Three heads nodded in unison and Bergmann came to his feet.

'Then we are agreed. Our story is that Admiral Krause made a foolhardy decision to attack the convoy and that British forces heavily outnumbered our small command. Certainly no-one had expected there to be an outlying patrol of five destroyers northeast of Iceland.'

He reached out to shake their hands, and sealed an unwritten pact.

When they'd gone, Bergmann settled down and wrote for an hour, revised what he'd written, and deleted a few unnecessary sentences. At the end of that time, he had a single, concise report that laid the blame squarely where it belonged, on Admiral Mathias Krause.

The report went out with the next batch of signals.

At Portsmouth's Semaphore Tower in Commodore Pendleton's outer office, Jennifer Farbrace answered the insistent ring of her telephone.

The switchboard operator said, 'Second Officer Thomson for you, ma'am.'

'Thank you,' she said. 'Hello, Mary?'

'He's back, Jenny. Thought you ought to know.'

For a few seconds, Jennifer closed her eyes, her heart thumping with relief.

'Jenny?'

'Sorry, Mary, do you know if he's alright?'

'Well . . . , he's not wounded, but he's been admitted to the base hospital. Something to do with severe headaches.'

'Oh,' she murmured, the momentary elation quickly evaporating. 'But not wounded you say?' She wanted reassurance.

'No, definitely not wounded, I saw him come ashore. He looked fine then.'

Quietly, Jennifer said, 'Thank you, Mary, thank you so much. Bless you for your kindness.'

'Don't be silly, that's what friends are for. But don't you dare forget my wedding invitation.'

Despite her concerns, Jennifer laughed. 'Not likely, I'll have him in harness before he knows it.'

It was Mary's turn to laugh. 'Sounds like you've got everything planned.'

'Yes, I made a provisional arrangement with the vicar. The village is on standby.'

'Good, that's the only way to pin 'em down. Anyway, at least you know he's back in one piece. I'd better say goodbye, I'm on duty soon.'

'Alright, Mary, thanks again . . . , goodbye.' The line disconnected and she sank back in her chair. Tears welled up, unbidden, the happiest tears of her life.

Richard Thorburn opened his eyes to find he was looking at a plain white ceiling and not, as he expected, the deckhead of his cabin. He lay on his back with his head propped on pillows and there was a strong smell of disinfectant in his nostrils.

A movement caught his attention and he focussed on two faces. One belonged to a man wearing a white coat, and the other a young woman with a starched white headpiece and a pristine apron.

The man bent towards him, a stethoscope swinging from round his neck. 'How do you feel?' he asked.

Thorburn thought about it before giving his answer.

'Fine.'

'Good,' said the man. 'I'm Doctor Hall and you're in hospital under observation. Your surgeon brought you in this morning, remember?'

Thorburn thought about that too.

'No,' he said, 'I don't remember Doc doing that.'

Hall nodded, his eyes serious, inquisitive.

'Guessed as much, you were out on your feet, unintelligible. We took you in to keep an eye on you. I think that wound to your temple has resulted in a bit of concussion, a hairline fracture. Had any headaches?'

Thorburn took his time to reply, guarded. 'Yes..., a few.'

'With nausea?'

'Sometimes.'

Hall straightened up, his head tilted in thought. 'Mmm,' he murmured, and Thorburn almost grinned. Typical doctor, a non-committal, vague reflection on the symptoms expressed.

'Right,' Hall said finally. 'I'm keeping you in for now, but I'll be back to see you again on my evening rounds.'

Thorburn stared at him, at a loss for words.

'I can't stay here, I've a ship to run,' and he moved to sit up.

Hall laid a firm hand on his chest, pinning him down. 'Not yet. The Admiral assures me that Lieutenant Armstrong can manage perfectly well in your absence.'

Reluctantly, Thorburn relaxed and resigned himself to enforced idleness.

'Alright, Doc, I'll behave.'

'Good,' Hall said. 'Now if you'll excuse me, I am rather busy.'

Thorburn held up a hand in apology. He'd forgotten that the hospital would be dealing with numerous casualties.

'Sorry, don't let me hold you up. I'll be fine.'

Hall glanced quickly at the woman. 'This is Nurse Chadwick. Anything you're not sure about, she'll have the answers.' He nodded briefly. 'Until this evening,' he said, and hurried out.

Nurse Chadwick picked up a file, made a note, and then checked the water jug was full. With a last friendly smile, she too slipped from the room.

Thorburn closed his eyes, grateful to be left in peace. He had to admit, he really did feel under the weather. The ache round his temple had become a persistent pounding, hard to ignore.

Adolf Hitler had by now heard of *Aldenburg's* deployment, and subsequent failure. He demanded an explanation from Grand Admiral Karl Dönitz, but by the time a full report became available, Hitler had more pressing matters to deal with. The Russians were advancing at speed on the Eastern Front, while Eisenhower and Montgomery had pushed the Allied Army to within a few miles of the German homeland.

Dönitz contacted Bergmann on the 25th of September, a telephone call before dawn.

Bergmann answered and was told in no uncertain terms that the crew of *Aldenburg* were to be broken up and distributed amongst the U-boats, thus helping to counter the ever dwindling number of recruits. The ship itself would retain only the gun crews and a skeleton engineering staff. Static operations against Allied aircraft were to be Bergmann's new priority. The surviving destroyers would be kept for inshore convoy protection.

Kapitän-zur-See Ralf Bergmann slowly replaced the receiver and leaned back in his chair. Although Dönitz had not officially cleared him of any misdemeanours, no accusation of wrong doing had been specified. He still retained command of the cruiser and might well see out the end of the war in relative obscurity. It couldn't be long in coming. To strip men from surface ships to man the U-boats, that he thought, was the beginning of defeat.

In the end, ten days elapsed before Thorburn heard he might be released, ten whole days of enforced inactivity while the medical staff carried out a wide ranging series of tests. The realist in him began to recognise the fact his sea going days might be at a fork in the road.

On the final day before his release, Thorburn was sat reading at the side of his bed. Nurse Chadwick came scurrying in and quickly tidied the bed, patting down the top blanket and plumping up the pillows. She looked flustered. Finally after carefully reading through her notes, she glanced round to see all was in order.

'What's up?' Thorburn asked quietly.

'There's an Admiral coming in, to see you.'

Thorburn put down his book and gave her

a warm smile. 'Not to worry,' he said kindly, 'nothing will happen. Admirals don't tend to take much notice of us little people.'

And just for a moment, she dropped her guard and he caught a glimpse of the girl behind the uniform, the young woman who could giggle at his poor joke. But then the laughing eyes blinked, and she became all official, straight faced. She blew out her cheeks and hurried from the room.

Long minutes passed before there was a discreet tap on the door and Thorburn looked up to find Rear-Admiral Lawrence T. Collingwood, walking into the room.

'Ah-ha, Thorburn!' he boomed, 'the very man. That Doctor of yours tells me you'll be out tomorrow.'

Thorburn came to his feet. 'So I understand, sir.'

Collingwood waved a hand. 'Relax, sit yourself down. I just wanted to congratulate you on a job well done. I had a long chat with your First Lieutenant, straight from the shoulder you might say.'

Thorburn protested.

'Couldn't have done it without the others, sir. They were bloody marvellous.'

Collingwood fixed him with those penetrating blue eyes. 'That's as maybe, but when you took on the *Aldenburg* you acted way beyond what might reasonably be expected.'

'*Zeus* needed our help.'

'Mmm..., but no man could have asked you to then start shadowing a damn great cruiser, least of all me.'

Thorburn squirmed, embarrassed, struggling to answer.

'Secondly,' the Admiral went on, 'you'll be pleased to know that the convoy arrived safely one day ahead of schedule, no losses. All down to you, Thorburn.' He paused, staring. 'And in this particular case, forewarned really *was* forearmed. It was your last signal giving *Aldenburg's* alteration of course and speed. That clinched it, and allowed *Stirling* to catch the enemy off guard. Turned tail and ran.'

'I'm glad the convoy made it,' Thorburn said.

Collingwood chuckled. 'So was Churchill,' he said. 'Well, you'll be rejoining Commodore Pendleton; he's been badgering me ever since I pinched you for that patrol.' He laughed loudly. 'I don't think I'm in his good books anymore.'

Thorburn had to smile. *Brackendale* had only been out of repair for one operation, and that had been cut short.

'No, sir,' he agreed, 'probably not.'

Collingwood stepped closer, and Thorburn stood as the man shook hands with a firm grip.

'Good luck, commander, you served your country well. God speed for the future.'

'Thank you, sir. Either way, at least I'll be out of here.'

Collingwood half shook his head, smiled again. 'Agreed, not my favourite places,' and with that the man was gone. Thorburn sank down into the chair. Tomorrow still seemed a long way off.

As promised he was duly released and returned aboard ship. Armstrong was there to greet him as he came up the Jacob's ladder.

'Morning, sir.'

'Morning, Number One,' he said, glancing around the quarterdeck. It appeared much as he'd left it, the pom-pom and galley housing still entwined together. 'Any news on repairs?'

'No, sir, but the flotilla has been officially disbanded. *Rosefinch* and *Pegwell Bay* are being sent south to Chatham for repairs, and *Brackendale* is ordered to Rosyth for a full assessment.'

'I see,' Thorburn said, 'doesn't sound very promising.' He felt movement beneath his feet as the ship swung to her mooring, and he smiled. 'Not to worry,' he said brightly, 'it'll all come out in the wash. Now, where's the gin?'

And together they headed for the wardroom.

26 .. All Change

Lieutenant-Commander Richard Thorburn, R.N., D.S.O., and Bar, stood outside the ancient door of Boxley Church and shuffled from foot to foot. It was almost eleven in the morning and sunshine bathed the timeworn grey flagstones that made up the small entranceway. He looked back at the old covered gate to the church grounds, and beyond that, The Kings Arms on the far side of the road. The two large gins had helped steady his nerves but even so he patted his pockets for a cigarette.

'She'll be late, mark my words,' Willoughby said, chuckling. 'Bride's prerogative.'

Thorburn lit a cigarette, blew smoke skywards, and managed a smile of his own. 'Probably,' he said, and turned to look at his best man. 'Who'd of thought it, Peter? Middle of a war and I'm getting wed. Not that many years ago I would have thought it impossible.'

Willoughby frowned in mock seriousness. 'Mmm..., and with a pretty girl in every port, it must have been hard to choose.'

Thorburn gave him a push and grinned. 'Don't hang your vices on everyone else.'

A car engine sounded from down the hill and they both turned to watch. What appeared was not what Thorburn expected to see. An Austin staff car in Royal Navy livery pulled into the side of the road and came to a halt. The driver jumped out and began opening doors. Three uniformed officers stepped down and tugged their jackets straight.

Thorburn stood transfixed. The nearest man glanced round as if getting his bearings, a stocky man sporting a full beard. Commodore James

Pendleton patted his cap into position and turned to wait for the others.

The 'others' turned out to be none other than Rear-Admiral Collingwood and Lieutenant Robert Armstrong.

Thorburn snatched a glance at Willoughby. 'Is this your doing?'

'Nothing to do with me, Governor,' he said, laughing.

Thorburn shook his head in mock dismay. 'I thought this was supposed to be a quiet family affair?'

'Well . . . , you know the Navy. Never were any good at keeping secrets.'

The deep base voice of Pendleton boomed across the drive. 'Richard, my boy,' he beamed, 'how the devil are you?' He strode up and offered his hand. 'Last few minutes of freedom, eh? There's still time to change your mind.' His laughter echoed through the church grounds.

Thorburn remembered his manners. 'I'm honoured, sir.'

'Ha!' Pendleton barked. 'Wouldn't have missed it for the world.'

Collingwood joined them. He too offered his hand and slapped Thorburn's shoulder. A broad smile softened his features. 'Good man, knew you'd make an honest woman of her.'

Thorburn nodded, disconcerted by all the attention. 'Yes, sir. Thank you, sir.' Armstrong hovered in the background looking a little ill at ease.

'Excuse me,' Thorburn said and pushed between the two senior officers. He put his hand out. 'Hello, Bob. Keeping rather posh company these days?'

'Not down to me, I blame your best man. Said I could have a lift, and I ended up with those two.'

Willoughby interrupted. 'C'mon, enough gossip, time we were inside.' He tapped the face of his wristwatch.

Thorburn nodded, took a deep breath, and dutifully followed Peter into the church. Nods and smiles accompanied them inside and they took their seats at the front. Ornate stained glass windows bathed the altar in a soft glow, dappled sunlight reaching into hidden corners.

He glanced round at his parents, his mother dressed quietly in soft lilac with a matching handbag. It had been years since he'd seen her wear anything other than a midwife's uniform. His father wore a dark grey suit, and *the* old regimental tie he reserved for special occasions. They both smiled and his father winked. It was as if to say, don't worry, son, we've all been there. He slowly closed one eye in return and grinned.

'The ring?' he asked.

Willoughby patted a pocket, then another, his face changing from a contented smile to a deep frown. And then he brightened and chuckled.

'Had you worried, didn't I?' He reached into his hip pocket and produced the finely engraved box. 'Safe and sound,' he said, and popped it back.

The organist, who up until that moment had been playing a quiet melody, suddenly switched to a lively rendition of "Here Comes the Bride", and Thorburn came to his feet. He turned to look down the aisle and watched in awe as Jennifer walked in, arm in arm with her father. The white of her wedding dress shone in the subdued light, a beautifully plain creation that fell elegantly from shoulder to floor. At her waist she carried a small bouquet of cream and pink flowers, colours that were reflected in the flowing dresses worn by two young bridesmaids. A fine veil made for a discreet covering over her face, but as she came closer he found her smiling eyes. Her father gently released her, arm and they finally stood side by side in front of the altar, the congregation falling silent.

The vicar, crimson faced and smiling, cleared his throat and the age old ceremony began. 'Brethren, we are gathered here . . . . . .'

A short while later, having made their vows, and with the wedding ring perfectly fitted, the beaming vicar pronounced them man and wife. He finished with a nod, looked at Thorburn and said, 'You may kiss the bride.'

They came together, lips brushing lightly. He pulled away, just a little, and met her eyes.

'Hello, Mrs Thorburn,' he grinned.

Jennifer smiled and curtsied. 'Hello, Mr Thorburn,' and they kissed again.

The vicar then ushered them into a small ante-room, and with both mothers in attendance as witnesses, the Marriage Register was duly signed. Formalities over, they returned to their respective places and finished proceedings with The Lord's Prayer.

And so, together, man and wife, they turned and slowly walked out to a chorus of good wishes and smiling faces. They emerged blinking into strong sunlight.

Thorburn stopped under the archway and for a moment his mouth fell open in surprise. Chief Petty Officer Barry falconer was stood smartly to attention in best uniform grinning from ear to ear. Beyond him, ten of the Ship's Company had lined up in pairs either side of the flagstone path.

The Cox'n took a half pace forward. 'Congratulations, sir,' he said very formally. 'And to you, ma'am.' He then took the same half pace back and turned to the sailors.

'Honour guard!' he barked. 'Caps . . . , off!' He paused briefly.

'Raise . . . , caps!'

Ten arms shot up to form an improvised archway, and Thorburn found himself grinning.

Jennifer squeezed his arm in delight, eyes sparkling. He patted her hand, took the first step and they both walked forward beneath the extended caps.

Thorburn recognised every man, thanked each one by name, and accepted enthusiastic congratulations. The wedding party followed and then everyone broke into small gatherings. Willoughby joined him just as Jennifer was whisked away into the middle of chattering women friends.

'Cigarette?' Willoughby asked, offering his pack.

'Thanks, think I need this one.'

Willoughby took one for himself and then Thorburn felt a discreet elbow nudging him.

'Who's that lovely in the wide brimmed hat?'

Thorburn looked round and saw Jennifer giggling, deep in conversation. The woman seemed to feel their eyes and glanced their way, just for a second.

'That, Peter, is Second Officer Mary Thomson, and I understand she's on the lookout for a good husband.'

Willoughby feigned shocked horror. 'Steady on, can't a man just sample the goods without having to buy?'

Thorburn grinned and drew on the smoke, interrupted by a voice calling, 'Make way, coming through!' and a photographer appeared carrying an assortment of professional looking paraphernalia.

'Where,' Thorburn asked, 'did he manage to get the film from? I thought that was one of the scarcer commodities.'

'Ask no questions, get no lies,' Willoughby said, wisely tapping the side of his nose, and they watched him set up in front of the church entrance. Thorburn then found himself front and centre with Jennifer, and the next few minutes were spent posing for the camera while the man then worked methodically through a preordained list of traditional groupings.

In due course, a wedding car pulled up beyond the gate, and Thorburn offered his arm to Jennifer. Walking out through an excited crowd of well wishers, they ducked through a cloud of confetti and made it to the sanctuary of the back seats.

The reception was held in an old barn at the home of Jennifer's parents. Their farm lay nestled in the valley below the village of Boxley and many of the local guests had contributed towards the preparations. Despite the severity of wartime rationing, for one special day, the years of austerity were put aside, forgotten. Importantly, there'd been no problem with the supply of alcoholic refreshment. The Royal Navy could be very resourceful when push came to shove.

Later after a succession of speeches, the meal devoured, and the traditional 'cutting of the cake', an accomplished quartet of amateur musicians launched into a waltz, and the Bride and Groom came together for the first dance.

For Thorburn, the next hour or so passed in a constant whirl of polite conversation with total strangers, but who, nonetheless, wanted him to know how pleased they were for the both of them. But eventually, with the coming of the blackout, it was time to leave. Family and friends spilled out into the yard and after a few final, fond farewells, the driver of the Royal Navy staff car closed the doors.

With shouts of 'Good luck' ringing in their ears, they settled back for the short run to Maidstone and the honeymoon suite of the Royal Star Hotel.

Their return to duty a week later was greeted with a call from Commodore James Pendleton. They were to attend his office at 10.00 hours that morning. What followed was not totally unexpected. *Brackendale* had been laid up in a repair yard and was unlikely to see active service again. The wound to Thorburn's temple had not healed as well as expected and after a thorough examination by a Senior Consultant Surgeon, the Admiralty had decided it was time for Thorburn to step ashore, his sea going days at an end.

Thorburn accepted the news without argument. He'd had a good innings and with *Brackendale* sidelined, probably for the duration, he didn't have the appetite to take on another command.

'I guessed as much, sir. Any inkling as to where

I'll be going?'

Pendleton stroked his beard and glared out of the window. 'Well now, that's the thing, Richard, the trouble is I'm not sure you'll like it.'

Thorburn frowned. 'Try me, sir.'

Pendleton sat very still, eyes averted. 'There's this vacancy that's come up in Operations. It needs an experienced Naval officer, someone who's recently been at the sharp end, hands on, so to speak.' He looked up. 'But I didn't know how you'd feel. It's not obligatory, there are other possibilities.'

Thorburn met his gaze. 'Who's in command?'

Pendleton looked away and blew out his cheeks. When he glanced round there was a twinkle in his eye.

'Me,' he said simply.

Thorburn pursed his lips and squinted round at Jennifer, but he couldn't read her thoughts, non committal. He dropped his eyes to the floor. There was really nothing to think about. If there was one man in authority he trusted, whose judgement could be relied upon, who'd stood behind him on numerous occasions, then it was Commodore James Pendleton. He slowly raised his head to meet the old sailor's waiting eyes.

'When do I start?'

Pendleton gave a broad grin and slapped the table in triumph. 'Good man! Hoped you would . . . , thought you might . . . , couldn't be sure.' He came out from behind his desk, hand extended.

'Welcome aboard, Richard.' He dropped the warm handshake and glanced at his watch. 'I've just got time to show you your office.' He looked at Jennifer and smiled. 'As for you, young lady, your in-tray overflows. Nothing like the present, eh?'

'Of course, sir, right away.'

'This way then,' Pendleton said, and led Thorburn out to the corridor.

27 .. Restless Seas

Lieutenant-Commander Richard Thorburn found his new surroundings on the upper floor to be surprisingly spacious, and his biggest concern, reams of paperwork, were in fact dealt with by a very efficient personal assistant and a well staffed typing pool. An unexpected bonus came with a commanding view over Portsmouth harbour that allowed him the luxury of watching the Royal Navy come and go as they went about their prescribed duties.

He and Jennifer took lodgings in a flat at a town house in the suburbs, and for the next five months he became thoroughly immersed in the day-to-day planning and execution of Naval affairs. His duties encompassed offensive patrols from as far away as Norway, and all through the Channel down to Brest. His final involvement came with the surrender of the Channel Islands, and concluded with the late capitulation of German forces in Alderney.

On the 8th May 1945, Victory in Europe became a blessed relief from the rigours of war on the continent. Pendleton visited the Admiralty in London more and more frequently, and eventually became permanently installed in the Navy Office for Forward Planning. By mid-August, V-J Day officially marked the end of the world wide conflict. Come Christmas, Jennifer announced she was expecting their first child and suggested they look into buying a home of their own. In the March of '46 they had arranged a mortgage and moved into an old thatched cottage set in an acre of mature gardens with a distant view of the sea. Jennifer left the Service and became a mother to a daughter they named Rosemary.

With the Royal Navy now in the process of slimming down, Thorburn decided to look to the future. He purchased a second hand ocean going yacht, and gave her the new name of *Lady*. Old Man Pendleton had always addressed Jennifer as 'young lady' and Thorburn thought it very appropriate. Not that he revealed the reason to anybody, least of all his wife. He had the auxiliary engine refurbished, and managed to secure a mooring in a nearby sheltered marina.

At the beginning of 1948, he retired from the Royal Navy and began the serious work of setting himself up in the day charter business. A second child, Christopher, came along in early July, and with bookings on the increase, Thorburn at last began to see a return on his new venture. His excursions around the Isle of Wight, advertised under the banner, "Windjammer Sailing", became *the* talked about day out in the more affluent circles of London's fashionable elite.

It was a fine autumn evening when a small green MG sports car roared up the drive and slithered to a halt outside the rose covered porch. From the sitting room window Thorburn watched it arrive and went through the hall to open the front door. A slim Royal Navy officer stepped from the car, and Thorburn grinned in amazement. Lieutenant George Labatt's boyish face broke into a familiar smile. Thorburn walked forward and reached for his hand.

'Hello, George, good to see you.'

'Evening, sir, hope I'm not intruding?'

They shook hands and Thorburn chuckled. 'Not at all, you're very welcome. And it's Richard now, I'm a civilian.'

'Yes, sir.'

Thorburn grinned again. Old habits died hard. 'Come on,' he said, 'come on in.'

'Just coming,' Labatt said, and reached into the back of the MG. He straightened up with a large flat parcel wrapped in brown paper and neatly tied with string. Thorburn led the way into the sitting room and Jennifer appeared from the kitchen.

'This is George, served with me in *Brackendale*.'

'Of course,' she said, 'and you've not changed a bit. Can I get you something? It's well past the yard arm.'

Labatt hesitated and Thorburn intervened. 'Gin and tonic I'm sure. I'll get it. You two take the weight off your feet.' He hurried into the dining room, found the Gordon's on the sideboard and rummaged through for tumblers and tonic. Back in the sitting room, Jennifer was telling him all about Rosemary and Christopher, already tucked up in bed.

Thorburn poured and added a splash of tonic, handed them out and eased himself into the comfort of his armchair.

'A toast,' he said, raising the glass. 'To ships and shipmates, old and new.'

Labatt raised his tumbler. 'And to *Brackendale*.'

They all took a mouthful and Thorburn said, 'She was a good ship.'

Labatt shot him a glance. 'Still is, sir. She's down at Dartmouth, training cadets in the art of handling destroyers. I've seen her.'

'I'll be damned,' Thorburn said. 'I thought she was headed for the scrap yard.' He took another swallow. 'So what are you doing now?'

Labatt gave a shy grin. 'Lieutenant in the *Ash-

anti. We're in for a boiler clean.'

'*Ashanti*, eh? Tribal class, that's a step up in the world.'

'Yes, felt like a battleship after *Brackendale*.'

Thorburn sipped his gin and wondered what other news he might have.

'Heard anything of anyone else?' he asked casually, making the query appear as offhand as possible.

'A few,' Labatt said. 'Bob Armstrong quit and took a position with Lloyds Shipping in London.'

Thorburn raised an eyebrow. 'Did he? I'll have to see if he can recommend a good yacht insurer.'

'And Bryn Dawkins apparently accepted an offer from British Petroleum, something to do with engineering at the Port Talbot refinery.' He thought for a moment. 'The Cox'n went back to Newcastle. Word has it that he took himself off to the Lake District. Became skipper to a pleasure cruiser taking sightseers round Lake Windermere.'

Thorburn nodded in thought. Time moved on, changes encompassing them all, everyone finding their own way forward.

Labatt frowned for a second, and then smiled. 'Your friend Peter Willoughby was promoted full Commander. He's stationed in Hong Kong, captain of a frigate.'

Thorburn chuckled, remembering his youth. 'The old China Station, eh? That's where we first met.' He glanced at Jennifer. 'He was always one for the ladies.'

She wrinkled her nose and raised an eyebrow. 'And you weren't, I suppose?'

He laughed and shook his head vigorously. 'Never,' he said, chuckling, and emptied his glass. 'Another?' he prompted.

Labatt nodded and Jennifer took his tumbler. 'I'll get these,' she offered, and waltzed off to the dining room. She came back and Labatt thanked her. Then Thorburn watched as he placed it carefully on the floor and reached to the side of his chair.

Labatt leaned forward and with both hands passed over the large flat parcel he'd retrieved from the car.

'This is for you, sir. Thought you might like it.'

Thorburn took it, rested it on his knees and glanced at Jennifer. She shrugged her shoulders.

He carefully untied two knots and placed the string to one side. Gently, he unwrapped the brown paper to find cardboard packing covering something flat. He eased them away, and then sat bolt upright, transfixed. He was mesmerised by a large, framed photograph of *Brackendale* moving at high speed through choppy waters. Her guns were elevated, battle ensigns flying, and the bow wave curled high over the fo'c'sle.

'My God, George, where did you get this?'

'I know a chap in Photographic Archives. We got chatting one evening and when I mentioned

I'd served aboard *Brackendale*, he showed an interest and rang me about a week later. Said he could get me blown up copies of the original. I also have one.'

Jennifer came round to stand behind Thorburn and he felt her hand on his shoulder. 'Is that you on the bridge?'

'Possibly,' he said. 'When was it taken?'

'On D-Day, by a BBC photographer working as a war correspondent. He was on the cruiser H.M.S. *Black Prince*. The caption read, "Royal Navy destroyer relocating after beach bombardment."'

Thorburn leaned back in the armchair with the picture propped on his knees. He shook his head, staring in disbelief at the image before him. 'Bloody marvellous,' he said, 'absolutely bloody marvellous.'

Jennifer went back to her chair and sat for a while, content to listen as they talked on about past exploits. They touched on light hearted moments, days ashore, and other times shared that only men who'd experienced such things could truly understand. Their conversation was not so much about the fighting, but more about the people, a bond formed across years at sea.

The laughter came easily and she realised their friendship had been as close as any. And Jennifer smiled behind the rim of her empty glass. This man, she thought, this once rebellious young captain with whom she now shared her life, this was the man who'd personally won the grudging respect of his peers. He never really mentioned what had motivated him to become such a leader, but in her heart, Jennifer knew without being told. Duty, honour, courage, all words he would ascribe to others and not himself.

From the hall, the muted tones of the grandfather clock struck ten, and she made her excuses and left them to it. She changed into her nightdress, checked on the children, and settled into bed with her favourite book.

The sound of the MG leaving the drive just after eleven brought Richard traipsing up the stairs to the bathroom before he finally came to bed. He lay half propped up on the pillow and she leaned over and kissed his cheek.

'What a pleasant young man,' she said.

'Yes, always enjoyed having him around. Brave too, when push came to shove.'

Jennifer quietly placed the book on the bedside table and turned off the lamp. 'Goodnight, then. Sleep well.'

'And you..., goodnight.'

She plumped up the pillow, turned on her side, and left him with his thoughts.

The next morning, Thorburn woke early, dressed quietly and crept down to the kitchen. He stoked the range with a fresh shovelful of coal, filled the kettle and popped it on the hotplate. While he waited for it to boil he wandered out into the back garden and lit a cigarette. Standing there in the warmth of the sun, he thought of the previous night's conversation. It had been good to hear Labatt's news, to know that others had moved on and reshaped their lives.

The kettle's whistle brought him back to the kitchen and he slid it to one side, the shrill noise slowly dying. He made a pot of tea, and as he poured one for himself, heard Jennifer coming down the stairs.

She joined him in the garden and they stood for a while watching the chickens pecking busily at bare soil.

'I think I'll take *Lady* for a short trip, need to check the jib. I have a family booking for Friday and Saturday.'

She slid a hand round his waist. 'Will you be back for tea?'

'I should think so, won't be going far.'

'In that case, I'll make some scones. Don't be late.'

'Not likely,' he smiled. 'With jam?'

She pushed him playfully. 'Go on with you, I've a lot to get on with.'

He turned away and made for the front door, and Jennifer waved from the porch.

Down at the boatyard he cast off fore and aft,

fired up the engine and eased gently out from the jetty. Once clear, he killed the motor, raised the mainsail and let the westerly breeze take *Lady* out into the Solent. A small alteration to port and he headed up the coast for Hayling Island. The breeze stiffened and she heeled over, taking the wind off her starboard quarter. He let her run until she drew level with the eastern headland, and then came about for the return leg. Pushing on through the short chop, Thorburn braced to the undulating waves. A drift of spray swept from bow to cockpit and he tasted that all encompassing familiar tang of salt laden air. He nudged the helm to port and *Lady* responded, lifting her stem to a roller.

Richard Thorburn grinned into the spray. Life, he thought, had turned out pretty well. He knew he was lucky, had survived the long years of war, and he'd never forget those who had fallen. But he'd been given the chance to make something of the future and had grasped it with both hands. No longer the rebellious young man of the past, but a husband and father with new responsibilities.

Lady twisted to an oncoming crest and Thorburn swayed with her, the consummate sailor born and bred, at one with the restless sea.

Novels by Graham John Parry

***

(World War II Naval Saga featuring Richard Thorburn)

The Waves of War

Man of War

When D-Day Dawns

Fighting Command

Printed in Great Britain
by Amazon